NOTHING IS
EVERYTHING

PRAISE FOR *NOTHING IS EVERYTHING*

"Simon Strantzas captures the creepiness of small town Ontario; there is something of Seth, of Alice Munro in his work, wonderfully tangled with the likes of Aickman and Jackson. Uncanny as a ventriloquist's doll, but with a real, beating heart."
- Camilla Grudova, author of *The Doll's Alphabet*

"Welcome to *Nothing is Everything*, the latest collection by Simon Strantzas. Taking the paths less traveled to the human heart and mind, and excavating the strangeness that abides therein, Strantzas is one of the most striking writers working today."
- Angela Slatter, author of the World Fantasy Award-winning *The Bitterwood Bible and Other Recountings*

"Simon Strantzas is Shirley Jackson-grade eerie, creating stories that are as unsettling as they are elegant."
- Kij Johnson, author of *At the Mouth of The River of Bees*

"'The unexpected has arrived, and has brought with it the unknown.' Simon Strantzas's stories arrive without warning, to offer those unknown gifts and sidelong glimpses that bring mystery close enough to touch."
- Kathe Koja, author of *The Cipher*, and *Christopher Wild*

"Simon Strantzas's compelling stories unfold across a liminal landscape of small towns and ordinary situations where encounters with the uncanny are often revelatory. With his latest collection, he further cements his place as a significant voice among a wave of writers who are redefining the boundaries of genre, blending a literary sensibility with a powerful sense of the possibilities for transcendence in the everyday."
- Lynda E. Rucker, author of *The Moon Will Look Strange*, and *You'll Know When You Get There*

NOTHING IS
EVERYTHING

SIMON STRANTZAS

UNDERTOW
PUBLICATIONS

PUBLICATION HISTORY
In This Twilight, original to this collection.
Our Town's Talent, original to this collection.
These Last Embers, previously published in *These Last Embers*, 2015.
The Flower Unfolds, previously published in *Nightscript 3*, 2017.
Ghost Dogs, original to this collection.
In the Tall Grass, previously published in *Shadows & Tall Trees 7*, 2017.
The Fifth Stone, previously published in *Nightmare's Realm*, 2017.
The Terrific Mr. Toucan, original to this collection.
Alexandra Lost, previously published in *The Mammoth Book of Cthulhu*, 2016.
All Reality Blossoms in Flames, original to this collection.

ALSO BY SIMON STRANTZAS

Beneath the Surface

Cold to the Touch

Nightingale Songs

Shadows Edge (as editor)

Burnt Black Suns

These Last Embers (chapbook)

Aickman's Heirs (as editor)

Year's Best Weird Fiction, Vol. 3 (as editor)

CONTENTS

IN THIS TWILIGHT

———————— ✄ ————————

Harriet Myers didn't expect to see someone lying against the far wall of the Greycoach station beneath the laminated bus schedule. He was dressed in a green army jacket that ended below his belt and was covered in a number of overstuffed pockets, giving him the lumpy appearance of an old rolled farmer's rug. The man was young and unshaven, his blond hair forming a faint halo around his indistinct chin. Beneath his head was a matching khaki pack he used as a pillow, and he made the faintest wheezing sound as he breathed. Harriet wasn't sure, but she thought he might be living there.

It was hard to tell sometimes. She'd grown up on the outside edge of Beeton, and though she was the first to admit it was a small town whose population tended to dress for comfort and convenience rather than fashion, her parents had instilled in her the notion that the way one looks reflects the way they're perceived. Thus, she always kept her poplin skirts pressed, and hung her silk blouses immediately after washing. She wasn't the smartest girl in her classes, nor the prettiest—not with the noticeable scar that ran from the edge of her temple to the bottom of her chin, only barely hidden beneath her bundle of wild auburn hair—but in some ways her averageness was her greatest strength. It kept people close enough to be friendly, but at enough of a distance that she didn't have to worry that they might ask what had happened. She'd gone away to school for the anonymity if nothing else, anxious to find a place where she could live her life without the specter of Martin Baxter constantly looming over her. The quiet also helped her think, and allowed her to focus herself on earning her music degree.

The young man lying on the bus station's floor appeared to be her polar opposite, and yet little different from the scores of boys on the University of Guelph campus. They all cared so little about their appearance, and about the classes they were ostensibly there to take. Drinking and midnight tumblings were all that interested them, and she'd already witnessed the fallout from that attitude. It was only halfway through her first semester and the third floor of gothic Johnston Hall was running at half-capacity. Her own roommate, Kimmy, a bubbly psychology student from Trenton, had dropped out the week before, disappearing while Harriet was at home over the weekend visiting her parents. Kimmy's bed had been stripped bare by the time Harriet returned that Monday, and the sight awoke something in her she thought might be elation.

Harriet hadn't intended to return home again so soon, but it was clear from the whispers through Johnston Hall that there was to be an impromptu floor party that evening, and she knew there would be no escaping it. She might be able to hide in the library or in the MacKinnon Hall practice rooms for a few hours, but eventually both places would close and she'd be left stranded, unable to return to her residence without braving the gauntlet of her drunken peers' solicitations and prodding. And, even then, once past the threshold, she'd be unable to fall asleep amid their braying laughter outside her door. It was better she leave—go home where she could relax in her childhood bed and wake to the smell of her father's Saturday morning blueberry-granola pancakes—than suffer such terrorism. With oboe in hand and a few study books in her neat blue backpack she took the Guelph City Bus down Gordon Street and into town, exiting twenty minutes later at the doors of the Greycoach station.

She'd never taken a Greycoach bus home before but was

determined to do so. It seemed simple enough: check the map, buy a ticket, ride to her destination. But she hadn't counted on the station being empty of employees, nor on the presence of the long lean vagrant (if that's what he was) who had camped beneath the framed schedule. She knew the bus she needed went through Orangeville, but couldn't get close enough to the posting to make out the tiny print of the departure times. The drab fluorescent lights didn't help; was the bus expected at six o'clock? Maybe eight? Did it say on the hour or twenty past? It was as though the schedule itself hadn't yet decided, the letters twisting with indecision. She blinked hard a few times and took a tentative step closer, all the while careful not to rouse the young man at her feet. If only the ticket booth were open, or anyone else were working at the station, but there was no one. The place was as empty as it was run down, and the only proof someone else had ever been there were the two small signs printed on copier paper and taped to the wall. The first commanded she buy her ticket directly from the driver; the second implored her to have exact change ready. Her scar puckered and tightened as she furrowed her brow and resolved to sit and wait. Surely it couldn't be that much longer, and from the middle of the station she ought to be able to see in all directions simultaneously. Should her bus arrive, she was certain she would know. And if not, she could always ask the driver of any bus that came through. He or she would have the answer, providing Harriet had exact change, of course.

She took a seat in the middle bank of orange plastic chairs, two bolted-down rows back-to-back along the length of the small station. It provided a vantage point of the entire north side and allowed her to easily swivel to monitor the south. Something as large as a bus would be difficult to miss. The floor appeared to have a patina of grime, so she kept her blue backpack close, placing it on the seat next to her, and across it laid her carefully-folded dark wool coat. Above her loosely crossed arms she surveyed the room, trying to absorb the essence of a place that she knew existed but never thought she'd have occasion to visit. In some ways what she was waiting for wasn't merely a ride back to Beeton, but the sort of new experience she'd left home to find. It was simultaneously nerve-wracking, illuminating, and exhilarating. And that was before the disheveled young man sleeping on the floor woke with a spastic jerk, knocking the bundle he used as a pillow across the floor.

He sat, blinking, and fiercely shook his head. Then he stretched both arms into the air until they quivered, and proceeded to unfurl a yawn that transformed his mouth into a hypnotizing chasm. Harriet saw past the teeth to the pink ridges that trailed down into his dark gullet, and when that wide abyss closed, she found herself unable to break the spell—not until she noticed his bleary scrutinizing eyes. His lips moved before she heard the sound.

"Hey, what time is it?"

Her wrist raised automatously as she stammered. "It's close to six."

"Already?" he asked, then yawned again, smaller, and she avoided another peek down his throat by focusing on the window. The blonde man stood and ran his hands over his face and through his nest of greasy hair, leaving the latter standing in odd directions. He scratched himself with fingernails both torn and dirty before clearing his throat and finally turning his attention to her. She shifted and focused on her lap.

"Hey, where are you going?"

"Home." She continued to not look at him.

"Obviously, home. Like, who isn't? No one comes through here unless they're on their way home, or on their way *from* home. You look more like you're going than coming. So where's home?"

"Barrie," she lied.

"Cool. Never been to Barrie. Is it nice?"

"Yes," she said, unfolding and refolding her arms as she glanced out the window. "Very nice."

He continued to study her, pinning her with his gaze, and she prayed he'd lose interest. If not, she worried what he

12

might be thinking, what he might do. Her brain shouted at her to disengage, to refuse to participate. If she did, maybe he'd leave her alone. Maybe.

It appeared to work for a few minutes. He didn't say anything, long enough for her focus to wander to when the bus might arrive.

"It'll be here soon," he said. "Your bus. Like, I can tell you're looking for it."

"I wasn't—I mean…"

"Don't worry. I don't blame you. I probably look like shit right now. Probably haven't looked that great in, like, a while. You know how it is."

"Not really," she snipped. But he wasn't dissuaded by her tone. If anything, he was amused.

"I guess you wouldn't. You don't really seem the type."

"No offense," Harriet said, "but I just want to wait quietly for my bus."

"Hey, I can do quiet. No need to tell me twice. I was just trying to make conversation."

With a polite smile and a perfunctory nod, she stood and moved to another seat, putting as much space as she could between her and the stranger without losing sight of the multiple bus stops. He didn't follow her. Instead, he put his hands behind his head and stretched his legs out across the floor. There were holes in his dingy sneakers, one big enough for his toe.

"So," he said. "Why do you seem so lonely?"

"What?" Her mouth went dry.

He pulled his feet back, put his elbows on his knees, and leaned forward.

"I'm right, aren't I?"

Harriet shook her head. This couldn't be real. She stood, walked to the glass entrance of the station. The place was still empty, and there was no indication that might change.

"Don't worry. Like, lots of people are lonely. Especially around here. Especially new students. I don't know what it is. Some people just never find their tribe, I guess."

"I'm not... I have friends."

He leaned back, put his hands back on his head, and stretched out his legs. A satisfied smile crawled across his face.

"It's okay," he said. "You don't have to tell me right now."

She remained by the glass doors, looking out at the empty stops. Every inch of her was irritated, tensed from the comical way she was being tormented. She had no idea who he was, and yet he was pushing her. If it were a game, it was a poor one. She caught her reflection in the glass and barely recognized it. Eyes cast in shadow, muscles around her mouth drawn down, she looked like some funhouse version of herself. The only feature she recognized was her scar, highlighted by the station's fluorescents. Was her reflection bleeding, or were those tears running down her face? She lifted her hand to check but it came away dry.

A bus that's twenty minutes overdue is a bus that's not coming. That's the sort of thing her mother might have said, but for Harriet it had become a matter of pride. To leave would be to admit defeat, and even if she weren't out of places to go, she couldn't bear the stranger thinking he'd driven her away. Harriet could see his reflection in the glass, with his cocksure smile and how at ease he was with himself. He rubbed his thumb across his bottom lip and she felt a shiver on the back of her neck. There was something about him, something she couldn't place. Something that worried her. But that worry was warm and its edges fuzzy.

"Where are *you* going?" she asked, pivoting her body at the apex of her inflection, as though it might catch him off-guard. He seemed as amused by her theatrics as she was embarrassed by them.

"I'm not going anywhere. I'm here for the duration. It's warm, after all. Safe."

"What? You live here?"

"Would it be so bad if I did?" He scratched his nascent beard. "You know, you should probably sit. I promise you won't miss your bus. I'll help you watch for it."

14

"No, thanks. I'll stand."

He moved his hands from the back of the seats beside him and brought them together in mock prayer.

"Please? For me? Your pacing is driving me nuts."

She accidentally gave him half a smile, then with reluctance sat down with her bags. He turned to face her.

"What's that?" he asked.

"What?"

"That black case. Is it, like, some weird purse?"

"This?" she said, holding up her leather case. "It's an oboe."

His eyes lit.

"Oh, play me something."

She shook her head. "That's absolutely the last thing I'm going to do."

"Come on, I want to hear you."

"No," she said. "I can't."

"Sure you can. Just do it."

There was a moment's hesitation as she briefly considered it. If she played, he might stop asking and maybe leave her alone. It wouldn't be that hard, would it? Play to buy herself some respite? But, no, she wouldn't. She couldn't. If she played, she'd only be giving in to his demands and encouraging his rude behavior.

"I'm not going to play," she said, and unzipped her blue backpack. The oboe case slid easily inside. He was disappointed, but she couldn't tell if it was because she wouldn't play, or because he'd failed to coerce her.

"What's the point of having an instrument if you don't use it?"

"I don't know," she said. "What's the point of anything?"

A smile curled across his face as he pointed at her.

"Now you're getting it."

Harriet couldn't believe how frustrating he was.

"Look, I don't know what you want, but I'm not interested in any company. I just want to be on my way home. I don't even know your name and—"

"It's Sear."

"I don't really care, Sear. Please leave me alone. Can you do that?"

"No," he said. "My name isn't 'Sear'. I said 'it's here'. Your bus. It's here."

"My—?" Harriet spun around. There, outside the windows of the station, was the silver panelling of an idling Greycoach Bus. The driver sat behind multiple panes of glass, impatiently checking his watch.

"I—I'm sorry, that's my bus. I—" She scrambled to pull her luggage together, and as she stood her purse dropped to the floor with a muted thump. Before she could move, her tormentor gathered it up.

"So I guess this is goodbye, then," he said, holding the purse lazily in his hands, just out of her reach. Harriet glanced back to ensure the Greycoach hadn't left.

"I guess so. My purse, please." She extended her free hand.

The fear of being late, of missing her bus, spiraled inside her. Harriet needed to escape Guelph—the school, the town, the bus station—and maintaining her veneer of politeness when that flight was being obstructed was becoming impossible.

"It's Hand. Charlie Hand."

"Who is?"

"Me. That's my name. Charlie Hand."

"That's good to know, Charlie Hand. Now, my purse?"

He smiled as he offered it to her, and that smile remained as she snatched it from his hands. The edges of regret replaced her anxiety instantly. She shouldn't have—

"You'd better go. You're going to miss it."

Harriet jumped. "Thank you," she offered reluctantly, then shuffled her bags and coat quickly through the door. A momentary glance back through the glass found Charlie Hand bending to retrieve the pack he'd launched earlier across the station floor. Such a strange man, she thought, then rushed to the bus's open door.

The driver waited at the bottom of the small set of steps,

16

a mustachioed man in his late sixties with tired beleaguered eyes. He spoke with a travelled rasp, and only to confirm the bus's destination was Orangeville. He took her payment without smiling, and once their transaction was complete he made no effort to help her as she boarded.

The Greycoach was nearly as empty as the station. There were a few occupied seats—mostly students travelling from other schools, or exhausted men in rumpled business suits. Harriet squeezed her way into a cramped seat near the middle of the bus and planted herself by the window, blue backpack resting on her lap. Finally, she'd escaped and was going home. Pressure and anxiety slid from her as she exhaled, leaving only weariness and fatigue. It was no mystery why Kimmy and all the rest had left Guelph, but that wasn't Harriet. She was not the sort to be defeated. If not in the aftermath of Martin Baxter, then certainly not due to the pressures of school. But even she needed time to reset herself. Reset, and restart.

With eyes closed she tried to let the hum of the idling bus soothe her. Vibrations travelled through the floor and her body toward the rivets and sliding frames of the widows. There they produced a rattle that needled its way into her tranquility. Passengers argued somewhere near the front of the bus, but Harriet refused to open her eyes and let their negativity infect her. She heard the rush of compressed air as the doors closed, felt the brakes release, and as the bus moved, Harriet couldn't help but smile.

"You don't mind if I sit here, do you?"

Her lids fluttered open. The bus's interior lights had been extinguished, but in the gloom she saw Charlie Hand seated across the aisle. Harriet recoiled, clutching her blue backpack to her chest, and prepared to scream. He raised his empty hands to calm her.

"It's okay, you're okay. See? I'm all the way over here. Nothing to worry about."

"I thought—" She relaxed her grip slightly. "You said you weren't going anywhere. That you lived in the station."

He shrugged. "Like, I don't even know you. Do you blame

me for being cautious? You never know who you're going to meet waiting for the bus."

His grin was meant as an olive branch, but Harriet found none of what was happening amusing.

"Are you following me?"

"What? To Barrie? No, no way. I have no plans to set foot there. Once we get to Orangeville I'll be getting off. That I can promise."

"Oh, I see," she replied, swallowing her dread. They were going to the same station, though thankfully he didn't realize it. But how would she exit the bus without his knowledge? She considered staying on and riding the bus to its next stop then doubling back, but quickly came to her senses. No, she would have to find another way. Maybe if she let him go first, she could ask the driver to wait a few minutes until it was safe for her to disembark. He would do that, wouldn't he? Didn't they have to take extra steps to ensure their passengers' safety? Especially women? Especially at night? She was certain that was the case. Maybe as the bus got closer to Orangeville she'd call her father to pick her up from the station.

They rode in silence, Harriet and Charlie Hand, the tires of the Greycoach bus jostling them down Woolrich Road and through Fergus on their way to County Road 3. Harriet tried to look out the window at the passing trees and farms in the distance, but the dusk light was draining too fast from the sky, and what was once dimly lit became a series of silhouettes. Lights from the rows of small houses ignited one at a time in the coming gloom, and before the bus reached the turn onto the narrow side road the world had fully donned its endless cloak of night, smothering everything outside the windows in absolute nothingness. Fully submerged, there was no more to see in the ink black.

"These windows might as well be painted over for all the good they're doing us," Charlie Hand said. Harriet glanced over as he rapped on the glass. "Did you ever see that movie, 'Salem's Lot'? I saw it on TV when I was a kid. Scared the hell out of me. That kid in his pajamas floating outside the window, knocking to be let in? Like, that's pretty twisted."

She smiled politely and dismissively before turning back to the window where there were no floating children; just her own blurry reflection staring back, scarred face repeated in both panes of the insulated glass, one off-set in the other. She squinted, looking for anything in the night outside to distract her, and found a tiny light barely visible, its exact location impossible to pin down. It might have been a few feet away or a few miles for all she knew. It followed the Greycoach for some time, flickering in and out behind trees and houses, and it was only when it finally vanished for good that Charlie Hand decided to speak again.

"It's so strange how grey everything gets at night. You look around and it's like you're in a black and white movie. Nothing seems real."

"It's the rods," Harriet said, unable to stop herself.

"What rods?"

She cursed herself for speaking, and for her inability to leave the question unanswered.

"Your eyes have these rods and cones. That's how you see. The cones are newer. More evolved. They work best in bright light and register colours. But when there's low light they don't work well, so you have rods. They only register black and white. That makes them better for seeing in the dark."

"Huh. Bizzare. I guess my rods are working overtime, then."

Harriet shrugged but didn't say anything, hoping it was the end of their conversation. But Charlie Hand wasn't done.

"So, like, how do you know all this stuff about rods and cones? I thought you preferred to not-play your oboe."

"I can play the oboe and still be interested in things. It's not one or the other."

"In other words, you contain multitudes."

He grinned wide at her and suddenly she wondered if he already knew all about rods and cones. Was he being polite by hiding it, or laughing at her? And was he still laughing? She had her suspicions.

"It's actually pretty impressive you know so much about how we see in the dark," he added. "Kind of weird, but impressive. Darkness is so fascinating, but like no one else ever notices. I mean, everyone sees the dark as this horrible thing, you know? I've never seen it like that. Sometimes, I feel like the only one who gets the truth. You ever feel like that? Like everyone else is blind to something but you?"

"No, never," Harriet said. Then, after a moment, with reluctance: "Maybe sometimes."

"Really? When?"

It was a long time before she spoke. In the silence, she wrestled with how much she wanted to divulge—and whether she was afraid Charlie Hand would become more interested in her or less.

"Sometimes at school. When I'm practicing, or I'm studying. Or just sitting in the University Centre, watching everybody. They don't care about anything. But they should. They should care about being the best they can be, and not give up on themselves. They shouldn't settle for being average. But that's all everybody I see wants, and I know deep in me that they'll regret it one day when it's already too late. I won't make that mistake. I can see the truth. I mean, I think I can."

Something in her gut twisted as she realized she'd said too much. The dark of the bus made it too easy, made her too confessional. Ashamed, she refused to look up, too afraid to see the expression on Charlie Hand's face.

"I understand," he said, and his voice was quiet and even and not at all like the voice he'd used before. It wasn't arrogant or judgmental or sympathetic. It was plain and human, and Harriet wondered if anyone had ever spoken to her like that before. Then she wondered if she'd ever given them reason to. When she finally dared to face him, Charlie Hand wasn't watching her. His head was tilted back and he was staring at the ceiling of the bus. Outside his window was the starless sky.

"How about you?" she asked, eager to alleviate the suffocating awkwardness. "What's the truth about the dark you think only you get?"

He didn't move, didn't blink; she wasn't even sure he'd heard her. Then, Charlie Hand took a deep breath and maybe closed his eyes—it was too dark to be sure. But they were open and bright when he looked at her.

"I bet you're like everybody else; you only see the dark one way. You see it as a negative. Like it's subtraction, the end of something. The light dies and fades to darkness. And it doesn't matter if it's light, or if it's life. The dark equals decay. A transition from something that *is* to something that *isn't*. Like a corruption of an ideal toward chaos and absence.

"I get it. Life teaches you to think that way. Everything you've seen in your textbooks and from your parents and teachers and institutions tells you to run away from the dark, from the void. The dark is nothingness, and nothingness means the end.

"But they've got it all wrong. Like, it's actually the opposite. In nothing is everything. Darkness is actually perfection, the most perfect state there is. It's not the decay of light or life. It's when there is so much light, too much life, all the life, that it transcends what we know and understand and becomes something more than we can sense. It becomes nothing because we can't possibly grasp it all. So much is summed up that it travels past the understandable and becomes darkness, becomes nothing. When you grasp the truth of the dark, it's like grasping at an understanding you can't really have—of what exists beyond everything. But it doesn't just go beyond it; it kind of makes it irrelevant at the same time.

"Like, okay," he continued, holding his hands before his beaming face, fingers spread apart, speaking faster. "Let me put this another way. Imagine the most beautiful song you've ever heard, yeah? Now imagine it's even more beautiful than that. Imagine it's like this perfect song, so perfect it actually *transcends* sound. It's so perfect you can't even hear it because it's beyond what you can experience. In that silence is the sum of every note.

"But it's not just every note. Now it's also every painting,

21

it's every word. It's every tree. Every person. It's everything. Think of the Big Bang. First, there was nothing. Then there was everything. Or the Bible. First, there was nothing, then God created everything."

He stopped abruptly and looked at Harriet.

"Sorry," he added, slower. "I get a bit carried away by all this."

"It's okay," she said. "It's...it's sort of a beautiful idea, I guess."

He snorted.

"I recognize that tone. You're humoring me."

"No, I—"

"I don't blame you. You've been programmed, and programming is really hard to break. But just because you don't see it doesn't mean I'm wrong. It just means you're not looking hard enough."

Was she really having such a bizarre conversation? It all seemed so strange. Maybe it was the dark of the bus, or the monotony of the road beneath them. Or the way he spoke, which was quiet, but not too quiet to hear—the edges she'd heard earlier in the station worn off. Or maybe it was everything, together, crowding her thoughts. She didn't know what to do but nod along as he spoke.

"But I think you get what I'm talking about, even if you don't know it. It's there, it's part of you, and you just have to learn to see it. Sort of like those rods and cones—maybe there's one more piece of your eye that you need to turn on."

"What makes you think I have any idea what you're talking about?"

"Do you remember what I asked you earlier while we were still in the bus station?"

Harriet thought for a moment. "I have no idea."

"I asked why you seem so lonely. You didn't tell me, but I want you to now. Think for a second, then honestly, tell me."

"But I'm not—"

He raised his hand.

"Think about it. Then tell me."

Harriet folded her arms. She wasn't going to tell him anything, let alone something so personal. But as he stared at her, waiting, memories of Martin Baxter floated unbidden to the surface. Memories she couldn't dispel.

"I don't really—"

"I know," Charlie Hand said. "But tell me anyway."

"I don't think of myself as lonely," she started slowly, reluctantly, unsure she wanted to tell this story to anyone, especially a stranger like Charlie Hand, but unable to stop. "But I guess it's been harder to make friends than I expected. When I was fifteen, I snuck out of the house with my friend, Janice Rinder, to go to a field party in Tottenham, just outside of Beeton. We met these two guys there who promised to drive us home. They were both nineteen, and just starting school, so they seemed older and more mature than anyone we knew. One of them, Glen something—why can't I remember his last name?—rode in the back with Janice. I rode in the front with Martin Baxter. I had no idea what I was doing. I'd never done anything like that before—my parents always taught me to be responsible, but I was just a kid, and I was tired of being responsible. I was tired of doing my chores and going home after school to study and practice. I wanted more and didn't know how to get it.

"So, the four of us were driving down Baedeker Road, just alongside Finnegan Lake, and Martin pointed up and said 'Look at all the stars you can see when there aren't any streetlights.' And I thought, if there's that many now, what would happen if there were no lights at all? So, I reached over him and I think he thought I was going to touch him because he didn't stop me, but instead of touching him I flipped the car's headlights off. I just meant to do it for a second. There was some yelling, but I was too busy trying to look out the window before Martin turned them back on.

"I don't remember anything else until I woke up in the hospital a week later, my face bandaged and my insides feeling like sandpaper when I moved. It was a few more days before I found out what happened. A moose had walked into the road when the lights were off, and Martin had driven straight into it. It was like driving into a brick wall. He was killed instantly—so was that moose—and though Janice and Glen were alive, they were still in the hospital and didn't want to see me. I never spoke to either again. I thought when I got to Guelph it would be easier because here I'm not the girl that killed Martin Baxter. Here, I'm no one, so no one stares at me when I walk by. No one judges me. Except, it still feels like they are. All the time. And it hasn't got any better.

"And it's all because I wanted to see some stars."

Harriet sniffled. Charlie took a few tissues from his lumpy pockets and sorted one out for her.

"How was that?" she spit, anger floating beneath her barely maintained composure. "Was it everything you hoped for?"

"I don't know about hope," he said. "But it proves to me I was right, that you're capable of seeing more than you think. More than people have let you see until now. I just have one more question: what did it feel like? Right then when you first put the lights out and it was just you alone in the dark? For that one second, where were you?"

"What kind of question is that?"

"A serious one. Just think about it. Just for a second. Where were you?"

"I was... I..." It was the last thing she wanted to think about, desperate to keep her distance from the pain, but she couldn't help but be dragged back.

"I..." She started to remember that night, the smell of the wind, the sea of tiny starlights. "I was someplace happy, I guess. From what I can remember, just for that second, I was happy."

"That's what I'm talking about. You do understand it, because that's a moment—a fleeting moment—that you transcended. You found everything inside that nothing."

Harriet was quiet, confused. He sounded like those first-year philosophy students who tried to impress each other during midnight ramblings at the Brass Keg, but there was also something in what he said that rang of another truth, one that filled her stomach with ice. The skin of her face tightened around the length of her scar, and she ran her finger along it to soothe the sensation before realizing Charlie Hand was watching her. She dropped her hand to her lap, but he continued to stare for a few seconds too long, then nodded as though reaching a conclusion.

But before he could reveal it, the driver slowed the bus and announced "Orangeville" over the Greycoach's crackling speakers.

"This is my stop," Charlie Hand said, removing his pack from the seat and slinging it onto his shoulder. "Listen, I'm sorry about your accident. That sucks. But, like, you experienced something most people never will, and even those that do won't ever really understand it. That's something special, regardless of whatever shit you had to deal with afterward."

He stood in the aisle, holding on to the back of the seats on either side of him as the bus made its turns toward the approaching station.

"How much further are you going, anyway? I'm not even sure I know exactly where Barrie is, to be honest."

"It's further up. Just off the lake."

He grimaced as the bus pulled into its spot at the station. "That's pretty far," he said. "It's going to be a long ride." At the front of the bus, the other passengers had stood as well, all preparing to disembark. "So, I guess this time it really is goodbye."

"I guess," she said, but Charlie Hand didn't wait for her answer. He had already turned around and was stepping off the bus. He did so without a glance back at Harriet, who was still sitting in her cramped seat, hugging her blue backpack to her chest. Through the window, she saw the station, saw the small number of future passengers milling and waiting. Within the sparse crowd Charlie Hand appeared, lumpy green jacket and khaki pack standing out among them. All Harriet needed to do was wait. Just long enough for him to leave the station so she might slip out behind him. Just wait long enough for—

The sour-faced driver was nearly knocked over by her blue backpack as she dashed from the bus. "Sorry," she called back, but was too frazzled to worry whether he'd heard her. It was imperative she catch up with Charlie Hand. She didn't know why, she just—she had to understand better what he had told her. What it meant. There was something, some truth she wasn't quite grasping.

The passengers in the station did their best to block her as though sensing her approach, but she pushed past their interference and searched for that army jacket, that khaki pack. What caught her attention first, however, was his halo of golden hair bobbing over the shoulders of the people that separated them. Harriet forced herself through as she struggled to catch up. When she finally reached him, she lay her fingers on his back and he turned around. Only then in her breathlessness did she realize she had nothing to say.

"Hey," Charlie Hand said, though his warmth quickly turned to confusion. "Wait, shouldn't you still be on the bus?"

"It's—" she grasped for words at the same time as breath. "It's my stop. Too. It's my stop."

"You're not going to Barrie?"

She shrugged, her panting slowing. "I don't even… know you. Can you blame me? You… never know who you're going to meet."

He laughed, put his hand lightly on her shoulder. Then lifted it to cup her face. Startled, she lifted her own hands to pry his away, but stopped. He ran his thumb over her scar. She closed her eyes.

"The accident?"

She nodded.

"Let me show you something."

He glanced around to ensure no one was paying them attention. Satisfied, he rolled the sleeve of his army jacket and then the sleeve of the old wool sweater he wore beneath before stretching his forearm out like an offering, rotating it under the halogen lights. What she saw could not be real. The flesh on his arm looked as though it had once been torn to pieces and then imperfectly reassembled, a web of shiny scar tissue woven over the length of his forearm. "Once I finally understood about the darkness and what it truly was, that understanding—like, I don't know how to say this in a way that will make sense—it was so powerful it literally ripped my flesh off. I was in the rear stacks of the McLaughlin Library, inside one of the study rooms, piecing the truth together, when suddenly it was *me* on the floor in pieces. It wasn't a dream; it wasn't a hallucination; it wasn't a vision. I was torn apart, experiencing an agony beyond anything I could have imagined, and that agony lasted until it didn't. Until I opened my eyes and found myself reassembled. But I'm not the same, and I'll never be the same, but I understand. This scar?" He ran his thumb over her wound again. "It's the same for you, whether you want to admit it or not."

Harriet's fingers tightened their clutch on her purse, on the strap of her blue backpack. Charlie Hand rolled down his sleeve without looking at her, though she couldn't help but look at him.

"I think you're right," she said finally.

He glanced up. Smiled. And his round blonde face was a sun inside the worn Orangeville bus station.

"We've come all this way," he said. "Now will you play me something?"

"What? Right here?"

"Yeah. Right here in the station. Right now. Don't overthink it. Just…" He held his hands in front of him and spread them apart in an arc. "Just, like, play."

Harriet glanced at the few people still loitering at the edges of the station or sitting in the hard green plastic chairs. She set her purse on a seat and lay her dark wool coat beside it. From her blue backpack she removed her oboe case and opened it. The reed was dry, as was her mouth, but she found enough saliva to moisten them into working. She touched the reed with the tip of her tongue, then stopped.

"I don't know what to play."

"It doesn't matter," he said. "You'll never see any of these people again. Just dig inside of you and play something. Whatever is right. You'll know what it is."

She nodded and put the reed back to her lips.

The notes came easily from the oboe—first slowly, then in a steadily increasing stream. As she played she saw them, little dark spots spilling from the bell, tiny motes circling her arms and shoulders in trailing wisps. The others in the station turned to look at her, some beaming as her notes carried. Charlie Hand sat cross-legged on the floor by her feet, hands on his knees as he swayed in rhythm, and as her fingers brushed the keys the station grew dimmer, the dark notes the oboe brought forth accumulating above, forming dense clouds that crowded out the lights. But the way the notes felt... it was as though they were desperate to be free, dancing as they cascaded from the instrument—from her—in fantastic waves, each one burning through her like a spark, each burning more than the one it followed.

The lights grew dimmer still, and in this twilight the past and future Greycoach passengers surrounding her were absorbed into the new darkness, became a part of it. But still she played. Even when the crowding night swallowed the headlights of the buses outside, she played; even when it swallowed the chatter of voices and the hum of the vending machines, she played. She played while the smell of stale floor cleaner and worn rubber soles and old plastic chairs slipped away. Played while the sunshine face of the smiling and elated Charlie Hand sank, too, into the darkness that encroached upon her. Harriet played for as long as she could, played until the sound of her music was gone; played until she could no longer hear her own breathing, her own heartbeat, and all that remained was dark; until there was nothing and that nothing was everything and it went on and on and on and on and on.

And when she finally opened her eyes, all she saw was light.

OUR TOWN'S TALENT

———————— ❧ ————————

It's always the final event of the school year, which means it's late June and it's hot and sweltering when we gather outside the gymnasium doors, dressed perhaps too informally in our summer skirts and blouses. Our children have been preparing for the annual talent show for weeks, though for some of us it seems no time at all has passed. No matter how early we begin to sew costumes or help practice routines it always feels as though we've started too late, and the date of the show is rushing too fast toward us. We are never as prepared as we'd like, but we've grown used to being in such a state.

With the children already ushered into the school for a final rehearsal, we use the time outside the green gymnasium doors to compare notes on our travails and laugh at how cute our daughters and sons look. Some of us show photographs to the other mothers, or display a talent of our own by re-enacting the moments of last-minute terror suffered by our littlest ones. We know from experience that the show will be tough for us to endure, with long stretches of boredom until our golden child is lit on stage, but those few moments in which they'll perform will be the subject of memories and recordings that will last forever on the digital tapes and in the boxes of photographs we'll store at the backs of our closets or in the furthest crooks of our attics.

When the time arrives, Mrs. Jaworski opens the green gymnasium doors for us to enter. Inside, we find walls covered in blue mats, and above them construction-paper art of varying quality decorates the room for the show. There are electric fans blowing from every corner, circulating the heat instead of dissipating it. We file between rows of folding plastic chairs and seat ourselves in small clustered pockets, designated by those cliques that have formed over time in our town. Such groupings are natural, but unlike what we've heard about the next town over, where the wives are often at odds with one another, our cliques are comparatively tame and relatively friendly. All the wives are polite with one another, and we hope this lack of animosity is due to more than how infrequently we have cause to meet—the annual talent show might be the only time the entire group of wives is together at once.

Few of us attended this school as children, but we all recognize it from our past. Gymnasiums, they are all the same, no matter where or when. They all smell of stale children and floor wax; all are covered in scuffs and scrapes, with painted courts chipped away by time and hundreds of rubber-soled feet. If we close our eyes, we can almost imagine being back at the one from which we graduated so many years ago, feel the pressure of its walls fencing us in, remember the way our voices reverberated off the painted concrete walls during school assemblies. Gymnasiums don't change, the people in them change.

The crowd settles into silence as we feel the electric anticipation in the air; the show about to start. Already, some of us have drawn our cameras from pockets and purses in preparation. Music plays through the loudspeakers, and we recall wistful memories of how it used to be, back when the student band was expected to perform some warmly out-of-tune standard.

A dour Mr. Peavoy takes the stage, wearing the same grey suit he wears to every parent-teacher meeting and every school event. We sometimes wonder what he must be like at home, if he wears that same suit to weddings and funerals, if there is a Mrs. Peavoy and if we might ever meet her. We wonder if she cuts his hair and looks at him with mischievous eyes. Or has he no wife at all? No one really knows Mr. Peavoy because he doesn't live in the town with us. All we can do is wonder.

Mr. Peavoy introduces the first child and we recognize her immediately. Little Jennifer Branston with her rusty hair and tightly-clustered freckles. She's wearing a bright orange sweater and green trousers, and on her head is an old floppy-brimmed hat, the sort we used to wear when we were young, just before we met our husbands, when we'd picnic in parks and laugh with our friends. When we wore hats like that, we wore them with the sort of seriousness reserved for French films and French cigarettes. When Jennifer Branson wears it, it's funny because it doesn't fit her apple-shaped face, and unsettling because it reminds us of who we once were.

Jennifer lifts the hat and three red and blue rubber balls spill out unexpectedly. They bounce across the stage, and she dashes to retrieve them while we laugh, unable to help ourselves. It's a darling scene. When she has them back under control of her tiny hands, she's panting heavily, and looks to the crowd only to become stunned by the faces watching her. We hear whispered reassurances urging her on, and from somewhere in the dark there is the flash of a camera. Jennifer Branston blinks her rusty eyelashes twice and then tosses one of her red and blue rubber balls into the air, and then another, and then the third. Round and round, little Jennifer Branston juggles them, concentrating as the gymnasium fills with applause. But she doesn't seem to enjoy our response as she's too focused on keeping those rubber balls aloft. The excitement dissipates quickly, the novelty of the act faded for us after so many years and so many children repeating the same routine, and it isn't long before Mr. Peavoy appears from the edge of the stage, clapping and smiling his same tired smile, as omnipresent as his grey suit. Little Jennifer Branston catches her balls and looks to him with confusion and no small relief. When he says her name we all smile warmly and clap, and she bows and dashes from the stage and to her freedom.

Mr. Peavoy introduces the next act, Jimmy Parker, whose parents moved to our town fewer than six months ago. They still have the air of the city about them, always rushing, always anxious, and Jimmy parrots them with his jittering hands and fierce blinking. Once Mr. Peavoy abandons him onstage Jimmy clears his throat and shifts from foot to foot, glancing above as though the instructions on what to do are written there. We grow uneasy, wondering if the show will derail itself on only the second child, and Mr. Peavoy's presence at the back of the stage, not quite hidden by the curtain, only further discomforts us. But before he can intervene, before we can't hold our breaths any longer, Jimmy's ticks settle down and he steps forward to sing a song we remember from our childhood summers, though we have never heard it like this. It's a talent show, after all, so none of us should be too surprised, and yet the voice that emerges from Jimmy's mouth seems incongruous with his perfectly round head and squinting eyes. Some of us even cry as we hear him sing, which is often a sign, though we aren't sure of what.

When the song ends, Jimmy exaggeratedly bows, and respectfully we clap, just as we do for the rest of the children that take the stage afterward, offering encouragement for all the talent that hides within our local elementary school. There is Leeann Grayson and her baton twirling, Susanne Costello and her rudimentary gymnastics, and Stephen Liebert with a guitar that is far more expensive than his talent or interest warrants. We know Stephen's mother well, and it inspires more eye-rolls than surprise from most of us.

The show takes two hours to complete, and culminates in a long line-up of all the participants, bowing again from the stage to audience's applause. Or at least the attempt is made, as it's clear to us that Mr. Peavoy's ability to wrangle that many children into a single task remains limited. Still, more camera flashes go off, and we hear soft weeping from the crowd as some of us are overcome with pride and love for our children. Once again, the annual talent show is a success.

But that success is short-lived. We typically don't hear or

say much about the talent show once the evening has passed, other than a few words in passing about how great it was to see each other again, and my didn't the Tavares girl look nice, before continuing on our way to run our errands or push a stroller through Brookbanks Park. Instead, this year, for the first time that anyone can remember, we hear rumblings that not everyone felt moved by the talent show. The whisper travels through the town, from ear to ear in the corner mart, between the stacks in the library, on the breeze through the local coffee house patio. Those of us paying attention hear it most outside the school when we're collecting our children, spurred by the pained expression Mr. Peavoy makes as he patrols the halls at the end of the day. It's more than marital trouble for once, we gather.

It's Mrs. Parker. We are not surprised to hear it, since she and her family are still so new to the town and unfamiliar with our ways, but the vehemence of her displeasure takes us all aback. To her, it appears her son's talents were not properly showcased by our "tar paper shack of a school" and, even worse, the notion that her son was not crowned the most talented child of the show was an insult of grand proportions. The word among us is that had she known there would be no winners, she never would have allowed him to participate. Perhaps not even moved from their unnamed coastal city to our small land-locked town. The words, even second-hand, are biting, and we all experience a mixture of embarrassment and anger upon hearing them. Our town is not wealthy, but it is *our* town, and we have chosen to celebrate all our children rather than pit them against one another. Mrs. Parker or no, we don't expect that to change.

But expectations are funny things, especially in the face of the unexpected. It doesn't take long before talk of Mrs. Parker and her distress over her son's experience at the talent show fades from our conversations, replaced with casual commentary about the weather and the ripeness of fruit at Edmund's Market. No one remembers the incident with the talent show at all. Or, at least, if they remember, no one thinks to mention it. It's done and in the past and we, the wives and mothers of the town, don't like to dwell on such distasteful things.

Which is why we find it surprising to hear about the other talent show. At first, it's difficult to even understand what that means. Is the school holding a second Autumn event, so close to the start of the school year? We eventually come to understand that neither the school nor Mr. Peavoy have anything to do with it. The other talent show is to take place shortly before Hallowe'en, in the acres behind Mrs. Parker's house, and all our children are welcome to participate. This is how many of us learn about Mrs. Parker's Talent Show—it is our children who tell us, all to a one excited there's another show coming where they might perform their newly practiced routines. We're wary of the unusual nature of such an event, not to mention the suggestion that our own event is somewhat lacking, but some of us make the case that Mrs. Parker should be allowed to hold any event she chooses, and wouldn't *more* community events be better than fewer? More chances to see one another outside our tiny groups and cliques, away from our husbands and household errands? We don't all agree, but even those who don't aren't able to discourage their children from demanding to be part of Mrs. Parker's show, and soon it seems that the unexpected has arrived, and has brought with it the unknown.

So we once again help our children prepare. We watch them practice and recite their lines. We sew their costumes and suffer their disappointments on the way to success, and when the day comes for Mrs. Parker's Talent Show we arrive at her house to find her acres decorated more lavishly than anything the school could have done. There is food laid out among whispers of caterers, and amid the fallen leaves there is a wooden stage erected that no doubt cost more than many of our husbands earn in a month. There is no Mr. Parker present, as the encroaching end-of-the-year banking requires his full attention, so Mrs. Parker stands alone among the folding chairs with a wide smile on her face, as close an approximation

34

to friendliness as we have yet seen from her. She thanks us each for coming to the show, then helps us herd the children away to prepare.

We mill and chat as we are wont, but this time there is an air of hesitant caution, of unfamiliarity, of confusion bordering on suspicion. We are not used to seeing one another in such surroundings, drinking punch and nibbling on finger food. We wonder what to expect from Mrs. Parker as this sort of display is unheard of in our town, but before we can form any conclusions recorded music begins to play through the rented speakers behind the stage. We all take our seats and watch with dread anticipation what Mrs. Parker has in store for us.

She emerges immediately, clutching a stack of note cards. She has donned a dark blazer tapered close to her narrow waist, as though it will add some formality to the proceedings. She does not remind any of us of Mr. Peavoy, other than by how much she differs from him, and by how strange it is to attend such an event in the middle of the day in the cool sunshine. Talent shows in our town have always been for the night, for the dark. It's just how it's done, and Mrs. Parker is doing it differently. None of us are quite sure yet if she's doing it wrong.

She introduces herself despite us knowing who she is, then she introduces the judges for the event. Mrs. Sisson, Mrs. Nixon, and Mrs. Ainley all look uncomfortable in their assumed roles, chosen for their impartiality and childlessness, yet likely wondering why they agreed to subject themselves to such a perilous job. They worry how we might treat them, but their worry is unfounded. We are too unsure of what to think about any of what we're witnessing.

When the first child takes the stage, we all brace ourselves for what's to come. Suzanne Kirby appears from behind the curtain, carrying with her a small box shaped like a miniature treasure chest. She is dressed in white tights and a violet ruffle around her waist like a skirt, and her hair is pulled back against her skull, bound in a knot at the top of her head.

SIMON STRANTZAS

She pads nervously to the centre of the stage and puts the box down before opening the lid. Gentle music plays, and it is louder than it should be from such a tiny object. Are the speakers amplifying the sound so it will reach us? It's a quiet, haunting tune, plinked out by metal tines, and to its rhythm Suzanne dances. Or, if not dances, then glides. It's as though her feet all but touch the floor of the stage as she sweeps back and forth, tiny arms periodically affecting the letter V, then O. She arcs her body at the waist and kicks her legs in the air as though it's water, sending her upward and away from the ground. She hangs long enough to spin her body like a top, the axis running from head to foot. It's the most amazing dance we have seen in the history of the town's talent shows, and we wonder how the extra few weeks have allowed Suzanne to transcend gravity. It's only on her final scissor kick that her buoyance dissipates and her tiny cloth shoes smoothly meet the floor. When she comes to a stop, Suzanne Kirby raises her head one last time and performs a closing bow with arms drawn to her side like folded wings.

We clap of course at the remarkable skill Suzanne Kirby has displayed. We agree it's like nothing she has shown before in the past talent shows, those put on by Mr. Peavoy at the elementary school. Perhaps, we mutter among ourselves between acts, Mrs. Parker's idea of a separate show has merit after all. We still find it distasteful that Mrs. Sisson, Mrs. Nixon, and Mrs. Ainley must judge which of our children is the most talented, but perhaps that competition is what sharpened little Suzanne Kirby's resolution to dance better. Our jaws remain agape as we wonder who will take the stage next, and how their talent could ever complete with what we've already beheld.

And when blonde Billy Brooks steps out from behind the curtain, our hearts quicken. Around his neck he wears the oldest and ugliest tie possible from his father's closet, and in his hands he carries a wooden dummy that nearly dwarfs him. The dummy's eyes bulge and rotate, and its limbs are strung loosely at the joints so its pendulous arms swing freely.

36

Otherwise, the dummy looks like Billy. It wears the same jacket, and its punched-in hair is styled just as Billy's is, though its colour is a shade too blonde. Billy Brooks's chubby head bobs and turns red as he heaves the dummy onto his lap and his wooden twin turns to address the audience.

The act startles many of us. Far from the conversational repartee we've seen from Billy Brooks at past talent shows—a mixture of vaudevillian jokes and simple songs—he has transformed the act into something closer to a mentalist routine. He announces the dummy's name is Billy Jr. before asking for a volunteer who might stand and repeat a simple innocuous phrase. Mrs. Ryan does so, and once the words are spoken Billy Jr. makes a rattling sound with its wooden jaw, pumping the neck up and down as though caught on a syllable it cannot speak. Then those large round eyes roll forward and the dummy announces a truth about Mrs. Ryan that is clear from her expression Billy should not know. Mrs. Ryan is visibly upset by the revelation, and by the reaction it causes in the audience, for we are all unnerved to hear it. Mrs. Ryan collects her things immediately and flees from the rows of rented chairs and away from Mrs. Parker's house. Billy scolds Billy Jr. and the dummy just laughs, though we notice it never takes its eyes from Mrs. Ryan as she flies.

We are all surprised by the chain of events, despite many of us doubting it was anything more than an elaborate ruse. Doesn't Billy's mother know Mrs. Ryan? None of us are certain. None of us remember.

We are anxious to discuss it, looking from one to another, filled with compulsive desperation, but there is no time. Before any of us can act, Mrs. Parker has returned to the stage, smiling and ushering Billy Brooks off while announcing her son's return. Jimmy strides out from behind the curtain, passing young Billy and his dummy without a glance. Billy does not turn either, but Billy Jr. does, its head swiveling around to watch Jimmy take centre stage. We feel restless.

Music plays through the speakers. It's not a song we recognize, but we agree it's beautiful, filled with sweeping woodwinds. It builds slowly while Jimmy remains before us, eyes closed, in a practised pose that suggests he's absorbing every note, and those notes are accumulating within him. When the song reaches the crescendo of its introduction, Jimmy appears incapable of preventing his mouth from opening and with eyes wide he emits a sound so heartachingly sorrowful all chatter stops, including that from any nearby birds. Everything quiets in the presence of the song he sings. What is strange, though, is none of us listening hears it the same way. For some, it evokes specific memories of our childhood, of sitting with long-gone parents in front of an old phonograph. For others, it reminds us of friends and loves long lost, of those taken by the flowing rivers of time. There are also some who remember none of these things or people, and instead have the empty holes within them uncovered, and who feel the ache of that emptiness bend apart their bones in an effort to escape. The song affects us all, including Mrs. Parker, who stands in the wings of the stage, openly weeping, smiling proudly if not happily.

And, still more children perform, each with a talent so honed it's as incredible as the one that preceded it. We watch amazed from the gallery with the knowledge that Mr. Peavoy's shows will never be the same again. They will remain the refuge of the youngest children, perhaps, too young to know better. But, the older children? There can be no going back for the older children.

Mrs. Parker is smug when all the acts are complete and the judges are deliberating. She stands apart from us and behind her son, both arms over his shoulders and crossed at the wrist, her chin resting on his head as she awaits the verdict from Mrs. Sisson, Mrs. Nixon, and Mrs. Ainley—who all have been comparing notes for a quarter of an hour while we watch and patiently wonder if the effort and expense was enough to buy Jimmy his award. Not that any of us believe it wouldn't be warranted, though we feel the same about all the children. Each of them accomplished the incredible and should be as rewarded. But we have always felt this way about our children, about awards, which is why Mr. Peavoy and the school do not issue them. How will the children react, we wonder, when one of them is singled out and the rest swept aside? There is not much longer until we find out, and it makes us as nervous as they, if not more. Yet it's also worse for us as we can see the long line of failures ahead that may spring from this decision.

It's Mrs. Ainley who clears her throat, rises from her folding chair aside the stage. She is not a tall woman nor especially large, but her voice is loud and firm and no one questions what she says is truth. Mrs. Ainley stands and puts the bridge of her glasses on the end of her sloped nose and speaks at us over the frames. We hold our breath and listen. She informs us the judges have reached a verdict. She admits it was difficult, because so many of the children were so good, so talented, and that the judges wish they could make each one of them the winner as they all deserve it. She asks us to applaud our daughters and sons for all their hard work and we do so. Even Mrs. Parker, whose smile has tightened into place. Mrs. Ainley goes silent again, looks at Mrs. Sisson and Mrs. Nixon who are both pale and nervous. Mrs. Ainley clears her throat and announces the winner is Billy Brooks. The crowd applauds again and Billy Brooks takes the stage, Billy Jr. in hand and scanning the crowd with unblinking eyes, but we have shifted our attention to Mrs. Parker in order to evaluate her reaction. She continues to smile, though much like Billy Jr. that smile is painted on. Jimmy Parker looks up at her, first turning his head left, then turning it right, unsure which way is correct, because they both result in the same thing, the same truth. Mrs. Sisson, Mrs. Nixon, and Mrs. Ainley will not look at her. They will not look at any of us, as though they know what they've done will likely drive the Parkers from our town. How could it not? Mrs. Parker will know and remember every day what happened. No matter where she goes, she will see us and remember. It's better for her this way. Easier. If she goes, everything may go back to normal.

Yet she doesn't go. And even if she does, it's too late.

SIMON STRANTZAS

Nothing will ever be the same.

Because Mrs. Parker sparked an idea. An idea so ludicrous none of us would have considered it a few months ago, before the town's talent show. Before Mrs. Parker's talent show. It's an idea that is so bizarrely out of step with who we are that when it first surfaces we think it's a joke. We tell our husbands at night, when they've returned from work and are staring blankly into the dinner they're scarfing down, and it sounds like a joke as we're saying the words out loud. So we laugh, and our husbands grunt and nod and affirm the ludicrousness of the idea, and then remind us of the work that they have yet to finish before they disappear from our tables and rematerialize behind the closed doors of their make-shift home offices. We don't disturb them and instead tend to the children, reminding them that Billy Brooks's win does not mean they are somehow less or he somehow more, then put them to bed and assure them that everything will be better in the morning. And, all the while, we consider that idea Mrs. Parker has given us. Mull it over, roll it this way and that in our thoughts, examine and test it. It is indeed ludicrous, and a joke, and bizarrely out of step with who we are in the town, but it's also an idea that is curiously fascinating and we all tacitly agree it's one we'd like to explore.

And, so, yet another talent show is born.

This is not a public talent show, however. There are no signs or flyers. There are no decorations or designs. There is nothing that says to anyone, anywhere, what we are doing. We are the only people in town to know what is happening— the collective wives, the quiet and hidden voices. Each of us understands something that we cannot put into words, that for our husbands' work and our children's play we must necessarily fade into the background. But a talent show, our own talent show, a secret talent show? There, for a brief moment, we might shine.

It is weeks later in the cold of the winter, in a small barn hidden at the edge of town behind the widow Mrs. Morgan's home, that we gather for our secret talent show. Unlike outside the school gymnasium, or Mrs. Parker's acres, we don't speak to one another. There are nodding heads and the hints of perfunctory smiles as we pass, but no words and no meandering. The air is too cold for it, but it's more than the weather that keeps us silent. Fear, perhaps. Nervousness. Or the pleasant dread of anticipation and suspicion that once the secret talent show is over, nothing will be the same.

There are long benches in the barn arranged in rows like pews, and as we file in we take our seats on them. The small cliques and groups we've formed in town hold no sway inside the barn, and are summarily ignored if not dissolved. We are all ourselves in this place.

With no one guiding the show, there is no one to call the performers to the stage, and that initially delays us as we struggle with how to begin. But Mrs. Havagal stands, brushes errant straw from her wool coat, and walks to the front of the barn—to the presumed stage. She doesn't ask permission or introduce herself because why would she? She's one of us. She has taken the first step for us all.

Mrs. Havagal closes her eyes behind her thick-rimmed glasses, brown hair in a bob, tucked behind her ears. Her tiny mouth shrinks to a narrow line as she concentrates, and none of us speak. She trembles, perhaps from the cold, and holds her trembling hands out to the sides of her wide hips. There's the sound of a hiccup or a gasp but it's so tiny it barely carries, and then Mrs. Havagal seems to grow taller an inch at a time. But, no, we all realize, not taller; she's not growing but floating. Mrs. Havagal has left the straw-covered ground, and lifts a foot into the air, then with a quick jerk it's two feet. She hovers, her legs dangling while her eyes remain closed, and then she moves. With limbs remaining still, she tilts slightly forward and her body follows, bringing her closer to us until she's five feet away, then four, followed by three. Those of us in the front rows do not react with surprise or fear because there is none left. We all knew there was talent inside Mrs. Havagal waiting to be unleashed, and we feel lucky to have seen it. After a few moments, she travels slowly back to where she took to the air and, just as slowly, allows herself to sink to the ground. Only when her feet are firmly planted do her lips turn from white back to pink, and she opens her eyes to find us staring back. One of us claps, so we all do. She is flushed, and retreats to the benches with a smile. As she passes, some of us squeeze her hand in gratitude.

She is followed by Mrs. Patti-Carlson, who carries with her a large roll of burlap. Once before us, she unfurls the roll across the floor and picks it up by two corners, showing us that it's a large sack, the sort we might use to store root vegetables in our cold cellars. Except in her hands it's empty, and as if to prove it she turns it upside down and inside out and shakes it so vigorously her grey streaked braid of hair bounces against her shoulder. We nod in union and understanding. She rights the sack and gathers the sides until it's a small circle, then lays it on the barn's packed dirt floor. She carefully unties her navy blue sneakers and removes them, putting the pair off to the side, and then steps into the centre of the burlap circle. Mrs. Patti-Carlson bends to take hold of the edges, and draws the rough fabric up with her as she stands. Some of us lean forward, curious what she's going to do, while others lean back, not certain they want to know. When the sack is fully drawn up, it reaches just below her neck, so Mrs. Patti-Carlson shimmies herself down until the material completely consumes her, hiding her from us. And without allowing us time to breathe or blink, the sack drops to the floor, empty.

None of us moves, none of us speaks, too stunned by what we've just witnessed to fully comprehend it; and even as understanding trickles in, still we don't believe. Mrs. Patti-Carlson has vanished as surely as if she'd been plucked from existence.

As the full truth washes over us, some of us in the audience twist our heads, scouring the barn for where she might have reappeared—for what's a disappearing trick without the final reveal? But Mrs. Patti-Carlson doesn't reappear. She doesn't rematerialize. Mrs. Patti-Carlson is simply gone, swallowed by that burlap sack that lies beside her navy blue shoes on the packed dirt floor. The applause lasts for two minutes before it abates when Mrs. Tomkins takes the ad hoc stage.

She does so empty-handed. It's just her, dressed in a burnt red knit shawl, her blonde hair shorn close to her skull except for a handful on her scalp that has been brushed straight back. The hoops in her ears are small and numerous, stacked along the outside length of her cartilage. Without a sound and with long fingers, she bends and picks up the empty burlap sack, then folds it meticulously and places it in the gap Mrs. Patti-Carlson left on the bench. The empty shoes, Mrs. Tomkins places on top. We stare with anticipation as she completes these tasks, and when she returns to the front of the room we find our stare mirrored back, albeit with rheumy eyes that gaze deep into each of us, one after the other. When Mrs. Tomkins is done, she straightens herself, opens her frowning mouth, and speaks. The words are sharp and clipped.

Agnes. Sherry. Linda. Margaret. Cheryl. Delphine. Kim. Amanda. Marcy.

She points at each of us in turn and speaks our name, our given name. The name we had before we were married. Before we had children. She says our names and they sound strange aloud. Like words from some long lost and forgotten language.

Julie-Ann. Rebecca. Heidi. Lisa. Monica. Olivia. Gayle. Sonia.

Each of us is startled when she points at us, but as the list continues to grow, we feel the tenuous strings extending outward from deep within us, weaving us together. The bonds strengthen, and the words that are our names become something else, something more powerful. We start to understand the talent Mrs. Tomkins—we mean *Miranda* Tomkins is showing us. Only it's not a talent. It's a gift. The gift of connection. Because with connection comes sight. And as though waking from stupor, we waver only slightly as we find ourselves revealed.

When Miranda Tomkins finishes speaking our names aloud, our true names, we are collectively weeping, as weeping

43

is all we can do in the face of such complete understanding. Miranda Tomkins doesn't remain at the front of the barn, but instead nods to herself, then simply walks back to the bench, retrieves Harriet Patti-Carlson's belongings, and continues toward the barn's door. She pulls it open and cold air rushes in, reviving us. Into that cold, she walks, and one by one we follow.

We walk out of the barn, and away from the widow Olivia Morgan's home. We walk down Piccadilly Street and past Haughton Hardware. We walk until the storefronts of our town fade behind us and the telephone wires strung above dwindle. We walk for a long time, for much longer than we can guess. Long enough for our husbands to grow concerned, long enough for them to pack our children into the backseats of our cars and drive out in search of us. Some drive past and we see our children's pale faces pressed up against rear windows, their tear-swollen eyes imploring us to stop, to return home. But we don't listen. We don't speak. Sometimes, one of our husbands will grow angry enough at our refusals and pull the car to the side of the road. He will then leap from the door and attempt to drag his wife into the passenger seat. At these times, our steady march pauses, and we descend on her husband as though he were our own. We descend and protect our sister, ensure he cannot take her. What this means, what we've done, none of us are certain, as the memory is forgotten as soon we are out of sight of the car and its screaming voices. We abandon it behind us somewhere on the endless road.

We continue on, a single long parade of women, leaving behind encumbrances with each step, forgetting one more piece of the anonymous lives we once led, lives where our hidden talents were subsumed, where our shows never celebrated us. But we have seen the truth now, and that truth continues to lead us forward, lead us in the direction of the next town only a few dozen miles away. The town where they too have an annual talent show such as ours, though not quite so large or so memorable. But that will change. We will bring them something more, something permanent. We will teach the mothers and sisters and daughters of that neighbouring town the lessons we have learned, and help them understand the talent they still have within them. And when they do, they will be one of us, a part of our special talent show. And in the end each one of them will remember that they have their own name.

THESE LAST EMBERS

———————————— �֍ ————————————

The rocks rattled off the bottom of Samantha's car as she drove toward her childhood home. It had been years since she'd last seen it; years since she loaded up her car and left behind a life so much smaller than she'd ever wanted. Yet she was haunted by her twin brother's sunlit face staring at her from the front window, inconsolably distraught that the person he'd come into the world with was leaving him behind. But Lemule was not as driven as Samantha was driven; her twin didn't feel the need to escape the shrinking walls of the house. And their mother and father had become strangers to her, no more than landlords with unreasonable demands about when she might come and where she might go. A double set of handcuffs, restraining her completely. Buying that car, driving away, was like some Houdini trick. She shook her wrists once and was free.

Yet she was returning all the same. There was no avoiding the orbit of her life. Not forever. She'd managed to escape for a few years, managed to make it to the city and live amid the steel and the concrete, managed to earn enough that she could afford to live unencumbered by those she left behind. She thought of home only in passing, called only on occasion, and told herself that Lemule would be fine without her.

They had been so close. As close as twins ought to be. She was taller, lankier, with straight hair the colour of sand. His had been so dark it looked like ink against his skin, and his

47

eyes were bored so deeply into his skull they were but pricks of light in the dark. He had been so serious with everyone else, but with her he smiled and laughed and danced. With her, she liked to think, the true Lemule bled forth. Bled forth and became her dark mirror.

When her job ended, so did her money, and with that, the dream of freedom followed. She held out as long as she could but eventually her choices dwindled. If there were one beacon of light amid the storm clouds, it was that she would soon see Lemule again. Would soon hold him in her arms and tell him how much she loved him. It almost scared her, that love, flooding back so sudden and so fierce, as though building pressure over the years, waiting for her to open the valve. When the day came to pack her apartment and return to her family home, the tears she cried were not easy to understand.

The house remained unchanged in her mind's eye. There, it was framed with her memories, both sturdy and bright. The paint on the porch looked as it always had, peeled away in the corners by a series of children's nails. The windows stayed large and bright, with wooden frames flanked by a pair of nailed-down shutters. And yet, when the car pulled closer to the destination, creeping up the stone drive, she saw the house in the light of reality and wondered if she'd made a wrong turn somewhere. But it was impossible. There stood the mailbox with her parents' name stencilled across the side; there grew the large tree in the front yard, shorn of those lowest branches from which she and Lemule had once swung so freely; there remained the swing set her father had installed where the grass was once thickest and coolest on her summer-warmed skin. Yet the shapes of the windows looked different, the colour of the roof altered, the front door frame replaced. And, changed most of all, the dark stain of fire that had turned the rear of the house black.

Samantha sprinted from the car, slowing as she reached the house. It was clear the fire had been intense but contained, warping the back windows until they were too rippled to see through. Her childhood room had been located in that rear corner, and beside it the fire's epicentre: Lemule's room. Part of her fell into despair, her head swimming with memories of her past life with her brother, hiding, laughing, praying for escape. Everything had been consumed by burning darkness. Samantha walked the perimeter of the house, trying to gauge the nature of what had happened, but it was too much. She could not reconcile it all.

Had her family left? Vanished without sending her word? She couldn't believe it, yet how could the house be habitable? Her once proud mother could never have stood for such a thing. There was light reflecting out through the muddy window; a single bulb, and nothing more, no other sign of occupancy. Samantha swallowed and stepped to the front of the house. The light flickered, a shadow floating between it and the window, then extinguished completely.

It was only then, standing before the locked front door, that she realized she no longer had a key to the house, and understood how telling that was and how clearly it encapsulated her distance. She had to knock on the door as a stranger might and wait and hope someone was there. But how could they not be? Would it have been so easy to leave everything behind? She paused, realizing it was exactly what *she* had done so many years earlier. Samantha put her hand on the wrinkled wood and wondered if she should be able to feel her parents inside, feel her brother's radiating pain and anger at her abandonment. But she felt nothing.

The air smelled tangy as she waited, as though a campfire had been lit somewhere close. Memories of her and Lemule running hand-in-hand through the endless woods, hiding and laughing, suddenly overwhelmed her, and her fleeting smile was crushed by time's weight. If the cracked door didn't open, she did not know where she was meant to go.

But it did open, and it startled her, revealing her mother's face. The years had multiplied the creases, and she had a long sallow complexion. Her eyes bulged when she saw Samantha, wide enough that the cataracts floated in the light. But, Samantha hoped, at least some recognition might be suspended there, as well.

"May I help you?" the old woman said.

"It's me, Mom. It's Samantha."

She looked confused, and Samantha saw the panic swiftly accumulate. Her mother's old eyes darted back and forth, unable to focus, and she retreated into the house. Samantha heard her father's voice from somewhere inside, as deep as ever but without its former power. He asked what was wrong, but as he turned the corner and saw Samantha, saw the state her mother was in, he faltered.

"Samantha. You're home."

"Dad, what's wrong with Mom?"

He shook his head and put his arms around the old woman. Her mother's anxiety dissipated as he gently held her.

"You might as well come inside," he said. "You're here."

He led her mother into the living room. Samantha marveled at how unchanged, yet smaller, everything was—the kitchen was still a sunshine yellow, photographs of vacations still hung on the walls. But she suffered a niggling feeling something was not as it should have been, and when she leaned closer to inspect those photographs, she realized what was missing.

"Where's Lemule?"

Her father looked startled, glancing furtively at her mother for a sign she'd heard, but the woman obliviously continued staring at the runner on the coffee table.

Samantha couldn't decide where she should begin.

"Dad, what's happened here? When did you have a fire? What happened to Mom? Where's Lemule?"

He stood from his chair. Samantha remembered it so clearly, even beneath its patina of smoky grime.

"You've been gone a while, Samantha."

"I have," she said. "But I've called... I must have spoken to you since this happened." She counted backwards in her head from the date, but the number seemed too high to be right. "I can't believe you're still here. My room looks like it's gone, and Lemule's—"

50

Her mother sat up, eyes darting as she fidgeted in her seat. Samantha's father touched his wife's leg, but it failed to soothe her.

"Please, Samantha. You're upsetting your mother."

The woman was agitated, looking at the two of them for comfort. Samantha's father stroked her mother's head to calm her. "I didn't tell you because there was nothing you could do. It was only the back of the house. We didn't lose much."

She shook her head.

"Dad, you guys can't stay here. The house needs to be torn down. It's not safe. There's probably all sorts of mold and stuff floating around." She fought the urge to cough. "Why didn't L— Why are you still here?"

"It's complicated," he said. "Your mother can't leave."

"What do you mean she can't?"

"I mean she won't."

"Why not?"

Her father looked pained as he stumbled for words. A cold realization took hold of her.

"Dad," she said, unsure if she wanted to ask the question. "Where are all the photos of Lemule?"

A scream tore the air. Samantha's mother clawed at her husband, struggling like a terrified animal to get free. His old hands could not control her. The aged woman broke loose and fled into the hall.

"Goddamn it, Abby! Come back, here!" He turned to Samantha angry and flustered. "Just stay here."

But Samantha wouldn't. She followed as her father gave chase.

The old woman was in the hall, hurtling forward on tiny tired legs toward what had once been Lemule's bedroom. She tried the doorknob before her husband could reach her, but did not succeed in turning it in time. When Samantha's father took hold, her mother fought back with all her strength. He shook her, the veins standing along his pale spotted arms, and Samantha watched horrified as her mother flopped like a cloth doll.

"Stop it, Dad! What are you doing? You're going to kill her!"

She reached out and put her hands on her parents, forcing them apart. Her father's eyes were blind, but once the connection was broken she saw that blindness fade, his clenched fists weaken. Samantha's mother pulled away, slinking back to huddle by the bedroom door.

Samantha's father panted, a tremendous weight on his defeated shoulders.

"You don't know, Samantha. You don't know."

"I know that's not how you treat someone, Dad. I know that's not how you treat Mom." Her father looked away, but he didn't look ashamed.

"You don't know," he muttered.

She turned to her mother, who had her hands on the bedroom door, trying to work the lock.

"It's okay, Mom. Let me open it for you," she said, and reached for the knob. Her father yelled something, but it didn't mask the sound of the bolt unlatching from the plate, or Samantha's mother's sob as she charged forward.

"Don't go in there, Sam!"

The sight inside the bedroom was unbelievable. Samantha didn't know how to process the impossibility that stretched out before her. Hundreds and hundreds of trees as far as she could see. Those closest to her poked their canopies out through the room's charred roof, but beyond that circle the trees simply grew into the air without interference. There had been no evidence of a forest when she'd been outside the house only a few minutes earlier.

"Dad…"

There was rustling, animals running, scurrying through the leaf litter. There was a breeze, similarly sooty, but also damp and earthy. Her eyes welled.

"Dad…"

"Help me get her back," he said. Samantha's mother had run nearly a hundred feet into the dense forest, then fell to her knees screaming herself crimson. Oblivious to everything else, she desperately called out Lemule's name until Samantha and her father put their hands on her. At their touch she fought for escape, and it took their combined strength to drag her back into the house. Samantha let go long enough only to lock the door, and once done her mother's struggling immediately ceased. But she continued to pant and fidget anxiously. Samantha's father, sweating and shaking, suggested she be watched while he got her medicine.

"And for God's sake, keep that door closed. We're lucky she didn't go further."

Samantha held her trembling mother, stunned by what she had witnessed. Her legs were still damp from the underbrush.

"After the fire, the trees grew."

Samantha helped her father administer her mother's medication and put her to bed. She looked at her lying there, the blanket pulled over her chest, feeble and exhausted, and wondered if that was the sight from which she had been running for so long. Her mother reached out her shaking hand and touched Samantha's face.

"I'm glad you're home," she said, then rolled on her side and shut her glassy eyes. Samantha switched off the light as she and her father left the room.

In the living room, with only the single lamp between them, her father sipped his watered-down Scotch.

"I don't know what caused the fire. If Lemule knew, he didn't tell me. Your mother and I were worried about him after you left. He didn't handle it well. Lemule never seemed comfortable in his skin, but at least when you were home he was happy sometimes. I don't think he so much as smiled afterward. He spent most of his time in his room, which was where he probably was when the fire broke out.

"Your mother and I were coming home from the Legion when she asked me about the light. I saw it flickering ahead of us on the dark road, but it wasn't until we were closer that I realized that little light was our house on fire. The trucks were already here, hosing it down, and Lemule was standing across the road, watching the black smoke rising.

"We stayed at a hotel, but Lemule seemed overly anxious, and in the middle of the night he disappeared. Your mother lost her mind until we found him back here at the house. He was sitting by his bedroom door, his clothes covered in damp soot, and he wouldn't do anything but stare at the doorknob. I thought he'd finally snapped. But when he looked at me, he just looked lost.

"We stayed in that hotel for two weeks, waiting for the insurance adjuster to come by, and each day Lemule left for the house and spent longer here, staring at his door. When the adjuster came by, neither your mother nor I were here. Only Lemule. I don't know what he said to the man, but when the insurance office finally got in touch they didn't offer us anything. They found a loophole. Pretty much like they always do. And we couldn't afford to do anything else but move back home.

"I was furious when I found out, and I came right back here to confront Lemule. I found him standing this time, his hand hovering over the knob. I didn't understand what he was doing. Not until I opened the door and saw."

"I still don't understand what happened," Samantha said.

He shrugged.

"The fire unleashed something. I tried for a while to rip the trees out, but they grew so fast they were a foot thick overnight. Lemule wouldn't leave the hallway for days, even though both your mother and I begged him. She was terrified, and I tried to put her mind at ease but it didn't do much to soothe her. I told her he wouldn't be like that for long. And he wasn't. One more morning he was gone, the door to his room wide open. Initially I was happy; I thought he'd come to his senses. But your mother understood.

"The next day, she was gone too. She'd run off into that forest in search of him. I heard her calling his name, though I couldn't see where she was, and I was terrified of going after her in case I couldn't find my way back. So I waited, called to her every few hours, left the door to the bedroom open and hoped she'd come home. And she did, a week later. But she wasn't the same. She's never been the same."

An oppressive wave of sorrow flooded Samantha's body, but when she looked at her father's face, she saw nothing there. No hint of emotion for the woman he'd lost.

"And Lemule? Didn't he ever come back?"

He closed his eyes as the warmth of the Scotch and the late hour rolled over him. When he opened them again it was as though he were someplace else.

"No, and after what happened to your mother, it's better this way. If he's still out there, he probably isn't Lemule anymore."

✼

She left her father sleeping on the couch, disturbing him only long enough to take the drink from his hand and the glasses from his face. Even after so much time and so much change she still felt as though she'd never left, and the sensation filled her with a strange cocktail of nostalgia, happiness, and restlessness. But mostly it was sadness on seeing how time had undone parents and how her absence had undone her twin brother. Everything was so much the same, yet so unalterably different. The fire-stained house only underlined it.

The pattern of flames on the walls looked like wings, spread outward from the depths of the hall. She passed her parents' room, heard her mother's gentle wheeze as she side-stepped the patches of warped floor between her and her old bedroom. She remembered her youth spent behind that door, so much time with secrets and games, with thoughts of love and jealously and hate. The whole house smelled of *then*, lost forever, consumed by those flames. She peeked her head in and saw the remnants of her childhood hanging from the broken walls. Trophies lay in the blackened soot, ribbons fluttering on a corkboard. A pile of cracked wood and fallen singed plaster where her small desk had been. The air still smelled of melted plastic and wood, an unsettling odour like an apartment building incinerator. Everything was in ruins, everything she had left behind destroyed. She took a step in and her childhood crunched beneath her feet. Near the closet still hung the mirror she stared into every day growing up, but the photographs of her and Lemule tucked into edges were burnt away, leaving the glass beneath opaque with dark clouds.

The damage was worst on the wall that divided her room from Lemule's, as though most of the creeping flames resisted the urge to spread beyond the fire's epicentre. She brought her knuckles to the bubbled wall and rapped on it once as she'd done when she was a child in that secret language that no one but Lemule knew. A game of twins clinging to each other—one to find a home for her restlessness, the other restlessly wanting to cling to home. Samantha paused as she heard unseen pieces of sheetrock drop in the shadows to become swallowed by ash, and resigned herself to the utter destruction of her past.

Lost in her thoughts, it took a moment to understand the sound of falling pieces had synchronized into a recognizable rhythm. Still, she had to hear it a second time to convince herself it wasn't an illusion born of grief and loss. It was the response to her knock, the reciprocation only her brother knew. She wasn't asleep. It wasn't a dream. It was Lemule.

Samantha dashed into the hallway to find the source. The night's shadows had gathered in its depths, congealing at their darkest by Lemule's room. There stood the remnant of the bedroom door like a slab of obsidian, the gate to the heart of the extinguished fire. Samantha put her hand on the door and impossibly it felt as though it were still burning. She stretched the arm of her shirt over the knob, and twisted it enough that the black door swung inward precariously on its hinges to reveal the thick of the tremendous forest stretched out beyond.

Samantha gazed deep into the woods, unable to tell if it were day or night. The sun glinted through the canopy that towered into forever, but the shadows were long and deep and dark near the ground. Shapes moved in the distance between the trunks, slipping shadows cloaked by darkness. "Lemule!" she cried. "Where are you? Can you hear me?" Only the muted echo of her voice returned, multiplied and fractured by intricate webs of branches.

Whereas her room had shrunken to a compressed void of darkness, Lemule's had expanded, a big bang of life radiating outward. Instead of ashes, there were trees as thick as Samantha's waist and as tall as the sky; instead of the odour of melted plastic and electricity, there was a cool breeze and rustling leaves. The fire had burned away the room's edifice and revealed the unlimitedness that lay beyond. A growing forest, consuming everything that had once been there, transforming it into something else, something inarguably better.

Samantha stepped between the trees, her hands on the corrugated trunks for balance, her finger wrapping around crooked branches for support. When she looked into the towering canopy she felt vertiginous, and forced herself to stare at her own bare feet, willing them forward as they sank into the dirt and underbrush. Lemule's room went on forever, and as she walked she felt the grip of the house behind her weaken and fade with each progressive step until it was gone completely. Only then did she look back, but the walls, the door, had vanished into the mist rising from the forest floor, leaving her alone and abandoned in her brother's room.

Even after being so close to him for so long, thinking of him every day, speaking with him late into the night, sharing every joy and sorrow of her unlife until the day she left, she had never fully understood, not until she stepped into that forest, walked directly into its density. Amid the oppressive growth, she knew her brother as never before.

Ahead, in the thickest of the trees, there was a light, lit as though just for her, beckoning. She felt its tug and wondered if it were possible.

The journey towards it was not easy. Stones tried to trip her, low branches attempted to scratch her eyes, and though that light flickered out between thickening trunks, she was convinced it wouldn't truly vanish. It was a piece of her being, calling her home. She had only known that sort of love once before.

"Lemule!" she cried as she slowly approached, foot over bleeding foot. "Is that you, Lemule?"

There was no voice, but amid the chirping and rustling she heard a knock, soft and distant, that repeated the pattern her heart made on the inside of her chest. She moved toward that light and that light too moved toward her, dancing as Samantha gained ground. It appeared from behind the trees, growing in size, in shape, sprouting a pair of arms made of fire, legs of ash. Its head trailed a plume of black smoke so thick and long it curled upward around the branches as it continued its slow ascent into the sky. And yet it was all so familiar. As though from a dream she couldn't recall.

Lemule had been so many things to Samantha in her life, so much a part of her, that his movements were seared into her memory. She recognized the stoop of his walk, the way he carried his overgrown limbs and the swing of his arms. When she saw the shape step from behind a tree, dancing, engulfed in white flames that burned hot and reached into the sky, she understood. She did not glance around her, she simply stepped forward into the endless forest, stepped forward to meet the pair of outstretched arms reaching for her. They hugged her close, and she felt the warmth of his brotherly love engulf her as she, too, burst into cleansing flame.

THE FLOWER UNFOLDS

———————— ✿ ————————

Candice knew two unassailable facts. The first was she looked every day of her forty-five years; the second was she would never escape her job. She was stuck there forever. Some days were bearable, when the rest of the office staff, all fresh from college and eager, forgot she existed in her tiny cubicle near the rear exit, and she was able to fall into her head while her hands automatically did their work. But the rest of her time was a struggle to avoid dealing with any of them. Each had the same look when they saw her—pity, irritation, a hint of disgust. They did not want her around, and though they did nothing about it, the message was quite clear: she was not like them; she was not one of them; she would never be welcomed by them. If there was any salve at all, it was that few would last beyond the first four weeks, and fewer still beyond the first twelve. By the end of the year, they would be replaced by an entirely new group while she remained a permanent fixture at the back of the office.

At least the elevator was close to her. Sometimes she heard its drone as it crawled up and down Simpson Tower, delivering loads of people to and from their offices. From her desk she heard every gear jump and cable slip. The elevator sometimes ground, sometimes squeaked, and always shuddered and hummed, but it was a reminder that everything moved, everyone went places, and she could too. It was as easy as pressing a button. Sometimes imagining going made it easier to stay.

When her telephone rang, Candice jumped, unprepared for the sound. The small LED on its face reflected a series of zeroes in an aborted effort to display the caller's number. Instead, all Candice knew was it came from inside the network.

"Candice Lourdes. May I help you?"

"I need you in my office," said Ms. Flask.

Candice's knees wobbled as she stood. They had started complaining only a few months before, but it had taken her some time to realize it was not because they were injured, but because they were no longer young. It caused her to shuffle slightly down the corridor, and though the effect would subside in fewer than two minutes, it was long enough that the front office staff had a chance to watch her pass. Most simply ignored her, treated her as invisible, and as difficult as that was to bear, it was better than the alternative, which was a series of scowls. She felt her appearance wordlessly judged: her hair was too flat, they'd whisper, too oily; she didn't wear enough makeup, or fashionable clothes; her nose was too crooked, her jaw too square... She had never been more than average, but she had once been able to coast on her youth. Those days had regrettably passed her by, and the woman that remained felt defeated and disappointed whenever the subject of someone else's glare. She did her best to skirt the bank of cubicles and remain invisible, but it was hopeless.

She knocked on Ms. Flask's door and entered. Her manager sat behind a large oak desk, the only piece of permanent furniture in the office. Her ear was to her telephone's receiver, and she motioned for Candice to sit. Flask's face was red and alive with complicated political manoeuvring.

Candice waited patiently. Flask's desk was covered in baubles and photos of her and her overweight husband, their overweight children. Candice could not stop herself from staring. The family was on a trip somewhere warm, though each was dressed in long sleeves and a hat. Sand was trapped between the folds of her youngest's arms. When Flask addressed her, hand cupping the end of the telephone receiver, Candice tried to react as though she'd seen nothing, as though there weren't any photographs at all.

"I need you to bring these forms up to seventeen. Silvia needs them for payroll." Flask uncovered the receiver and spoke angrily into it. "You tell him he better unless he's looking for a big change." It took too long for Candice to intuit she'd been dismissed. She stood and picked up the stack of pages. Flask scribbled furiously on her legal pad, then paused before unleashing a tirade of profanity upon whomever was unlucky enough to be at the other end of the line.

Candice slunk through the glass doors at the front of the office. The receptionist didn't bother lifting her head as she passed. Candice did her best to put it out of her mind as she walked across to the elevator and pressed the call button, pleased to be the only one waiting. The glass between her and the office acted as an impenetrable barrier, and having passed its threshold she felt somewhat better. Any break from the deadening office atmosphere, if only for the time it took to deliver files to another floor, was heartening and helped replenish her reserves.

There was the normal hum and clanking of metal as she waited, and when the elevator arrived and the doors parted Candice's heart skipped. The car was empty. She exhaled the breath she'd been holding and stepped inside.

No sooner had she done so when there was a shout from down the corridor instructing her to hold the doors. She did nothing, but a giant, suited man appeared before her just the same. Well over six foot tall and smelling faintly of rosewater, he slipped into the car and smiled through the curls of his beard before pressing the button for the top floor. Candice ceded the car's space, pushing herself into the rear mirrored corner in hopes she might vanish, all the while keeping her eyes trained on a small circular stain on the carpeted floor. The large man spoke, but she could not hear him. In the trap, all sound was muted and distant. She closed her eyes and willed herself to calm down. She could ride the elevator two floors.

Two floors, and then she would have arrived and could escape. Only two floors to freedom.

But the trip was endless. She waited an interminable age, hugging the files to her chest, her lungs throbbing beneath, desperate for air, and when she finally heard the gentle chime she worried it was her ears playing tricks. The car slowed, then shuddered to a stop, and the opening doors flooded the car with brightness and the odour of soil and flowers instead of the expected stale air of floor seventeen. Candice opened her eyes a crack as her giant companion disembarked, and realized she had travelled to the top floor. Had she forgotten to press the button for the seventeenth? The question lingered only until she opened her eyes wider and saw her destination.

The Botanical Garden spanned the entire top floor of Simpsons Tower. Stepping into the faceted glass enclosure was as stepping into paradise. The rooftop garden was divided into rows of plants and flowers, a cascade of colours and scents that overwhelmed Candice, wrapped her in warmth. With uncharacteristic abandon she walked the aisles, past small benches set out to rest upon, ignoring the handful of other people that milled about the greenery, and looked at a variety of plants in turn while a gentle breeze brushed her face, tickling the small hairs on her forehead.

The sun caressed her skin through the many windows, and she turned toward it and closed her eyes. Dots appeared behind her lids, a flutter of coloured lights dancing in strange patterns. When she finally turned away and opened her eyes she wondered for a moment where she had been transported. Everything appeared unreal, hyper-coloured, all except one section of the garden that lay beyond. It was trapped in the shadow of a neighbouring building, and at the end of the aisle an archway stood, wrapped in clinging vines.

"It's beautiful up here, isn't it?"

Candice shook. Beside her stood the large man from the elevator, his chequered blazer reflected in the wicker baskets hanging above. Sunlight haloed his soft creamed hair, his beard hinted with grey. She collapsed in on herself, shrank from his scrutiny, pulled the files close to act as a barrier. But he would not be so easily dissuaded.

"I've been coming up here for months. Usually, I have my lunch just over there." He pointed lazily across the rooftop. "Why would anyone want to be anyplace but here? It's a mystery."

Candice would not look at him. She wanted to flee, but was too terrified and self-conscious to do anything but remain perfectly still. Only her heart moved, and it pounded.

"I don't think I've seen you up here before. I'm Ben Stanley."

Candice stared at the ground.

"Lourdes," she whispered.

He leaned his enormous bearded face toward her.

"Come again?"

"Candice Lourdes."

"Well, it's nice meeting you, Lourdes, Candice Lourdes. There are some lovely orange lilies over on the south side of the garden you should smell before you go. They've really opened up in this air."

He placed his hand on her shoulder gently, briefly, before walking away. As he did she marvelled she'd let him touch her at all. Her body did not rebel. Nevertheless, once she was certain he had gone, Candice moved as quickly as she could to the elevator to escape the garden and deliver the wrinkled files she had crushed like petals between her fingers.

By the next day, Candice had promised herself two things: the first was to never return to the top of Simpson Tower; the second was to stop thinking about Ben Stanley's warm hand on her shoulder. Yet neither was as easy as she'd hoped. In the morning haze that accompanied her sleepless night, she had unthinkingly selected her nicest skirt to wear despite it being tight across the hips, and tried to wrestle her hair into a style that did not appear damp. Her mind idled on the subway, taking the elevator up to the top floor to meet Ben Stanley among the flowers, and the smile it brought to her face evoked strange glances. Yet when she arrived at the office the only comment made was by a young temp who asked, aghast, "What are you *wearing?*" Candice did not speak. As soon as she was able she sneaked off to the washroom and wiped off her makeup. She then retreated to her office and put on an old sweater that covered her bare arms.

When Candice's lunch hour was at hand, she found herself defeated before the elevator doors, finger hovering over the buttons, unable to decide which direction she should travel. She felt the gentle draw of the flowers and plants on the rooftop, yet knew also the danger the visit posed. Taking the elevator down was safer—she knew what to expect. Her heart raced as she watched her finger drift toward the familiar and practised route. The safer route. But she found she could not press the button. Her body was betraying her. Instead it drove her finger into the other button, the UP button, summoning the shuddering box from the depths of the tower so it might propel her skyward.

When the doors opened, she felt an uncomfortable relief and unbearable disappointment. The car was empty. Completely and utterly empty.

She closed her eyes and inhaled. Perhaps it came from the elevator shaft, perhaps from the building's ventilation, perhaps it was mere imagination, but Candice smelled the summer flowers, felt the warm breeze, tasted happiness as it wafted past. It lasted forever. She opened her eyes and stepped into the empty elevator. It quietly hummed as it ascended.

The rooftop garden was busier than Candice remembered. Men in pressed suits spoke with women in blazers and pencil skirts, walking, sitting and laughing, while elderly ladies in neon colours inspected the plant-life, small white purses hanging from their scooped shoulders, faces unfathomably loose. Candice stood on her toes and scanned the crowd but saw no one of unreasonable size, no one with a beard so thick it was like a bush. The sweat at the base of her spine was cold, and a hinted dizziness unmoored her—both multiplied by the mixture of floral scents.

As she explored the rooftop garden she realised every

sound was distorted. The giant windows overhead reflected noise in odd directions, bouncing it off the floor or the metal struts, causing some corners to be so quiet they might be miles away, and others so loud it was as though people were yelling directly into her ears. The echoes stretched and bent around the aisles of flowers and greenery, intersecting with the potted autumn clematis and the reed grass that gathered around their warted stems. But Candice didn't mind any of it. In that space, she was free in a way she was not when inside the office, or on the street awaiting her relay of buses. Or even at home, alone in her cramped one-bedroom apartment. Every moment of every day was planned out for her, controlled. But there in the garden, she felt unburdened. And after a few minutes, she couldn't remember having ever felt different.

"I see you're back," said the amused voice behind her. Ben Stanley stood there, barrel chest near her face, dark beard hugging his chin. Perhaps she imagined some shadow dancing there.

"I—I just wanted—I mean I only came—"

He waved his hand to silence her.

"There's nothing to be ashamed of. We are all up here for the same reason. We all deserve to explore ourselves whenever we'd like."

Candice nodded, though she didn't understand what he meant.

"Would you like to join me?" he asked, and pointed to the bench on which he'd been sitting, a bench she had somehow overlooked. Along the seat was an unfolded blanket and a plate of green olives and cubes of yellow cheese. "I have more than enough for two."

Candice didn't speak, and Ben Stanley did not wait for her. He swooped his hand to indicate she should follow, then took a seat. His tiny glazed eyes poked out over round cheeks as he looked up at her, and all she could smell were the lilacs from two aisles away.

She fought her urge to flee. His smile curled around his temples.

"Fruit?" he asked, opening a small cooler hidden behind the bench. A pair of ladies in their seventies strolled by, sagging heads pushing out of their chests, and Candice waited until they were gone before taking some grapes with a polite smile. She held them over her trembling hand and ate them one at a time. She blinked slowly, then swallowed, and immediately regretted it. They tasted gritty and bitter, and she felt ill.

"So, Candice Lourdes, tell me: Do you work in the building?"

She squeaked, her throat constricted from terror. She coughed to clear it, but only managed to loosen the muscles enough for sound to squeeze through.

"Yes," she said, her voice tiny, her eyes trained on the shadows.

"Well, don't make me guess. I imagine it's on the fifteenth floor? Where we first met in the elevator?"

Her face flushed with fire and she had to turn away in case she wept. She saw aisles of flowers all bent towards her.

"I've always thought of the fifteenth floor as 'our' floor—we've had such good times there."

She looked at him, forgetting her fears in her immediate confusion, and he bellowed a laugh. All the glass above rattled.

"You're a joy, Candice. A joy. Here, have some cheese."

He held up the plate for her, but she didn't feel like eating anything more. It smelled as though it had gone off. She felt overwhelmed by the heat, by the muted sounds, by the stream of passing people, by the omnipresent floral smell, and by the sheer mass of Ben Stanley, who impossibly grew larger the longer she stayed.

"I—I have to go." She attempted to stand but her legs buckled, and before she knew what happened Ben Stanley had her in his arms. She wondered idly if she might also fit in his palm.

"Are you okay? Do you need some water?"

"No, no," she protested, wondering if her voice was as slurred as it sounded. "I just need to get back. My break is over."

"Let me walk you to the elevator," he said, and did not let her protests deter him.

The doors opened as soon as they arrived, and Candice wondered if she'd missed when he pushed the button, or when the other passengers had walked out. Ben made sure she was safely deposited inside the box, then pressed the fifteenth-floor button for her.

"You be careful," he smiled. "I hope I see you soon."

She nodded impatiently, jabbing at the CLOSE button until the metal doors slid shut. Trapped suddenly and unexpectedly in so small a space, Candice's stomach convulsed, and she could not keep it from reversing. It pushed its contents up her throat in a rush and she vomited in the corner, blanketing the stain she had studied for so many years. She wiped her mouth, humiliated, and stuck her jittering hands in her pockets to quell them. She did not look at the chewed green grapes floating in her sick.

The succeeding week followed the same routine. Candice refused to go in the elevator, instead making the gruelling climb up the stairs to the office. She couldn't afford to be in that small box again. Her shame over what had happened neutered any inclination to explore the garden, to encounter the strange Ben Stanley again. He was simply too much for her in every way—too present, too intrusive—and she found it suffocating to even think of him. It was much safer to eat only at her desk, hiding in the back office, nibbling her homemade sandwiches while in the break room the younger staff made a ruckus. When her telephone rang with an internal number, she avoided answering it, and no one bothered to find out why. Ms. Flask likely found someone else to torment into running errands, leaving Candice to drown herself in work until night came, at which point she descended the echoing stairwell as quickly as she could. No matter how she tried to mask it, though, the scent of the botanical garden flowers lingered— first in her clothes, then on her skin, and soon enough her every thought was corrupted by a wide field of flowers, the scents of lavender and ground roses in the breeze. She left stacks of work on the edges of her desk and huddled with her dry sandwiches and water, fluorescent bulb above humming erratically. She watched the elevators and waited, but when those doors slid open no one ever emerged looking for her.

Sometimes, it felt like aeons since she'd last spoken. Her days were a series of stairs and hidden cubicles, flickering fluorescents and vacant-eyed commuters adrift in underground tunnels. She woke, worked, dined, slept; over and over again. At times she was curious if she still had a voice, but could not gather the nerve to test it. Instead, she closed her mouth and felt the pressure of her depression dig in its weighted talons. Soon enough, even sleep was denied her.

Having woken without anything to occupy her frazzled mind, Candice left for work a half-hour early, her trip unusually silent. The subway car she travelled in was devoid of other passengers, and when she arrived at her destination platform it too was unpopulated. It would not be long before the sun rose and rush hour arrived, flooding the tunnels and streets with drab business men and women sprinting to nowhere.

The windows of Simpson Tower were frozen when she arrived, frost turning them opaque and milky. The hydraulic doors still functioned, however, and inside the lobby was warm and newly lit. The entrance to the stairs, however, had yet to be unlocked. She tried the handle with as much force as she could muster, a tiny panic growing as she did, but there was no movement at all, and no indication in the empty lobby of anyone coming to unlock it. Even the security desk was vacant. She wondered if she should leave and return later, but there was nowhere to go. She swallowed and looked at the elevator doors, then around in vain for another option. Any option at all. But there was only one.

Her stomach rolled in protest, her mouth dried. Her hands trembled as she pressed the button to summon the elevator toward her. The car shuddered and ground, moving slowly from floor to floor, the pale display's lit orange number decreasing incrementally. When the car reached the lobby, she felt its gears slip before the doors staggered and wrenched apart. The mirrored walls inside were murky with grime, and it was not until she bravely stepped in with held breath and turned to press the fifteenth-floor button that she noticed the familiar stain on the carpet was gone. She stared at the void the entire way up.

The office was vacant and locked. She inserted her key, the heavy bolt sliding back with a satisfying snap, and merged with the dark. No one else would be there so early, and the air in the dark was queerly muted, the carpet muffling her footsteps. Candice visited each area in turn, flipping light switches in succession, ignoring the flicker and buzz of the fluorescents gradually warming. Soon the sound was joined by a random chirping, so faint she was not certain where it emanated from, nor what she'd done to initiate it. Perhaps that insectan drone had always been there, masked by the noise of office bustle, but in the quiet of morning the sounds were deafening, and she put her hands over her ears to silence them. It made no difference; they would not diminish.

Candice frowned, then shuffled to her desk and slipped into her worn leather chair behind it. Her computer rattled to life, vibrating as the drive spun, the fans revolving. A pale green cursor faded into view, blinking slowly as though taking breath, before the computer screen displayed line after line of unreadable code, paging rapidly. Candice mashed the keys, hoping to stop the flood, and though she saw those letters she typed appear in the intervals she typed them, none slowed the cascade or remained on screen for more than a few seconds before the wave of garbage data swept them away.

She pounded the keyboard but it made no difference. Coming in early and immersing herself in work was supposed to distract her from thoughts of Ben and the garden, but without access to the computer network she was helpless to prevent their invasion at every unoccupied moment. She tried to focus on anything else, tried to ground herself in the present to break the spell. She touched things around her, one at a time, calling out their names to fix them in reality, and she alongside. "Desk. Chair. Computer," she said. "Wall. Stapler. Telephone."

It was no use. Details about Ben Stanley filled the quiet seconds in her mind, flashes of him sliced between thoughts; his towering figure, his floral scent from the garden, that deep laugh, the warmth of his touch. His eyes, though small and recessed over protruding cheeks were mesmerizing, and she found herself remembering those black stones more than anything else. How they glinted in the daylight. Her fear was immense, but for the first time it was a terror that invigorated her. It was like nothing she had experienced—not like her father, overbearing and reeking of sweat; not her mother, timid and perfumed. Not like the sweating students she had been so removed from, or the worn leather adults that took their place. All these people stood too close to her, tried to grab her and push her. From all their flesh her skin recoiled. But from Ben Stanley's, it heated. She could feel it in her face. She could feel it between her legs. Her mouth lined with cotton.

A chime drew her from her reverie, so familiar she did not realise at first it had sounded, and when she did she wasn't certain she hadn't imagined it. The humming drone returned, amplified somehow, a double sine wave that rattled the small bones in her skull. She padded out of her office toward reception, wondering if Ms. Flask or an eager staff member had arrived, despite it being impossible without her hearing. But when Candice reached reception she saw the elevator doors standing open beyond the office glass, dim light spreading outward.

Candice tested the lock, yet could not shake the feeling someone had managed to sneak into the office. Why else would the elevator car be there, its doors open? She hadn't summoned it. The car waited, beckoned, drew her toward it, and Candice hesitated, then turned the office lock. The bolt fell heavily, and when she opened the door the smell of flowers overwhelmed her. The world swayed and her mouth once again dried. She staggered forward with closed eyes.

It seemed to span no longer than a blink, but when

Candice was once more aware of herself she discovered she was seated against the mirrored wall of the elevator car, skirt pulled up across her doughy thighs, a foot-long run in her hosiery. She shook her head and rolled onto her scuffed knees, fearful someone might summon the elevator and see her there, dishevelled. She trembled as she reached up and took hold of the railing.

Had she pressed the button for the top floor in her stupor? She must have, as it was lit dull orange, but she had no memory of doing so. Something wrong was happening, something that brought her to the edge of hysteria, but she managed to tamp it down, convinced herself there was an explanation, if only she had time to work it out. Breathing slowly helped, and when she felt calm enough to function again, the first thing she tried to do was step off the elevator. But the closing doors prevented that, and with a short buzz the car lurched into ascent; it would not be stopped no matter how many times she hit other buttons. It headed toward the top floor where the botanical garden waited.

The doors opened on the unoccupied garden. The lights were turned to a dim low, the giant thermal windows making up the polygonal dome brushed with a layer of frosted ice, refracting the rising sun's light. Each window became a haloed fractal, and the odd angles sent curious shadows down the aisles of closed flowers, petals folded gently inside, pistils turned downward. The potted vegetation edged toward her impossibly, though it might have simply been those shadows cast by the overhead sun against towering skyscrapers. The atmosphere was filled with restrained potential—every inch of the garden asleep, its dream seeping outward in a hazed umbra. Candice worried she might be asleep as well, her limbs slowed by the weight of the fragrant air as she lifted them to stab at the fifteenth-floor button. But it did not light up. She was trapped in the too-sweet miasma of the waking garden. It would not be denied.

She stepped out and was immediately confronted with the cloying odour; she closed her eyes, inhaled deeply, a rush of nostalgia flooding her senses. Instantly, she was transported to her childhood in the park, lying by the small creek, listening to wind blow through the grass. She could still taste the tang of it. But the resurrected memory was not as peaceful as before. The leaves were skeletal from insectan mandibles, the creek bubbled viscous foam, the wind carried with it something rotten. She felt a presence there in her waking dream, something that loomed over her, a shadow heavy enough to pin her. She shook her head but it took all her strength to do so, the waves of dislocation like stagnant water. She shook and shook and shook, flailing to be free, and when she finally managed to wake herself she did so with a gasp, sucking in air to refill her suffocated lungs. Yet as she remained bent, struggling for breath, the sensation of a looming presence intensified. Candice cleared her throat, fearful of what she had to do. "Hello? Is there someone here?" Her wavering voice echoed on the buzzing glass, and the sound discomforted her. Something strange was occurring. She withdrew into the dim aisles. "Please say something."

But no one spoke. Another rustle. Like a bird among branches. Candice spun but saw only plants. Honeysuckle. Cotoneaster. Dark Beauty toad lilies. The plants lining the aisle all were absolutely still, and yet Candice felt cold, as though they were deliberately still. The flowers... there was no other way to explain it: They were *watching* her. Coaxing her. Whispering to her. She pulled her blouse closer to her chest and retreated another step.

She travelled the aisles one by one as though confined to her daydream. Movements dragged, reactions delayed, and when she struggled to cohere her muddled thoughts and make sense of the puzzle, it proved impossible. There was something about the garden that she could resist when seated a few floors beneath, but in its presence cast too strong a spell.

Part of her hoped she wasn't alone. She kept looking around, searching for Ben Stanley among the empty benches and closed flowers. But why should he be there? Other than the fact that he simply *belonged* there, belonged in a way

Candice did not. His beard, his height—he seemed a part of the landscape, another tree in the forest, the swirls in his hair and beard repeated in the swirls of garden branches and vines. It was Candice that was the interloper, stumbling over roots she could not see, scratched by wisp-thin branches. But in her haze she felt unquestionably welcomed; the garden's arms were open, ready to embrace her.

Under the arch strange shadows moved, and though it could easily have been a reflection on the glass beyond, Candice wondered. It seemed so alien, so different from any world she had ever known, ever imagined. She took a step closer and the images moved, unfolded, opened to reveal more of themselves. She felt lightheaded but continued down the aisle, breathing heavier as she got closer. The heat of the garden had risen with the sun, and beads of sweat formed on her forehead. Candice's body vibrated gently with every step she took toward the archway shaded from the morning sun. It was a tickle at the base of her neck which became a warm river flowing downward along the channel of her spine. The slow hazy world took on a different appearance, one where her eyesight was heightened, showing her each pattern of budding petal, each dew-covered thorn on those plants surrounding her. And the vibrations continued as she entered that dark aisle. They washed over her neck; numbed her arms, her chest; sped her heart. They flowed downward until they met the warmth from her back, a spiralling eddy between her legs. She bit down on her lip, bent over and gasped. Her mind flooded with images of Ben Stanley, now twenty feet tall, reaching out and enveloping her in his massive arms, his face the landscape of the desert, his eyes the expanse of the sea. He reached down and plucked her from where she stood and she screamed as the sky turned vibrant and everything exploded outward in streaks of crimson flame. Stars and suns lit her vision, colours streaming over her eyes, an eternal cascade bathing her, invading her, transforming her. It continued for aeons, and yet ended too quickly, abandoning Candice to the dull realities of the physical world. The botanical garden faded back into view, one unfurled flower at a time, and she stumbled upon entering it once more. The archway before her filtered the light from rising sun, burned clean of any shadows that had once gathered there. Nothing seemed amiss about it any longer. She heard behind her distant voices shouting something, but whatever words they spoke were transient in her decaying memory.

✂

Ms. Flask was unimpressed. The financial reports due on her desk before her weekly teleconference had not appeared, and for the first time since assuming her position she was forced to make excuses to the board. It made her appear weak, incapable of running her team, and that she could not abide. It was enough that they snickered about her weight, called her names, but until that moment they could never have claimed her incompetent. It would not do. Not at all.

Candice had been missing for three days, and in that time no one knew where she had gone. True, she was hardly irreplaceable—Ms. Flask would have done so immediately if possible. But Candice had been there long enough that only she understood how to extract the numbers Ms. Flask needed. The reporting of those quotas was perhaps more important than those quotas themselves, and ever-dependable Candice was key. Except she was not quite so "ever-dependable" any longer, and that was a problem too large to solve over the telephone. She had to be made an example of.

Ms. Flask stormed through the office toward Candice's cubicle, quietly enjoying the terror that spun around her as she cut a swath through the office. The newest employees rattled in their seats, the rest kept their heads down and feigned work, too afraid to look at her. When she faced down Candice, it would be with the power collected from their aggregate fear.

But Candice was not as Ms. Flask expected. The woman sat at her desk on the telephone, and offered no more than a half-smile in her manager's direction. Ms. Flask was impotent with rage as she watched Candice's brightly painted nails clicking on the desk, but all she could do was wordlessly broadcast her irritation. Yet Candice's smile never faltered. When she finally hung up, Ms. Flask's power felt strangely flattened. It was a foreign sensation and one she did not care for.

"Ms. Lourdes, where have you been?"

"I took some personal days. All the forms have been sent to HR."

Ms. Flask made a mental note to verify that when she returned to her desk, and to ensure no errors were committed filling out those forms. "That may be, but you had reports due this morning that never arrived."

"That's weird," Candice said, her brow furrowed unconvincingly. She checked her watch, then pushed her loose hair behind her ear. "I came in early today to catch up on everything."

"Well, I received nothing."

Candice shrugged. "Would you like me to send them again?"

"Yes, of course."

Ms. Flask remained in the doorway, staring as the unperturbed Candice lazily checked her watch. Everything about the woman was wrong, and it was far more disconcerting than the missing reports. Ms. Flask could not put her finger on why, but it made her uncomfortable.

"Do you have somewhere else you have to be, Ms. Lourdes?"

Candice laughed incredulously at Ms. Flask. She laughed like sparking steel, then crossed her smooth bare legs.

"Not yet," Candice said, and touched her tongue to her lips.

GHOST DOGS

———————— ❧ ————————

Who was the sandbag who first called them *ghost dogs*, anyway? I mean, it's not like they're ghosts and they're probably not like dogs, either. They're just things that live in the skirts and seem to enjoy keeping me from falling asleep on those hot nights when I already can't stop sweating. Do they all get together in a circle somewhere in the nothing that surrounds Whitby and agree to keep me awake for as long as they can?

I'm not sure why, but they've always had it in for me. No one believes me, though, even after I tell them the ghost dogs have already tried to get me twice. The last time I was running home from Jody's place. I never actually saw them, but I knew they were there, which is why I ran as fast as I could through the stretch that connects White Abby Court to Lupin Avenue. My feet were numb and my chest felt like my belt was tightened around it and I was crying because of the wind in my eyes and nothing else. The ghost dogs didn't catch me though, and when I got home and used the last of my energy to dash by Mama and into my room, do you know what I found? There were about a million brush brambles clinging to the cuffs of my yellow cotton pants. What I'm saying is the name 'ghost dogs' is like one of those brambles—I'm not sure where it came from but it's stuck and it's not going anywhere.

I tried explaining all this to Jody and Dennis, but they never listen as much as they should. Dennis is too trapped in his head to pay attention, and Jody's too busy trying to get into mine. I've hung out with them a lot this summer mostly because I like getting away from Mama and the chores she wants me to do. She's too fat and lazy or drunk to do them on her own, and if you think I'm being cruel, I'm not. She's the one who calls herself those names whenever she wants me to do something. Just this morning she said: "I was too fat and lazy and drunk to have a girl of my own, so you're going to have to sweep the porch even if you're too slight and stupid to do it right." Mama is a real good motivator. She can motivate me right out the door. The best way I've found to avoid having to do everything for her is to get on my bicycle and ride as far away as I can. One day, I'm going to ride right out of Whitby and into the skirts and keep on riding until the sky turns from blue to orange. Jody tells me the more orange the sky, the further away I'll be. I don't know if it's true, but I like believing it.

And it's not like Mama's my real mom anyway. My real mom got sick when I was young enough that no one thought I'd remember what she was like, but it's the one thing I can't forget. I can't forget how thin she looked, like a dying branch underneath a sheet; I can't forget the feel of her twig fingers on my face and stroking my hair one last time. That stuff is clear to me. What's not so clear is what happened to my dad. He ran off somewhere after my real mom died, crazed with grief, and never came back. When people ask, I tell them the ghost dogs got him, because why not? They don't ask again, which is nice. About the only part that isn't nice was being sent to live with my real mom's sister, Selma, who has my mom's face only it doesn't fit her quite right, like it's the wrong size. She makes me call her "Mama" even though I don't want to.

Not that spending time with Jody and Dennis isn't work, too. It's just different work. Mama makes me sweep out the dirt that always comes back, run errands like carrying home our water rations from the station, but it's all easy stuff. Go here, do this, do that. With Jody and Dennis, it's much more complicated. It's like one of those love triangles from the old books my real mom left behind when she died, those few I managed to keep before Mama threw them away, except I don't know how you have a triangle when the sides don't connect. I don't mind Jody because she's my friend, and I don't mind Dennis for the same reason, but I don't feel about either of them the way those books talk about, and I know Jody doesn't either because she'd tell me. She can't not tell me. Dennis, on the other hand, keeps lots to himself, even if I already know what he doesn't want me to. Still, when it comes to how he feels about me or Jody, I can never tell, even though he gets all red and stammery when it comes up. It probably doesn't help that Jody and I can't stop laughing at him when he starts to fumble. I don't care how mad he pretends to get; I know he's not angry because he starts smiling with those chisel teeth. You can't be mad and smile at the same time. It's a known fact. I'm sure I read that in another one of my real mom's old books, but even if I didn't I still bet it's true.

Still, it's weird that Jody's mom doesn't want her near me or Dennis. With Dennis it kind of makes sense, I guess, seeing as he's a boy, and even though he's the least boy-like boy I've ever met, Jody's mom still doesn't trust him. But me? Why wouldn't she want Jody near me? I know there are stories floating around but most of them aren't true. It's all just rumors and gossip and Jody knows that, which means her mom should, too. But sometimes grown-ups have narrow minds when it comes to that kind of talk, and they'd rather believe the wrong stuff than accept the right stuff. It's not like anybody has any proof of their suspicions, but you can't change people's minds if they don't want them changed, so Jody's mom keeps on worrying about Dennis and me and hating us, and Jody keeps ignoring her and sneaking out of the house anyway whenever we ask her to. It's not a great system, but we make it work.

That's why it's a surprise that Dennis, quiet Dennis, who would be afraid of his own shadow if the sun ever gave us a break for a minute, is the one who decides he wants to see a ghost dog. "Aren't you even curious?" he asks while the three of us lie by the edge of what's left of Massey Creek, our bikes in a heap, Jody's feet languidly toeing through the damp silt. I'm still tired from the night before—so tired I keep hearing ghost dog howls when no one else can.

"Not me," I say. "My luck's going to run out if I get chased again. And I'm surprised you're curious, considering."

"Yeah, I don't want to go either," Jody says, though it's hard to be sure if that's what she wants, or if she's just agreeing with me. "Besides, my mom wouldn't like it."

"Oh, we should totally go, then," I say, but I don't think she appreciates my joke.

"Neither of you ever wanted to see one?" Dennis seems to shrink. His first idea, and we stomp all over it. I get the feeling it's about more than curiosity. It's about his mom, and it's dangerous. "I bet they aren't even that big."

I sit up. "Big as a horse, at least," I say.

"No way." His shrinking stops.

Jody nods, smiling. "You're right. And those are just the pups. A grown ghost dog is more like an elephant."

Then I add: "Yeah! Like a whole herd of elephants. And when they run, you can feel the ground shaking like an earthquake. Like this!" I leap to my feet and stomp the packed ground as hard as I can. Trails of dirt rattle down into the empty creek. "Only you know where it's coming from because you can hear them coming after you. It'll shake your teeth out."

Dennis folds his arms. Turns away. "You guys aren't funny."

"Yes we are," Jody says, and then we both fall on our backs and cackle. Dennis waits patiently until we're finished laughing at how funny we are. I could actually keep going, but I haven't seen a cloud in days and it's too hot to be rolling around in the dirt for no good reason.

Everybody's afraid of fire in Whitby. We use it for cooking

when we have to, and there's a furnace two blocks over for smithing, but it's a dangerous thing to keep around. Mama's always warning me to stay away from it, and at school tall, bald Mr. McIvory taught us what to do if we see one, but most of the other kids stopped listening years ago. They say it's because it's so hot most of the time it feels like everything's on fire anyway, but I think they're too busy worrying about ghost dogs to worry about fires. They only have so much worry in them to go around. I guess that's because we hear the ghost dogs howling all the time, and people keep going missing. When it comes to fire, the really dangerous kind, most of the kids have never seen one.

I have, but only once. But at least it was a big one. The Parkway Fire. It started at an old house that wasn't causing anybody any trouble, so no one really knows how it happened. Mama thinks it was kids, but she always thinks that about everything that goes wrong. I remember seeing the column of black smoke spewing into the sky and being mesmerized. I was with Jody near the school, so the two of us hopped on our bicycles to get a better look at what was going on. There were more people there than I'd ever seen before, women and men of all sizes working their shovels, digging a wide moat around the house as fast as they could. No one stopped to look at us; no one cared. All they cared about was digging. That's the only way to stop a fire, Mr. McIvory told us later. You've got to isolate it. Make sure the damage can't spread. Sometimes, they'll even knock down good houses that people are living in if it means keeping a fire separated. He also said that they used to use water to put out fires like that back in the old days, which still makes me laugh. Why would anyone waste water, pouring it on a house? It's the stupidest thing I've ever heard. It would make more sense I think to take all the sand they dig up from their moats and pour it *over* the house, but I can't figure out how you'd throw it far enough, or what you'd do with the half-buried house after. At least when a fire burns something down you can shovel away the ashes and start again. There's something cleaner about that.

But I still remember that Parkway fire. That beautiful, hypnotizing fire. As that old house burned, the air buckled and rushed and sounded like whispers that I thought I could maybe make out if I tried real hard. But I couldn't, and neither could Jody, though I kind of suspect she didn't really try. She probably just told me what I wanted to hear. But that's okay; I don't blame her. I shouldn't have been so close to the fire anyhow. Mama wouldn't have liked it.

I find I can't stop thinking about what Dennis said. About seeing a ghost dog. The idea doesn't scare me like it should, like it scares everyone else, but I've never thought about it before. I guess because we've always been told to keep away from the skirts and anyplace else they might be, I went along with it without thinking, which was dumb and makes me angry. I hate looking in the mirror and seeing a sheep.

The thing is I should probably be scared of ghost dogs more than most, considering how twice I've come close to being taken. The other time it happened, the first time, I was still a kid, and I heard howling when Mama and I were walking down the street, back from the house of Mrs. Piggly who had just fitted me for a new skirt even though I'd never had an occasion to wear one. I never liked Mrs. Piggly: she used to snuffle as she held the straight pins in her mouth, and it sounded like no animal I'd ever heard. Still, it was nothing compared to the sound of the ghost dogs. That was so much worse. I'd heard them howl before, but it was louder this time with Mama. I know because I remember covering my ears and crying. It was sort of like thunder, where you see the lightning then hear the rattling sheets of metal a few seconds later. Only there was no lightning first, and the metal made a screeching like it was being twisted in two directions at once. The sound was like a block of ice on my neck, and my little legs quaked so bad I thought the ground under them was coming undone. But Mama, she didn't care about my legs. She was shoving me so hard I almost fell over, and she kept on shoving me until we were inside the house and the door was closed. I'd been in such shock I went where she told me, but once the door bolts were slid and chains drawn, I started to wail and blubber like you only do when you're a kid. I'm not sure what Mama was doing—she was really just a blur, scurrying past me back and forth—but I knew when she stopped in front of me because I felt the inside of her closed fist strike my face. My real mom had never hit me, and Mama hadn't either before then; I stopped crying instantly, too shocked to continue. We looked at each other forever, me and Mama, my face slowly starting to burn while hers remained cold, at least until everything stopped shaking and those howls got further apart and farther away. Then a change came over her, like she only then understood what she'd done. She lunged at me and I shrank, but not in time to escape her arms. They enveloped me, pulled me so close I could smell the drink rising from her skin. My eyes started to water, and without warning I was balling again while she clumsily and half-heartedly tried to console me.

Dennis is right: we need to see a ghost dog. We both need the closure. It won't be hard convincing Jody; she's always listened to me, ever since Mr. McIvory first sat us next to each other in class. He probably thought she'd be a good influence on me or something. But it didn't work like that because it never does. She didn't show me what life could be like; I showed her what life really was, and instead of Mr. McIvory getting two smiling eager pupils he got a pair of secretive connivers. I bet it drove him crazy, but no matter how many times he pulled his hair out trying to intervene, no matter how many times he warned her mother to keep an eye on her, slowly Jody slipped away from them and closer to me. And when we met Dennis? Well, that sealed it. There was no stopping us.

Jody didn't take to Dennis at first—she got mad when it stopped being me and her and started being me and her and him—but it was clear pretty quick Dennis wasn't a threat to anyone but himself. He's who I'd be if I cared how Mama and Mr. McIvory and all the rest felt about me. But Dennis is different; he's not unwanted. He wears long sleeves in the summer like I do, but his dad loves him and his mom probably would, too, if she hadn't disappeared. There's no reason to do the things he does to himself, which is why I like him being around. He reminds me that none of this makes any sense. That sometimes things happen and there are no reasons, so there's no point in wishing things had gone different. Different is no guarantee of anything.

We plan our expedition in the middle of Willowfield Park, which we now call Willowfield Dust Bowl. I don't even know if it was ever a park like you see in books or photographs—no one ever told me and I never bothered to ask. But it's the only place we can meet where nobody can sneak up on us and find out what we're planning. No one sneaks up on you when there's nothing to hide behind. Of course, nowhere to hide means no shade, and it gets so hot so fast that by the time we're talking the sweat is sizzling on my scalp like hog's grease. I put my hand on the hottest spot; I enjoy how it makes my hair feel like it's on fire, but it's too much, even for me, so I settle on standing my bike between me and the sun, then crouching down in the small shadow it traces over the dirt. The other two do the same—we don't have to worry about ants because even they aren't dumb enough to be out when it's this hot—and with wagons circled we lay out our intricate plan.

"Finding a ghost dog won't be easy," I say. "Otherwise someone would have done it by now."

"How do we know nobody ever has? Someone must have at some point."

"Don't be a sandbag, Dennis. We'd know. Everybody would have talked about it. They probably would have thrown a parade."

"Yeah, Dennis," Jody adds. "Nobody has seen one. Nobody who's lived, at least."

Jody looks at us, horrified, like she's done something wrong. It takes a second before I realize she's remembered what happened to Dennis's mother, what happened to my father. Or, at least what I told her happened. I wouldn't be bothered either way but I pretend to be for a moment. I'm not sure why. Dennis, however, recoils and withdraws into himself, like

Jody has punched him right in the face worse than Reinhold or Merchant ever has. It's worse because at least with them he knows it's coming. Jody just hit him straight out of nowhere. "I'm sorry, Dennis," she says. "I wasn't thinking." And he nods like he believes her but you can never tell with Jody what she means and what she pretends to mean. Because remembering what happened to Dennis's mom shouldn't be that hard for her. Even I remember and I've got my own things to worry about. Jody would never admit it to me—and if she wouldn't admit it to me, she wouldn't admit it to anyone—but I think she does this stuff on purpose. Like, she's mad at something else that's not Dennis, and because she won't talk about it she punishes him instead. It makes things uncomfortable because now I'm the one who has to broker peace, and I hate doing that. I'm not good at it.

"Let's get this over with so we can get out of the dust bowl. I'm already sticking to myself." I pull a wad of paper from my back pocket, and concentrate on unfolding it so it will take my focus off the heat for a few seconds. Just a few is all I need. Still, my sweating hands make it harder than is should be. "I made a list of everything we know about the ghost dogs. Here's what I came up with."

I read off the list of points, saying each out loud so there's no confusion about what awaits us. I mention we think they're as big as wagons and always travel in packs. Also, that they have long nine-inch claws, and hunt only at night, and prefer the skirts, past the scrub, though if anyone knows that's not always certain it's me and Dennis. What we don't know, what nobody really knows, is how many people have they taken and killed.

Sweat drops from my face on to the flattened list on the ground, and it makes the paper wrinkle. The word 'claws' gets all blurry. I have one more point and I pause before I say it in case I don't.

"They might be invisible, too."

That shuts Jody and Dennis up, and it gets so quiet you can hear the heat baking everything. It sounds like nothing, like the sun has burned all the noise away. I don't look at Jody or Dennis. After all the times we've talked about ghost dogs, whether or not they can actually be seen is the one idea I've resisted bringing up. I don't think either of them is ready to admit it's possible, but if we're going to go looking for a ghost dog they need to be prepared. I can't baby them anymore.

"Can you two think of anything else?" Dennis sits cross-legged, inspecting his fingers. Jody's stare burrows through me. It's as uncomfortable as it is irritating.

"If they're invisible, how are we going to see one?" she asks. Dennis looks up then, looks at her, then at me, then at her again, but Jody looks only at me and never stops. She stares, wanting an answer. I'd like someone to stare at, too, but as usual I have no one.

"I've got some ideas about that," I say. "But we've got to find one first. And the only way we're going to find one is if we go looking."

"Go looking for something invisible?" Dennis asks, the words drawn out as he puts the pieces together. I nod and then he nods and Jody looks from one of us to the other.

"I don't know," she says, twisting pieces of her sun-bleached hair. "My mom won't want me traveling to the skirts. Not right now."

"Why? Why not right now?"

Jody scratches her head, brushes dirt off her knees.

"It's just—it's too far away. And the sun would cook us before we got anywhere close."

"Sure," I say, and when Dennis won't look up I know he understands. I'm not surprised—he's always been quicker than Jody. "That's why we aren't going when there's going to be any sun. We have to do this at night. When they're out hunting."

Jody's face turns the kind of white that reminds me of my real mom. I wonder if she'll drop dead right there.

"You want to find a ghost dog. At night. In the skirts. Are you crazy?"

I shrug. "I don't know what's so crazy about it. When else

are we supposed to do it? What's your better plan? Or yours, Dennis?" I wait for either of them to say something, but now it's them who won't look at me. It's kind of disappointing.

❋

Jody, Dennis and I lay out our plan, though I don't think Jody likes it very much. She's quiet the whole time, and when I suggest she and Dennis leave their bicycles at my house—behind the old stone wall at the side of the property, because it will be easier to sneak out that way—she shakes her head and doesn't speak. It makes me angry, so I don't talk to her when we're riding home and talk only to Dennis. He's uncomfortable, I can tell, and doesn't want to be in the middle, but that's too bad for Dennis. Sometimes, when you're friends with more than one person, there are going to be times like this. Times it's not easy. Jody seems pretty upset about the whole thing. When we're coming close to her street, she asks me, quietly, if we can talk a minute. She says she has something she needs to tell me, but I don't want to listen. I've only gotten angrier during my silence, and don't think I can put up with hearing what she has to say. So, I pretend I can't hear her. I don't feel bad about it, even when she pulls away from me and Dennis and rides slowly off. Dennis stops his bicycle to watch her, but I keep going. I have other things to worry about.

❋

The day comes for us to go looking for a ghost dog and unsurprisingly Jody isn't at school. It's unsurprising because of how Jody's been treating me since we made our plan—she's barely spoken to me, and even when she has she sounds sad and exhausted. I asked her once, and had Dennis ask her twice, if she was still coming to find a ghost dog and she said she was, but I could tell something was wrong. Jody's been mad at me before when I haven't paid enough attention to her, so none of this is new. I have to remind myself it'll pass eventually.

The best way to speed that up is to continue doing everything we said we would. Sticking to the plan is what's important. So Dennis and I keep to ourselves and talk like nothing is wrong, even though Jody isn't there. It works for a while, and keeps Dennis from worrying too much about her; that is, until Merchant and Reinhold and some of the equally ugly older kids appear and knock Dennis on the back of his head as they walk by. They laugh among themselves, so I shoot over my nastiest glare. Their laugh becomes the swallowed kind people make when they want to pretend they aren't worried. But if I'm glaring at them, they usually know they should be plenty worried. Reinhold touches his ear as if to reassure himself it hasn't already been bitten off.

Dennis doesn't want to talk about them, though. Which is sort of disgusting. "Can't we just go over the plan for tonight? I want to make sure we don't die."

"We won't die. Don't be a baby. And don't let those sandbags make you question yourself. No one likes them. Anyway, the plan is easy. You already know it. You leave your bicycle at my house behind the wall, and then tonight we meet up and go get Jody so we can all ride through the scrub to the skirts and find ourselves a ghost dog."

"I don't know," he says. "I'm worried."

"Are you backing out? This was your idea."

"I said I wanted to see one. I didn't say I wanted to die."

"I already said you're not going to die."

"You can't know that."

"I can. You won't die. I give you my word."

He shakes his head again. It's getting boring, so I stand to keep from kicking him. "Well, if you don't want to go, you don't have to. Jody and I are going and if something happens to us I hope you can forgive yourself."

Then I walk away. It's the most impactful thing I can do, and I know it will get him thinking. I don't want him to see me look back, but I sneak a glance anyway to be sure my words landed. He's still there, starting into his lap, shivering in the heat like an exposed nerve. No wonder those sandbags see him as such a target.

Here's the thing about Dennis: he wears those long sleeves all the time because he doesn't want to be who he is anymore. But you can't be someone different, can you? I mean, not really. You can make some outward changes, maybe stop doing things you used to do, but you can never stop being you. You're the only you that you can be. I know how stupid that sounds, but I still think it's true. You're stuck with who you are. So no matter how much Dennis wants to be someone else—someone who doesn't feel so much all the time while also feeling nothing at all—he has no choice. He has to be Dennis. And Dennis would not abandon Jody and me. I've never doubted it and I never will.

I scrub the dishes twice after dinner because I'm too nervous to concentrate, and because Mama found a spot of sauce on the underside of a bowl. As a punishment, I'm not allowed to wait for the ashes to cool before mixing them with the scrubbing sand to make the pomis, so everything is going slower than I want, and having my hands in hot pomis makes the stifling kitchen air feel that much thinner and harder to choke down. We have the doors open and the dust screens down, but there isn't a breeze, so the heat accumulates in the house. I'm supposed to be done, and Mama is supposed to be asleep, but my punishment must have invigorated her, because instead of collapsing in a chair she's peeled the paper off another stone for the vaper. I shift from foot to foot as I expect Dennis or Jody to appear right in Mama's line of sight on the other side of the widow, which will cause problems when I want to avoid problems. I know, it's funny, right? Me, trying to *avoid* problems instead of causing them for once.

The pomis cools enough to use by the time I'm finishing the scrubbing. My hands have gone bright red to the wrist and feel like they're on fire, but I don't see any blisters and I can move the fingers well enough to know they're okay.

It's only when I'm balancing the last plates to put them away that I notice the hissing. Outside, in the dark beyond the dust screen I see Dennis's round face peering in at me, eyes like a pair of fireflies on the netting. I fumble the plates but pride myself on not losing control of them, letting them clash or make a stray sound. Maybe I say "My..." or something, I'm not sure, but if I do it isn't much, and it isn't loud. Once I realize who the floating eyes belong to I wave him away from the door and lean into the front of the house to see what Mama's doing. She's still sitting slouched over the table with her vaper in hand, snoring in that way that used to leave me suspicious that she might stop breathing at any minute, and disappointed when I eventually realized she wouldn't.

"Mama," I say. "Why don't you go lie on the couch? I have to clear the table." I'm very careful how I speak to her in case she thinks I'm telling her what to do. After vaping a few stones, she's liable to get offended. But she doesn't move, so I walk up to her and put my hand on her shoulder. I'm repulsed just doing it, like my hand is pressing into something old and sharp, but Dennis can't hide outside forever, and we have a schedule to keep if we're going to meet Jody. When I shake Mama her sloppy hand tries to wave me away.

"Mama, time for the couch," I say, and push on her slightly.

She mumbles and her frowning brow lets me know exactly what she thinks of being disturbed. "Mama, I have to clean up," I say again. And, surprisingly, if reluctantly, she starts to push herself up from the chair. It's hard for her considering one hand is still wrapped around her vaper, but she manages to get to her feet and stumble over to the couch. Once she's down, I know she'll be down for the night. I don't bother crossing myself since it probably won't do any good, but to be on the safe side I spit into the corner of the room before draping a blanket over Mama's lumpy body. It's a relief to know there's one thing I can count on in the world. I don't know why, but I kiss her once on her sleeping head, sort of like what my real mom used to do for me. At least, I think she did. Who can remember?

I race back to the kitchen as fast and as silently as I can. There's no one at the dust screen. I press my lips against the

tiny wires, and whisper: "Dennis." It takes a minute, but he
finally appears.

"Yeah?"

"Go wait by the bicycles. I need to get something."

He jogs off, and I creep to my room and pull my backpack
from under my bed. I've already packed it with everything we'll
need for the trip to the skirts, including the taped paper bag I
had hidden in the pantry behind the sack of oats Mama hasn't
opened in forever. Still, looking at my backpack, I worry I've
forgotten something I'll regret not being able to come back
for later. I shrug. If I did, it's too late to do anything about it.
I take a final look at my room and try to memorize it as best I
can before turning out the lights.

Dennis is waiting behind the wall right where I told him
to, standing with a bicycle in each hand. I take mine—neither
of us saying a word—and then we both swing our legs over
our crossbars and start riding toward Jody's house. It's a few
minutes later than I'd wanted to leave, but if we pedal hard I
figure we can make up the difference. Dennis stays close the
whole way.

Jody's whole house is dark when we get there, which
isn't that strange considering how late it is—we were hoping
everyone would be in bed, not just her mom—but what *is*
strange is that Jody isn't waiting for us on the street out front
like she's supposed to. Like she normally would to keep from
getting caught.

"Where do you think she is?" Dennis whispers.

"Let's give her a minute. Maybe she had trouble getting
out."

We sit on the edge of the street, shielded from view by
the torchglow bushes her family wastes water maintaining.
The bushes are dusted with sand like everything else, which is
weird; I've never seen them like that before.

"Did you bring anything to eat?" Dennis whispers.

"What? No, Jody's bringing the food. Didn't you eat
something before you came over?"

He shrugs and looks at his feet. I shake my head, then

91

peer around the torchglow. Dennis does the same.

"I'm going to see what's going on," I say. "Wait here with the bicycles." But as I'm getting ready to go looking for Jody, a ghost dog howls from somewhere nearby. Its growl is deep enough that I feel it in my chest.

"That ghost dog's too close," Dennis says, his back so straight he looks like a prairie dog in its burrow. "We should call this off."

I think about Mama passed out on the couch. It might not be so easy to get out of the house again, not with the bundle of everything I'm carrying. Besides, this was Dennis's idea. He's the reason all this is happening. I don't want to give up on my plans because he's lost his nerve. I'm not going back.

"Let's find Jody first, then we'll decide."

The two of us leave our bicycles under the torchglow and creep up to the house. We stick to the shadows as best we can, though there aren't enough to hide behind. I keep glancing at the windows for movement, whether it's Jody signaling us she's coming down, or her mom signalling she knows we're there and we're going to be in trouble. Dennis is even more nervous about it than I would have guessed, which is probably why he doesn't speak. I hear his heavy breathing trailing me as we pick our way forward.

When we get to the house, there's still no Jody or anybody else, so I cup my hands to the glass patio doors and look in. I stare at those shadows a long time before I understand what I'm seeing, and when I do I transform.

"What's wrong?" Dennis asks.

"She's gone."

Dennis's eyes dart as his face pales.

"Did, did the ghost dogs get her?"

"What? No, you sandbag. I mean she's gone. Everybody's gone. The house is empty."

He looks stunned, so I tap on the glass and point. He puts his hands up to the window and peers.

I can barely control my anger. They've left. All those years of effort I put into Jody and me gone like everything else in forgotten Whitby, centre of drought and dust. I'm mostly mad at myself, though: I should have known, should have guessed. All her weird behaviour, it was all her getting ready to bolt.

Dennis pulls away from the glass, still not fully recovered, still stunned.

"I can't believe it," he says. "Her mom must really have hated us to move them away like that. Where are they even going to go?"

"Don't be a sandbag. Jody's gone because she didn't want to be here anymore. She didn't want to be our friend. Otherwise, she would have told us she was going. We could have helped her."

"But how—?"

"By getting her away from her crazy mother. By stashing her somewhere. We could have done it. We would have because we were supposed to be her friends. But she wasn't ours. She was a liar and always was one."

The anger makes me angrier. It pumps through my body, pushing switches I didn't know I had. I kick the door of the house as hard as I can, over and over and over, as I shout all the curses I know. But I don't know enough curses to feel better. It would take all the curses in the world and there aren't that many left. I don't start calming down until Dennis and I are back at the bicycles, his hand locked around my wrist, dragging me. I wrestle it free and wipe my eyes. Jody is such a waste of water.

"We have to go," he says. "Can't you hear it?"

I listen and hear the howling. I can't tell anymore if it's one cry or many.

"You shouldn't have done it. You shouldn't have ruined that house so no one else could use it, and you shouldn't have made so much noise. We're probably going to die now because of you."

"Stop shivering about it," I say. "I promised you we wouldn't die and we won't. Now shut up a minute." I listen again to the ghost dog's howls. They haven't died down. "It doesn't sound close. It's not coming after us."

"How do you know?"

"I've gone through it before. I know what it's like. This is nothing like that."

That seems to calm Dennis, which is good because I don't know what other lies to tell him. The truth is I have no idea if it's coming for us or not, or how close it really is. It's a ghost dog: the whole point of calling them that is because we don't know a thing about them. But I can't remind Dennis without causing him to panic. Only one of us is allowed to be scared, and since I can't afford to be and still look after Dennis, I stay angry. I stay really, really angry.

"You know what we should do? We should burn the house down. Raze it so it was like that liar Jody was never here. Burn it and grind its ashes into the dirt."

Dennis stares at me, probably because setting an on-purpose fire is maybe the worst thing anyone could do. It's certainly the stupidest.

"No, we can't burn it," he says plainly, for once not eating his words. "It's not the house's fault you're mad, and burning it will attract ghost dogs. I don't want to be here if that happens."

"I thought you wanted to see one."

He shrugs.

"Maybe someday," he tells me. "But I don't want to wait by a fire for it to come get me. We already know there's one close by somewhere. Who knows if there are more? It isn't safe."

I imagine Jody's house burning. Imagine the orange and yellow flames pouring upward out the windows, licking the soffits and eaves. I imagine how high it would get, the thick smoke spiralling into the air in a giant column, announcing itself to all Whitby and maybe further. Maybe all the way across the world. It would be a fire as bright as the sun in the middle of the night, and, yes, it would attract the ghost dogs. Of course it would. Why wouldn't it? Something like that should attract everything and everyone from miles around in every direction. People would try to contain it, choke it until it died, but it wouldn't work. Not this time. This time it would burn and burn forever. It's already burning forever inside me. I can feel the sparks and embers.

"I guess so," I sigh. "It's not like we have a flint rock and steel anyway."

Satisfied, he takes hold of his handlebars and brings the bicycle to a stand.

"We should go home now before any ghost dogs show up."

"I don't know," I admit. "I kind of feel like this is it. This is the time. If we don't keep to the plan and go to the skirts, we never will. Things are already different and it's only been one night. If we turn around, it will all have to start again. We'll say we'll plan and then we won't. And then something will happen—maybe Mama will get too angry and break my arm, or you'll cut too deep and bleed too much, or Mr. McIvory will catch on to what we're planning and tell someone, or maybe one of us will disappear like Jody did. Then who will be left?"

I look over my shoulder at Jody's house and I'm not even angry anymore, not really. I'm scared, and for once it has nothing to do with Mama or the ghost dogs. It has to do with me.

"I don't have much left," I say.

"You have me, " Dennis says. "And we're going to see a ghost dog one day, I promise. But tonight we better leave before it's too late."

I shrug and pick up my bicycle.

"I'll race you home," I say. And he smiles, big and broad, his teeth an overlapping mess that cut his face in two. He's so happy I'm back with him, so happy I'm agreeing with him for once, that he's on his bicycle and pedalling as fast as he can to keep up with me, faster than I ever thought possible. Dennis's bicycle is all spinning wheels and jumping chains, and he keeps neck and neck with me, then somehow he passes me by, and as he does I can actually feel the grin breaking across his face even though I can't see it. I keep that feeling with me as I stop pedalling and let my bicycle slow down, come to a stop. I stand and watch as he keeps going, pedalling like mad into the dark, until he slips away into the night without once glancing back to make sure I'm still with him.

❁

When you're about to travel, there are a few things you always need to bring with you. I imagine my dad had them before he disappeared, because that's what fathers are supposed to do when they leave: be prepared for anything that might keep them from coming back home. I like to look out the windows of Mama's house sometimes and pretend that's where he is right now: trying to find his way back to me. I don't believe it, though. Nobody does anything for anyone, especially come back. If there's one unwritten rule of Whitby, it's that once you leave you leave for good. You leave forever. So even though I told Dennis and Jody we were going to find a ghost dog, what we were really doing was leaving everything behind. All the dust and depression and hopelessness. I want it all gone; I want it replaced by something else.

That's why I packed so much. I packed clothes and a book and what little food I could get out of the pantry without Mama noticing. I also packed the flint rock and steel because I didn't know if we'd need to cook anything or if at some point the blanket of heat that kept pushing down on us would break and we'd find ourselves too cold to go on. And we couldn't huddle, since I don't like people that close to me.

But Jody turned out to be a liar and Dennis didn't really want things to be any different anyway, so I'm on my own, and the only thing I know for sure is that I can't turn around. Not even if I want to, not anymore; not once everyone in Whitby finds out what I did. Dennis will probably tell them it was me eventually because why wouldn't he? He'll realize I'm not coming back for him, so there's no reason to lie. He might even think the ghost dogs got me like they got my dad and his

mom—that they'd come to see the flames leaping off Jody's
house and found me close by, alone in the dark. That doesn't
happen, of course. I wait for them, but the ghost dogs never
show. Nobody does, not for a long time, so I watch Jody's house
as the fire takes it, foot by foot; watch what's left of the paint
bubble, turn black, become a cloud of thick smoke while I
stand bathed in the orange light, in freedom. I stand there not
thinking, not about anything at all; I just exist in that moment,
try to hold onto it for as long as I can, try to climb inside and
live in there forever, but it doesn't work, and when I hear the
anxious screaming I know it's time to put my backpack on and
ride away. I pedal as hard as I can in the opposite direction
from Mama's house, from Dennis, from school, from Whitby,
and head toward the skirts and the great unknown. A ghost
dog howls to applaud me, and I feel so weightless I think I
might lift off the ground and float into the clouds.

There aren't too many paved streets outside Whitby. The
sun cracked the concrete and asphalt a long time ago, leaving
everything twisted and uneven. And where the roads are
broken everything is covered in dust and dirt at least a foot
thick. The only way I even know the roads are underneath
is because of the abandoned street signs for places that don't
exist anymore. Places like Budea Crescent and Armitage Drive
are painted on blue flags that poke out of the ground on bent
metal poles. Most of the time, we use the signs as markers
to know how far out we've gone, and when I pass Trestleside
Grove I know I'm saying goodbye to the sandbags of Whitby
for good and slipping into that no man's land scrub before
entering the skirts proper.

Riding in the dark is hard, and breathing in the dry
sweltering air doesn't help. The night's even hotter than the
day, if that's possible, and I wonder if the moon's light is
worse than the sun's. I'm also thirsty, but I'm always thirsty
and don't worry much about it. You can't be free if you're too

worried about what you don't have, and there's lots I don't have anymore. I don't have the liar Jody or the coward Dennis, and I don't have Mama hanging over me, making sure I do things the way she wants and hitting me every time I screw up. I don't have any of them and no matter what I told anyone before, I don't need them. All I need I have on my back or under my feet, and that's all I care about. That, and seeing a ghost dog before I leave this sand-filled crater for good.

Because the ghost dogs, all they are is freedom, right? They go wherever they want, and no one bothers them, no one stops them. No one has ever caught one or seen one, yet they're always there, outside Whitby, waiting for someone to stray too far. I'm amazed as much as I'm terrified by them, and the longer I'm out in the dark, in the scrub and the sand, the more amazed I become. They're not dumb animals; they're something more, something beyond animals. And I don't know if it's the exhaustion from riding or the exhilaration of knowing I'm never going to see Mama or anyone from Whitby ever again, but seeing a ghost dog is the only thing that means anything to me anymore. Even if I don't know exactly what it is that it means.

Eventually, I can't ride anymore. The roads are too far gone, the sand and the dirt are too deep for my wheels to get any traction, so I stow my bicycle behind a drift that was probably a car once, or maybe a rock. The bicycle all but sinks into it, and the grains falling over the drift's slope look how I imagine those old waterfalls did. After I'm sure there's no way my bicycle will be found, I cinch my backpack straps against my body and keep heading south.

The dust storms start up after I've been walking for a while. First it feels like waves of heat rising from the ground, but soon the sand is racing past as though it's trying to outrun me. I turn around, worried it might be something else, but there's only one set of footprints, and they go back fewer than twenty feet before the dancing sand fills them in.

As the storm worsens, the blowing dirt stings my face, and I spend more time spitting it out than breathing. I have an old scarf that used to be my real mom's, so I tie that around my face so I can keep going without getting sand burns.

In the skirts the world is burnt and forgotten. A giant desert, an empty wasteland of dried out farms and buildings. There's nothing for anybody so far outside of Whitby. Mr. McIvory likes to say nothing lives this far out because nothing can. Nothing but the ghost dogs, I always want to correct under my breath.

The storm fades so dawn can peek through the clouds of settling dust, but I'm so disoriented I don't know where I am or where I'm heading. I check the horizon for a column of dark smoke—maybe I can use Jody's house to steer me—but either I've gone too far or everybody has already descended on the fire and put it out. A part of me suspects a third option: that the night I walked through was actually made of that thick black smoke. Like, as if it spread out from Jody's house and then curled around the world and filled the sky. But that's probably the dehydration talking. I've gone a long time without anything to drink, longer than I ever have before, and it's suddenly dawning on me that I may be in trouble.

I can't help thinking about Dennis, probably heading to school right now, wondering if I'll ever come back, while Reinhold and the rest watch him while their mouths water. In one night Dennis has lost both his friends, his only friends, and without us I don't know how long he'll last, or even if. I hope maybe he'll pull himself together and draw some lines around him, but if I had to guess I'd say the only lines he's going to draw will be deep red ones down his arms. And then it won't matter that Jody and I are gone. Nothing will matter. Whitby will just become that much smaller.

I also think about Jody, living somewhere new, lying to new people about new things, while her mom smiles and feels pleased she kept her beautiful daughter from associating with the wrong people. But if people like me are wrong then why is it we survived when all those people in the books my real mom left behind are so long gone that I'm not even sure they were ever real to begin with? Sometimes, it's as hard to believe as it is in dinosaurs—like it's all a big story made up to trick us when we're kids so people can laugh at us. Jody's mom is probably still laughing; laughing and negotiating more rations than her share so she can find another torchglow bush and nurse it to health. I shudder to think what life with her must be like. No wonder Jody lies. I'd lie too if I was stuck there, having to pretend I was happy.

By the time I get around to thinking of Mama, the morning sun has already heated up and it boils off my sweat faster than I can make it. My brain starts to sizzle in my skull, and it gets harder to remember that I'm walking through the remains of a dust storm, and not sitting around home, talking to Mama. She's trying to tell me something, but I don't want to hear it, whatever it is. She grabs my arm and shakes me, except I don't feel anything. I look down at my arm to see it's fallen off and sand is pouring out of my shoulder. Just waves and waves of sand falling and piling up on the ground. I try to put my arm back on but it won't fit, not with all the sand in the way. And Mama keeps yelling at me the whole time like it's my own damn fault.

And then I feel like I'm buried under sand, and the fleas are nibbling my fingers and toes. I pry my eyes open as best I can and I'm staring at a cloudless blue sky while still half-stuck in a dream, with arms and legs so heavy they might really be filled with sand. I can barely move, but I manage to roll myself over onto my side. My situation is not good. It was a huge mistake coming to the skirts. I'm in the middle of nothing—nothing is all there is. Everywhere I look is nothing, and that nothing is everything. I force myself to sit up, even though my head doesn't like the idea too much, and struggle to choke down my dry heaves. I can't risk losing any more water.

I slowly strip off my backpack, unsnapping the clasps even though it takes forever for my fingers to remember how. I deliriously look inside for a bottle of water I'm convinced I have, but there's nothing. Just the paper package I stole from Mama's pantry hidden among clothes stuffed inside of clothes which I pull out one clenched handful at a time. Eventually they're all spread across the sand and I'm clutching the paper-wrapped package to my chest because I'm weaker and more confused than I've ever been. This is the moment, right when I lie back down on the ground, that I realize this is it. This is the end.

I have no idea why I open my eyes again. It's not a howl or a voice from beyond urging me to keep going. It's not the memory of the way Dennis looked at me like there was nothing I could do wrong, or all the times Jody followed me into something crazy knowing that we'd always somehow make it back home. It's not some desire to see Mama again, or the fantasy that my real mom and dad wouldn't want me to die here in the skirts, bones bleached if I'm lucky, torn apart by ghost dogs if I'm not. I don't think it's any of that stuff. Instead, I'm pretty sure I open my eyes out of pure stubbornness, and maybe disbelief. Plus, I barely have any idea what I'm doing anymore.

But when I open my eyes I see them. Right there, in the deep blue sky that's so clear it looks flat: pillars of smoke. And they're rising out of the kinds of big houses from my real mom's old books—ten times taller than anything I've seen before, made of brick and windows. The smoke is wispy, and nothing like the thick black smoke that billowed out of Jody's house. It's pale. A pale imitation, like Mama would say. But, I don't know, it still looks familiar, and I wonder if I've been walking in a circle all night. Is this Whitby? Even as I struggle to get onto my feet and stay up, a little voice says that's impossible. It can't be Whitby, because Whitby isn't real any more. It's past. Done. Gone. Whitby's like my real mom and my dad: it loved me for a time but now that time's over. I don't belong in Whitby anymore. I'm no more wanted than a ghost dog. I try to cry, but I'm so breathless that all that comes out is dust. At least I'm not sweating anymore.

I don't remember standing up or walking toward the smoke. Time is acting funny all of a sudden, or maybe it's the ache in my head crowding everything out. When I realize what's going on, I stop to look at all those things I threw in the dirt, but they're gone, left somewhere behind me. The only thing I have is the paper package cradled in my arms like it somehow still means something out in the nothing.

That's when I see the ghost dogs. A whole pack, standing out in the dirt maybe five hundred feet ahead of me, not invisible at all. The air bends between us, and they're too far away to see clearly anyhow, but there's no mistaking what they are. It's the way they stand, and the way they watch me stagger forward. Light glints off them like their eyes are glowing, even though I know that can't be real. But the howling, that's real. I hear it clearly, only its rougher, shriller than I'm used to, and as I get closer it starts to sound different from how it did before. Stranger and more metallic, like the sound of a wheel that needs greasing so bad it screams. And the howls repeat themselves, over and over in a steady rhythm like an old clock. Or a siren. But I'm not afraid of the ghost dogs anymore, so I keep going. I keep walking. I'm not afraid because I've realized something on my walk through the skirts. I've realized that maybe it's okay that Jody is a liar; maybe I don't mind that Dennis expects me to solve his problems. Maybe none of that stuff matters, and what does matter is that they were part of me, part of my own pack, and I turned on them. Turned and burned everything down. Maybe it's not the ghost dogs that are the monsters. Maybe it's been me all along. And if I'm the monster, then there's no sense in being afraid of a bunch of ghost dogs.

My lead legs shuffle me closer through the haze, and it's so hot I can barely make sense of what I'm seeing. I always figured the ghost dogs would look sort of like dogs, even if they weren't actually. But they don't. They look like people. Standing near the smoke, a row of five all pointing at me, talking into boxes in their hands, shouting at each other about gates. Which is a weird thing for a ghost dog to do, I have to admit, but it also kind of makes sense. None of them are howling, though. That sound comes from a ghost dog somewhere behind them that's being amplified from the other side of the gates and smoke. I open my mouth to greet the pack and introduce myself, but what comes out of my parched throat is more like a squelched cough.

"We've got another," the one ghost dog says, the one who looks like a woman, but not like the second woman. There are three men with them, too, and all five look like they're dressed in light brown pyjamas while they cautiously walk toward me, hands out. They're all wearing helmets except the woman-dog who's still talking to me, who has already thrown hers into the dirt. They stop walking when I stop, but they've already spread out to try and circle me. I crouch down on my haunches, paper package hugged against me. I know I'm tired and thirsty, but I'm not crazy. I know to not stop watching them.

I'm surprised I understand what they're saying. Then I wonder if it's because the transformation has already begun.

"Kill the sirens," she says, and the man-dog closest to me speaks into his box. As soon as he does the howling from the ghost dogs I can't see halts. Now everything quiets down. So quiet I hear the blowing sand scraping across the dirt. It's louder than the howling ever was and I cover my ears. When I reach my hands up, all the ghost dogs flinch. I've startled them. That feels good.

The other woman-dog holds her hand-shaped paws out in front of her, mumbling something I don't really understand. None of the other ghost dogs move. She reaches into the bag slung across her shoulder, slowly, very slowly, and pulls out something that looks like a mirage at first. Even when she tosses it at me I don't know what to do. It lands in the dirt in front of me with a thud, sending up a cloud of dust. I glance at it then back at the five ghost dogs staring at me; then, again, back at the clear bottle on the ground. The sun shines through it like it isn't there at all. I know I should be watching the woman-dog who gave it to me, but I don't.

"Drink," she says, and though I'm wary I can't help myself. So much water, so close that I can't think straight. I try to control myself in case it's a trap, but before I know what I'm doing I've dropped my paper package and I'm pouring half the bottle into me.

"Careful," she says. "Drink slowly." I glance up and see her in the corner of my eye—see them all—inching forward. I shimmy back, dragging the package with me. The bottle is still clenched in my hand. The woman-dog has long hair, chestnut, with a curl that reminds me of my real mom, of the only photos of her Mama would let me see, but I know it's not true. This woman is not my real mom. It's a good try, and they did a good job trying to fool me, but now that I'm not as thirsty and my head's not as hot I can see the difference. It's in the way she acts. Like she's actually here and not in my imagination.

"We don't want to hurt you." She points past the rest of her pack at the fence behind her. That fence goes on and on in both directions, and behind it are those big houses spewing smoke. All safe and secure and separate. I sniff the air and it doesn't have that savory smell of burning wood, but instead is kind of gritty and maybe a bit greasy. I don't know why there are ghost dogs hiding behind the gates. I don't know why I can still hear the echo of their steady howling.

The woman-dog who is not my mother is close enough now that when she snatches out at me she actually grabs hold of my wrist like Dennis did before, except she's bigger and stronger and less afraid of me even though she should be. I figure out then that her pack is not a pack of ghost dogs at all but instead of regular people, because if they were ghost dogs I'd know it. I'd smell it on them. They're nothing but stupid people, and this place is full of too many stupid people. When the others come closer to help her, I know they're coming to cage me, but they don't know I can't be caged. Not by anybody. Everybody, even stupid Reinhold back in Whitby knows that. But these people don't so I have to show them.

I'm not sure how deep into her hand I get when I bite down, but I think I can go all the way through. I only stop because the bite is a warning to let her know what I am. The woman who is not my real mom and not at all a ghost dog screams and the others stop coming at me while the sick look on their faces tells me they aren't sure what to do. I keep my jaw clenched down until her fingers go limp and she tries to pull away from all my teeth. I release her a second later than I should to hammer in the point, and as she's bringing her hand to her face to inspect the damage everyone can see how dark and red her arm is getting. They're all confused, not sure what to do, so I pick up the paper package I've been carrying all this time, the one way I can think of to see a ghost dog when they don't want to be seen, and even though these aren't real ghost dogs I tear it open anyway and throw it at them.

A cloud of flour billows out of the package, carried by the rising heat, and covers the stupid people, clogging their glinting eyes and making them look more like ghosts than like dogs. It's a funny sight, or probably would be if I stayed long enough to see it. Instead I'm slipping between their blindly grabbing hands and sprinting across the sunbaked dirt and old concrete in the opposite direction. I've still got that half-bottle of clear water locked in my hand and the taste of blood on my curling lips when I hear the sirens behind me, whooping and howling like the largest pack of ghost dogs I've ever heard, except of course they aren't ghost dogs either. They've been tricking us. I bet no one from Whitby has been eaten or savaged or swallowed. Everyone that's gone has just been taken and locked away behind that metal fence. Everyone except my mom and dad. They're the only two who are definitely gone for good. Maybe they got Jody, and she's inside that cage; Dennis, too, if he survived long enough. Mama, they probably left with her vaper to rot where she was and I don't blame them.

I find what's left of a CNR overpass that has so much dust and dirt build-up underneath there's only a narrow opening that's nowhere near big enough for any person to fit through. But I'm not a person anymore so I burrow in fine, even if it's tight. It's cooler than out in the sun, and it keeps me hidden when I hear the voices of men and women shouting, see the dust kicked up as they run. I get a glimpse of one of those cars I read about in real mom's old books but never thought

I'd actually see, not in real life, and it's louder and smellier than I ever imagined. It's like a thousand flies in my head and I have to cover my ears to keep them from exploding. Dirt from the overpass falls down all around me so I close my eyes tight. The rumble of the wheels is in my chest, a great vibration rising up from the ground. But the sound doesn't last long and soon enough the voices and the shouting go away and even the howling disappears and I'm left under the bridge with nothing but my half-bottle of water and whatever I'm wearing.

I wait until it gets dark and quiet before I crawl out from my burrow into the skirts. The sun hasn't finish setting yet—there's still a single sliver above ground, but it colours the sky the deepest purest orange I have ever seen, and it reminds me of what Jody told me once. I can hear the ghost dogs howling faintly from the distant fenced-in town, only now I know the sound isn't ghost dogs, and the nearer rumbling is from the teams of people hunting me. Still, I'd rather be hunted than found, so I'm careful to stay out of sight, even as I make my way back to those gates. I've had a lot of practice hiding—from Mama, from Mr. McIvory, from Jody's mother—and when those rackety old cars start closing in fast, I hide from them, too, lying face down in the dirt, disguising myself as just another piece of debris. It fools those sandbags completely.

I feel both free and a prisoner at once. The truth has released me. The problem is I never planned on what to do after I discovered it, and I'm not sure what happens next. A part of me always thought I'd be like Dennis's mom and so many others and the ghost dogs would take me like they tried to twice before. Or, I guess, *three* times, if you count today. Three times, and they never got me. I never realized how strange that was, but now I get it. It's because they aren't real. I never would have stood a chance against a real ghost dog. But a bunch of sandbags in pyjamas too stupid to avoid getting bit? I'm much too smart for that. My real mom always said there's more to me than people assume, and I think about that a lot, about how people underestimate me. Maybe it's time I show them how wrong they are. Maybe it's time I show those people in their tall smoking houses that they made a mistake. I feel a smile coming on. I know because the dried blood on my face is starting to crack.

Avoiding the people hunting me is easy enough once that sliver of sun finally disappears and the night sets in. The sirens that were howling before are gone and the skirts are a wasteland of animals looking for smaller animals to eat. I sit on my haunches beside a dried yucca bush as a pair of mice wrestle at my feet, not realizing what I am. The muscles in my arms twitch, but I stay calm. My focus is on the town ahead of me leaking wispy smoke into the dark sky. It's nowhere near as beautiful as the site of Jody's house in flames.

The town's gates are taller than anything in Whitby, and around them are more people in light brown pyjamas, some holding crackling boxes or carrying hunting rifles. They're searching the skirts for someone or something, and I wonder if it's me they're afraid of or someone else. Maybe it's *something* else. I try to make out their faces to see if I recognize any of them, but it's too dark to be sure. It doesn't matter: I know if I wait long enough their attention will start to wander and then their eyes will do the same, and I'll be able to get closer to the gate, close enough to squeeze through without being noticed.

That's when I should do something, though for once I'm not sure what. If this were one of my real mom's books, it would be the part where it turns out I still have the flint rock and steel with me and maybe the glass bottle my not-mother ghost dog threw at me. I would use them—together with some gas I'd somehow siphoned from a car—to make a Malted Cocktail bomb. I'd then sneak over the gate or past the checkpoint and lob it at the town to instantly start a big beautiful fire, bigger than Jody's house and the Parkway fire put together, bigger than the whole of Whitby. And while everyone was digging dirt to fight it I'd sneak in and find Jody and Dennis and everybody who'd been captured and release them all. I'd maybe find my dad in there, too, and we'd meet up with my real mom who actually *was* that ghost dog woman the whole time and we'd escape together. Maybe somehow all this would lead to some rain, and the plants starting to grow again in the skirts and everywhere else. And something would happen to Mama, too, I guess. All because of me and how lucky it was I never lost the flint rock and steel.

But it's all a crock. Life isn't like my real mom's books. You know how I know? Because in order for all that to happen, you'd have to assume a bunch of other things. You'd have to assume I'm still part of this world or even want to be. You'd have to assume my transformation hasn't already begun, and that I haven't already forgotten Whitby and everyone in it. Really, what you'd most have to assume is that any of this means anything to me. It doesn't. Not anymore. If it ever did. I don't belong here and it doesn't deserve me. That's the lesson I've learned over and over again, the lesson that keeps me going. But there's another lesson that comes and goes when I try to think about it, and sometimes, like now, it escapes me completely. But it doesn't matter: I don't need lessons anymore. So, instead, I wave goodbye with one finger to the fences and gates and columns of smoke and pad away from this burning town and the errands and the people of Whitby. I have no use for them anymore. I pad away from everything that brought me nothing worth having and dash off into the skirts. I escape everything I hate and try not to remember how bad I used to feel about hating it all before I realized I don't anymore. I just don't.

The only thing I care about is how unburdened I feel. Dashing past search parties I sniff at the dusk air and I can tell it's going to be cooler soon. Ahead of me is the emptiness of the skirts, and once I'm beyond them who knows where I'll go. All I know is it won't be Whitby—I'm too big for Whitby now; like a giant, dwarfing all the houses and the people—and it won't be a caged-in town filled with pretend ghost dogs. Where I'm going only real ghost dogs can go. Only sad ghost dogs. Only unwanted ghost dogs. Or maybe only the ghost dogs who don't want anything from anyone. Who only want to howl and roam and eat. Not quite ghosts, not quite dogs. Who are something else. Yeah, that's where I'll go.

IN THE TALL GRASS

❊

When Reiter is awake, Heike sits at his side, entwines her fingers with his, sometimes strokes his hair. But when he's asleep she steals out to the tall grass at the edge of the farm and finds a spot deep within it to kneel. She doesn't know what she prays to—there's nothing to believe in anymore—but she prays all the same. She prays because deep in the tall grass, far away from the house and from Reiter and from everything she knows, the world is softer and more malleable. She's closer to something she has no name for—be it God or Fate or whatever. No matter how foolish it might be, she hopes if she prays there she will be heard. Reiter will be saved and the two of them will be happy forever.

But she isn't heard and Reiter is gone by the time she returns.

He's buried in the tall grass because that's what he wanted, but she never visits him. She can't go back to where her world ended. Without him, she is untethered. Those crow's feet in the corners of her eyes eventually stretch farther across her broad face, and her red hair turns to a grey like water tinged with blood. The woman in the mirror who returns her furrowed-brow glare looks as though she's forgotten everything Reiter taught her about being alive.

She doesn't notice Baum in the grass because he takes his time arriving. At first he is no more than a shoot between the seed-heavy blades, a thin reach of green that grabs hold of whatever it can to climb its way into the sun and open a lone pink flower to the light. It's during the subsequent autumns and winters and summers and springs that Baum grows and blossoms, getting larger, stronger, until he is finally able to uproot his twisted legs from the soil and find himself steady enough to tramp forward.

Baum emerges from the grass while Heike works on her truck, shirtsleeves folded to above her elbows. She hears the snap of a thousand twigs and turns her grease-smeared face to find Baum crying, crooked arms spread wide. The smell of new green wafts from him while light diffuses through his foliage, dappling shadows over her face.

Baum attempts to speak, to tell her he has watched her move past windows, from the door to the garage; watched her sit on the back stoop in the cool evenings with only a cigarette and a mug, and watched her rub her face and the back of her neck alone in the dark. But there are no words, only a quiet and fluttering rustle. Only in this moment does Baum realize Heike might be unreachable. His round knots well with tears as his crooked limbs stretch farther out. The wind picks up, blows through the leaves, and Heike wordlessly puts her wrench on the truck's running board, then pulls Baum to her breast. Her heart makes a sound like knuckles on a hollow door.

There were never children between Heike and Reiter, and his clothes were given away long ago, so Heike has nothing that will fit Baum's irregular shape. She makes any alterations she can to her own old clothes using nylon thread and stiff-backed perseverance. It's not the easiest solution, or the swiftest, and Baum's small round eyes stare unblinkingly at her the entire time, but eventually Heike is able to fashion a rudimentary pair of trousers to envelope the trunks of Baum's legs, and a jigsaw shirt that makes room for the blossoming pink shoots along his grooved skin. When she is done and Baum is dressed, the noise is like the whistle of rain-soaked leaves. Baum lights up, and Heike recalls how it feels to smile.

The two sit by the dried up pond, soaking their bare feet in memories. Memories are all Heike has of Reiter—the two of them cooling off by the water, laughing and teasing one another. Sometimes she thinks she can see his weathered face reflected back in the remembered water. Other times, she can't see the reflection at all, no matter how long or hard she squints. At these moments, there is nothing in the pond but sunbaked mud, its cracks as deep as the grooves on Baum's flesh. Slowly, they spiral outward.

The farm is no place for a boy. The days are long and hard and Heike likes it that way because it keeps her from remembering Reiter. Remembering his wasting face and body and jaundiced skin. But Baum needs more than that. He is alive and Reiter is not and he needs to learn more than Heike can teach, see more than Heike can show.

Baum has never heard the knocking sound before and even after Heike explains it's a visitor at the door he still lumbers away to hide. The front door opens and unfamiliar voices mumble in the other room. One he believes is Heike's, but the woman is so taciturn Baum cannot be certain. The second is not familiar at all, and leaves him unhappy and apprehensive. Dry twigs break as he shifts, scratching the worn floor. Leaves fall. If he remains motionless perhaps he will fade to safety.

The tutor, Ana, is not prepared for what she finds when she turns the corner in the faltering farmhouse. She has taken odd assignments before—she hasn't had much choice; there are too few tutors so far outside the city, and yet too few students needing help to discriminate. Ana took the job with Baum because she had to, but also because the cousin she remembers most from childhood wore an oversized hearing aid and a single thick-soled boot. That boy went out of his way to treat her well and demanded nothing in return. She hopes helping other challenged students will in some small way assuage her guilt.

But when Ana turns the corner she understands this is not her cousin. This is nothing she has seen before, and for a brief moment the world is completely still, and she is staring at Baum who is staring back with round shimmering eyes, Ana convinces herself it's a joke of some sort. A hoax. A horrible statue posed in a dark house to surprise her. She glances around for her husband and her friends who will soon emerge to laugh at her discomfort. It is only at the end of that second, when the horrible statue moves and she understands it's alive and looking right into her that she gasps and turns away.

There isn't much to say after Ana flees, bags pressed against her chest, eyes darting madly, but Heike does her best to find words to comfort Baum. A rivulet of tears runs along the grooves of his face. It doesn't matter what Heike says, however. They both understand perfectly. Ana, the tutor, has done exactly what she was hired to do and more. She has taught them an unforgettable lesson.

Nothing is the same afterward. Leaves darken. Dry. Fall and crunch underfoot. Pink shoots wither. Baum becomes sullen, withdrawn. Heike does her best to talk to him, but Baum shrinks from the feel of her gnarled hands on his corrugated flesh. When he speaks, if he speaks, it's with branches thrashing and cracking in thunderous resentment. The farm is too small, its fences a prison of constricting walls. He lashes out and storms through Heike's life with wind and fury. Baum wants to escape, but where can he go where he won't be judged or mocked or studied or shunned? Heike doesn't know. But she must do something.

The farm is so far from the city she and Reiter had to stay overnight during each of his treatments. She knows it will be the same for Baum. She has spoken to the county hospital and there is no specialist closer than Dr. Meyer. But this is what Baum wants. He wants to be normal. Through Baum's winter branches Heike can see those knotted eyes and thinks not for the first time there is something of Reiter in them.

Baum never believed he would ever see what lies beyond the tall grass, but Heike's truck sputters and pops, and the air smells as though it's on fire, and he doesn't worry about memorizing that moment because the smell will always remind him of sitting in the truck, branches scraping the bare metal cab. The farmhouse shrinks behind the grass, then the road, then the world itself, and where Heike is taking him is filled with bright blue sky and nothing more for a long time.

Baum's angst withers when the trees come into view. Towering giants marching over the horizon, they grow with each passing moment until they eclipse the sky, laying a veil of shadows over the road and Heike's truck. Baum presses his grooved face against the window but still cannot see their dark canopy. All he sees are the hundreds of trunks woven together on each side of the road, two impenetrable walls ushering the truck toward the wavering sun bursting orange as it approaches the horizon.

They could make it to the city if they drive into the night, but Heike doesn't want to push the truck too hard. The engine needle is already creeping higher than she'd like, and the radiator is guzzling water like Reiter once his kidneys failed. Heike doesn't like thinking about his yellowing skin or cracking lips, so she turns off the highway at the first neon sign she sees. It has become night so swiftly, so completely, it's as though a switch has been thrown, and Heike hopes the dark will keep passers-by from noticing Baum waiting in the car as she pays for their room. He doesn't deserve whatever strangers at a rundown motel might heap upon him.

But she needn't have worried. There is only one person who walks by. He introduces himself through the truck's grimy window as Waechter. Impossibly tall and slender, his coats are black and yet the tie he wears is the colour of summer soap bubbles. Waechter peers at Baum with eyes just as slippery, just as mesmerizing, that make his face look as though it has recently caught fire. The brim of Waechter's hat is large and folded and beneath it Baum can see the rows of gleaming teeth and the pink flower he wears in his lapel, its petals radiating like a starburst. Waechter taps a long finger on the car window, and Baum's branches tremble as he shifts in his seat. He searches for rescue but cannot find Heike.

Baum chirps nervously, the hitch in his voice like a bustle of squirrels caught in autumn branches. Waechter sizes him up while simultaneously looking past him. Then he speaks with a sonorous boom and asks Baum why he is in the car. Baum doesn't know how to respond. Is fear stifling the answer, or is there no answer at all? He is travelling with Heike westward. Branches creak.

Waechter understands. Baum is a prisoner.

Baum protests, but Waechter ignores him, taps his long finger again above the lock. Baum looks at the door, then up at the man's broad smile and slow nod. Leaves blanket the car as Baum trembles. Heike will help him, he repeats to himself. When Heike comes, she will help him.

But Heike does not help him. Heike is inside the motel office, impatient for paperwork to be completed by the stout clerk in thick glasses, wondering how her life twisted so strangely. Everything has been familiar since leaving the farm despite it being years since she's seen any of it. Every inch of road, every curve of hill on her trip through her memories has been a reminder of how far that journey has taken her only to end up in the same place. The only difference being Baum beside her instead of Reiter. Afterward, when Heike leaves the office, room key in hand, she takes only two steps outside then stops. The truck is where she parked it, but the passenger door is open, and the solitary light from the motel flickers blue neon and illuminates the empty passenger seat inside the cab.

Cold creeps up Heike's spine, dries her mouth, disassociates her. She floats a half foot above herself, watches from the aether as her body goes on, always a few seconds delayed. She hears herself call out Baum's name, sees herself jog to the truck. There are leaves and twigs on the cab's floor, something like sap on the handles. Heike looks in every direction while her mind tries to understand something that's just beyond her. She calls out with more volume, moves more frantically.

The neon buzzes then clicks and light shines on the edge of the parking lot. There is a familiar rustle, and Heike turns to see the shadow of branches swaying in the periphery. No less frantic, Heike swallows her concern and approaches Baum who stands on the edge of the paved world and who stares into the darkness of the arboreal.

Heike puts her calloused hand on Baum's rough bark. She

thinks of Reiter.

Baum doesn't turn, but he too thinks of Reiter. His hand is twisted into the shape of a fist. He creaks and moans and wonders where Waechter has gone. A few minutes later, Baum looks at Heike but he can't see anything, his knotted eyes engraved by the forest. Heike guides him back to the truck, then into their rented room. During the night the neon buzzes and clicks and neither Heike nor Baum are able to sleep for the thoughts rattling in their heads.

In the morning Baum is more or less himself, although quiet, and Heike does not want to push him. Instead they gather their things and drive off in the direction of the city with a burst of exhaust and the rattle of a truck unused to meeting its limits. If anyone from the motel has seen Baum, there is no effort made to get a closer look. Baum looks for Waechter, but if he once was near, he has long since retreated into the woods.

And the two drive on.

The jagged cityscape rises from the horizon as the forest had, but with concrete taller than trees and lights brighter than fireflies. It looks grand and endless, but Baum finds little excitement in seeing such a vast monstrosity. There are loud and sudden noises, and the air grows harder to breathe the closer the truck gets. Baum looks at Heike and sees her aged hands turned pale as they tighten around the steering wheel. She turns her head a fraction and her grip eases. The corner of her mouth offers a smile. Reassured, Baum turns back to the window, and the sights there bend his rough bark into a frown.

It's nearly noon when the truck, overheated and thirsty, finally pulls to a stop in the small parking lot adjoining the hospital. Baum has never seen a building so large, and it makes him feel insignificant. His problems are nothing in the face of the gigantic. He puts his hand on the concrete wall to prove it's real, and it's cold and rough and splinters catch on it like brambles. He can't put into words why he isn't surprised, nor explain why he pretends not to notice Heike watching.

Dr. Meyer's office is on the fifth floor. They take an elevator, and Baum cannot help inspecting every inch of the small room. It makes Heike weaken, but she says nothing and wonders again if she was wrong to hide Baum from the world. But what choice did she have? Heike does not like the city—too many reminders of Reiter in the curved streets and looming buildings. Avoidance had served her well, and would have continued to do so had Baum not needed her more than she needed herself. The understanding makes Heike stagger, but she doesn't falter. Instead, she pushes the realization aside. It won't help her where they're going.

When Heike and Baum arrive, the receptionist purposely avoids reacting to Baum's corrugated face. Instead, she hands them a clipboard with a pen tied to it by a piece of frayed twine. The form must be filled out, and she asks them to sit in the waiting chairs while they do so. Heike struggles for the words to describe her relationship to Baum, afraid to write what she knows is true.

A nurse with tight brown curls leads them to a room only slightly larger than the elevator and has them wait behind the closed door. Baum is nervous and timid, but once the nurse has gone his inquisitiveness resurfaces. Heike watches him probe the room and test the world. Baum wraps vines around drawer pulls and leafs through a stack of forms, but with each investigation he comes away disappointed and soon disinterested. Whatever he was looking for, he can't find it.

There is a clipped series of knocks on the door, and before either Heike or Baum can react Dr. Meyer has entered the room. Energy crackles off him as he speaks, lightning-eyed and curious in a way that Heike doesn't trust. But she never trusts anyone who is too curious, and since Reiter's passing she trusts doctors least of all. Dr. Meyer introduces himself but Heike doesn't pay much attention. She's too busy looking at Baum to see how he's reacting. Limbs shake as though there are rodents scurrying between them, the sound like a crashing river. Baum's knot-holed eyes have sunk so deep into his phloem that they are hidden. The only evidence they are there at all is the teary glint of light from deep within the recessions.

Dr. Meyer reassures Baum it will be okay, but something about his manner concerns Heike. He acts like a pig waiting impatiently by the trough.

Baum nods when Dr. Meyer says he needs to run a few tests, and asks if Baum can be brave for him. He feels as though birds are nesting in his branches, their weight slight but aggravating, and knows the only way to dispel the sensation is to shake them out. He does this obsessively three times to be sure they're gone, and when he looks up again through the rain of dry coloured leaves floating to the ground it's only Heike's smile that is no longer there.

Dr. Meyer finds it hard to contain his excitement about such an important autosomal case, and is nearly skipping as he leaves the subject in the small room, promising to be back shortly with more information. But leaving was only to give him time to process the intensity of his excitement. Dr. Meyer looks at the nurse, aware of the broad smile on his face, and sees her eyes are already alight. She, too, has never seen anything like this. *Epidermodysplasia verruciformis*, in all its glory. It's a find that could, if coordinated properly, mean solving the riddle of HPV and potentially more. There is so much good they can do. When Dr. Meyer gets to his private office, he places a call to the Research University, then waits as he's transferred to the dean. Above his door hangs a framed novelty Time magazine cover with his photo, and above the headline reads: "Doctor of the Year". Dr. Meyer smiles and puts his feet up.

But in the middle of explaining his find, there's an urgent knock at Dr. Meyer's door. He puts the receiver to his chest as the nurse rushes in with the news. It's the last thing Dr. Meyer wants to hear. It takes a moment to catch up with his thoughts. He tells the dean he'll have to call him back.

Getting to the car again is more difficult than Heike had expected. There are too many people rushing through the streets, and if they make Heike feel uncomfortable and claustrophobic, she can only imagine how they are affecting Baum. There's no point in going back into the hospital—no one there is interested in helping. Heike urges Baum to hurry as she notices passers-by slowing. She can see it in their mannerisms: they are beginning to question if what they're seeing is real, and instinct is prompting them to advance. Baum notices it, too, the slow migration toward him, and he shrivels in fright, branches shaking off his last straggling leaves. Heike is helping him into the truck as the first curious gawker arrives.

What is that? he asks. Some kind of costume? And Heike won't look at Baum because if she doesn't maybe Baum won't have heard anything. But Heike hears. She hears twigs scraping the roof of her truck, back and forth the sticks worrying the old metal, and Heike grows irritated, angry. She puts her hand flat on the chest of the man trying to peer through the truck's window and shoves him. Tells him to mind his own damn business. The man corrects his twisted shirt; looks hurt and annoyed. He was just asking about the costume, for Pete's sake, and Heike teasingly imagines for a second—for less than a second, for a fraction of a second—slamming the man's teeth into his face to show him and all the approaching gawkers that they can't say these things about her son.

Baum. Her son.

The idea frightens her. She looks through the window at the trembling Baum and understands how much Reiter would have loved him, and he Reiter. Death robs so much from everyone, stopping only when there is nothing left worth taking. Heike turns, unsure if she means to hug the man or beat him senseless, but it doesn't matter. He's already gone—back up the street to rejoin the gawkers who now keep their distance, who have decided they no longer need to see the freak—and the end of the afternoon feels closer than ever. The wheat is probably ripening at the farm as she stands on the dark asphalt of the hospital parking lot, so far from her centre, from where Reiter waits patiently for the day she will inevitably join him. She'll be there soon, she thinks. Home with Baum, home with Reiter close by. She feels better when he's near. Closer to being complete.

Baum doesn't speak as the truck pulls out of the parking lot, finds the long road toward home. He watches out the window, tendrils on the glass, as the world passes by; as the crowds on the streets thin, as office buildings become storefronts become houses. The truck crawls from the depths of looming concrete to surface on the flat landscape of grasses and rocks. And all the while, Baum doesn't speak, not even as the city fades in the rear mirror, taking with it the last of Baum's hopes. There's nothing left for him now. The roughness of the road vibrates from the tires into the cab but Baum doesn't feel it. He doesn't feel anything. Disconnected and untethered, he is starting to float away. He turns to Heike, though he's not sure if it's for help or to say goodbye. What comes out of his mouth is the long sorrowful creak of a branch about to yield from strain.

Heike looks at him, at his grey bark, at his softened grooves and ridges, and she knows she's made a mistake. She's made so many—running from Dr. Meyer, bringing Baum to the city, hiring Ana—and she wonders how far back it goes. Where did it start? Was there a single choice from which all her mistakes sprang? If she could change that one thing, maybe everything would be different. The answer comes almost immediately, and it makes her so sick she can barely form the thought.

If she'd never met Reiter. Maybe if she'd never met Reiter then...

She glances at Baum.

I ever tell you about the day I first met my Reiter? He was seven; I was nine. His aunt lived in the house next to mine, so he'd sometimes visit there. Once, he was visiting because the aunt was sick, and when he was shooed outside I was already there playing. So he joined me and we played till the sun went in. Then his aunt died and his family took him away and never came back.

That's the story he told me a year after we married. Didn't remember it then. Don't remember it now. But it makes sense it happened like that. Reiter and me, we belonged to each other from the very beginning. No bad luck or hardship or nothing can change that. Not even him dying. Those people back there who stared at you, all the people you hide from? They don't get it. They don't get belonging. It's not about pushing away things that are different, it's about finding how things are the same. It's about finding your place. I found mine and a piece of me is still with him underground, wrapped in a sheet. Forget those people. Forget Dr. Meyer and the rest. Just worry about where you belong.

Baum stares unblinkingly at her, each bump on the road shaking his bare branches. Heike twists her hands on the wheel, frustrated the words came out wrong. She wanted them to make Baum feel better, to reassure him. They were the wrong words. But before she can fumble for the right ones, he reaches out and gently touches her hand.

The forest materializes out of aether and mist. It isn't that Heike doesn't recognize the highway as it takes them into the woods, but that the day is late and her back is hurting from the bent spring in her seat, so everything appears slightly distorted and foreign. Trees look older than they had earlier in the day, thicker and balder, and they glare down at the truck passing beneath as though they've been expecting this return. Heike leans forward, looks up at the imperfect canopy, and considers how bizarre it is that such a sparse mesh can still snare so much light.

She has no plan beyond reaching the farm as soon as possible, driving through the night if necessary, but all Heike's fight drains once the truck enters the thickest section of the forest. The endless shadows overtake the truck, clawing it back as the fading day stretches time to its thinnest strand.

Heike feels the drag of exhaustion slowing her movements, filling her arms with sand, and she knows she won't be able to drive much farther. At least Baum is slowly shaking his stupor. Once among the endless web of trunks and brush he stirs, presses his face against the window, and looks intensely into the woods for something.

If the clerk at the motel recognizes Heike from the morning, she doesn't show it. Or, perhaps it's a different clerk at a different place. Heike cannot be sure when every motel looks like the one before. Bored, irritated without obvious reason, the pudgy woman slides Heike the key and turns away before Heike can retrieve it. Heike staggers back to the car in a race to get to bed before the sleep hurtling towards her arrives, wondering how much of what she is experiencing is real and not waking dream. The truck wavers in the lot and she feels a chill when she sees it, sees Baum's face behind the glass; his ashen, leafless face molded with an emptiness Heike cannot define any better than she can her own.

They settle in the room for the night, speaking little to each other. Baum sits by the open window, watching the forest outside while Heike sits on the edge of the bed, staring down at the wrinkled photograph of Reiter she carries with her. Between them lays nothing but worn and dirty carpet. Eventually, exhaustion comes for Heike, but she doesn't question its source for fear of the answer. Instead she pulls the covers up to her chest and turns out the light. Baum remains in the window, so Heike watches him—his leafless branches fracturing the rectangle of sky that's cut into the room's darkness—and listens for his breathing. It's slow and steady and mirrors her own. When sleep comes, and reality softens, a moment before Heike succumbs she wonders if Baum's breathing is so familiar because it's always only been hers. A reflection in darkness. She rolls over before she can wonder more and the thought is gone.

There is a solitary light on the highway, illuminating a small circle of road and those few leafed branches that reach for it. Baum watches them sway in the night breeze, dancing or beckoning, he doesn't know which. Tall and without burden, they just exist, growing forever into one another's embrace. They belong, so why doesn't he? Tears fill his grooves, travel a long way down until their momentum dissipates. He remembers his life in the tall grass, remembers how it nourished him. Now he slowly drifts away inside a cheap room, unable to feel that grass or those woods beyond the highway. Baum runs his splitting vines on the glass to clean a blemish, but it doesn't move, and he realizes the spot is something else. Something more, hidden among the trees. Baum leans forward, his trunk creaking, and witnesses the trees part like a curtain. From the void between steps Waechter. He is dressed in pink now—pink shirt, pink linen jacket and trousers, all dingy to the elbows and knees—and his legs look strange, as though bent in the wrong direction. Like the legs of a goat. His toothful mouth emits no sound, but it laughs all the same, his head bobbing in time. He mouths a word Baum cannot make out, but the sound... he has heard it before. It is the sound of the forest, and Waechter speaks for it as he beckons Baum onward while retreating into the darkness between the trees, fading into the tall grass where the world is its softest and most malleable.

Heike is thrown from bed and onto her feet before she is fully awake. Somehow, it's mid-morning, and the late day and lingering grogginess induce a vertigo she can't fully tamp down. Baum is no longer at the window, but he is not in the bed, either. Heike checks the bathroom, then opens the front door. Beyond it is the gravel lot, followed by a narrow asphalt strip of highway with cars that whizz too fast. On the opposite side, the world full of trees. A thunderstorm of panic swirls inside Heike, but it's suppressed by an inchoate layer of something else—something cold that keeps it at a distance where it is unable to affect her. It is a form of shock designed to help her displace her terror and keep moving, though there's a whisper that tells Heike that it's all she will be able to feel from now on, forever and ever. It's the feeling of leaving the world behind.

The first place Heike goes to is the pond, but when she arrives there is no Baum, and there is no pond. It's as dry as the one on the farm. She looks into it, but does not see the reflections of memories, does not see Reiter or Baum or anyone else. What Heike sees is nothing. Nothing but an empty vacant hole in the ground. No, not empty, she realizes. There's something in the middle of the dry pond, something small and bulbous. She carefully gets to her knees, ignoring any pain, and throws her legs over the bank one at a time before sliding in. When she reaches the bottom, she realizes the dried mud belies the wet muck beneath, and her feet sink five slowly-filling inches. She trudges through the mud at the centre of the dried pond and finds the fibrous pod waiting for her there, small green vines clutched around it. She bends over, her back already sore from strain and picks it up.

Baum is gone as though he was never there. Heike spends the day walking through the woods, calling his name, but he never appears and the cold never dissipates. It stays, seeping into her flesh, pricking her skin. About an hour into the tangle of trees she finds a small Redbud covered in pink blooms. Its branches hang low, and dangling from them are strips of dingy cloth like a shirt Baum once owned—though they could just as easily be pieces of something else.

When she emerges from the woods the sun's orange has leaked across the sky. Heike's throat is hoarse from calling for Baum, and mud has caked her arms and legs. She crosses the highway without a cautionary glance in either direction, and gets into her truck. She places the pod on the empty seat beside her, using the strips of torn shirt to form a nest. The truck's engine starts with a hollow, distant cough, and it jerks when she puts it in gear and drags it onto the road. Heike leaves everything behind, heads back to where she came from. She doesn't look at anything beyond the road, doesn't do anything but drive. There's no reason to.

It's only been three days since she was at the farm, but she barely recognizes it. It's like entering an old photograph, familiar only at a distance. Heike parks the truck and turns off the engine, and stares at the culmination of her life. She wonders: if not here, then where? She exhales, deflates, and takes into her hand the pod she remembers as being much lighter. The walk into the tall grass—the grass she has not looked at, or visited, or acknowledged in years—is long, and the blades have grown to her waist. But they reach higher, catching her with barbed ends, like fingers trying to pull her close for an embrace. Heike pushes them aside, unwilling to be slowed, as she searches through the overgrowth for what she knows is there.

A lifetime has passed, but not long enough to hide where Reiter rests. She finds his marker not by sight but because she nearly trips over it. He is where she left him, beneath the small stone monument that announces his passing. Heike kneels and touches the stone with her gnarled wrinkled fingers, runs them over the carving, uses her nails to dig out those letters obscured. She cleans the stone as best as she's able while her heart knocks on her chest and the sweat loosens her glasses from the bridge of her nose. She tells Reiter everything: what's happened since he left, how Baum entered her life and how he left. She empties her heart, and though she expects a number of times to cry, she does not. When she's done unburdening herself, she lifts a divot of dirt from the ground and places the seed pod underneath. Then Heike does her best to stand and tamp it with the flat of her shoe.

Heike waits, looking at what lies at her feet, and somewhere inside her the clouds she didn't think would break do, and a torrential thunderstorm rushes through her. It seems never-ending until it does, and when she wipes her face she finds the ground soaked and the divot of dirt has produced a small shoot that gingerly tests the sky. She sniffles, smiles, and watches as the tiny stalk reaches upward and catches the rough weave of her cotton trousers. Watches it cling, then wrap itself around her leg. She watches leaves slowly unfurl and open to the light while the shoots grow longer, thicker, stronger, intertwining with her limbs.

And she continues to watch as time splits the seams of her shoes and fibrous roots appear, then sink into the soil. Her skin hardens, her wrinkles deepen, become grooves.

In her hair, shoots blossom, silky pink with yellow pistils. Soon, there is little difference between her and the tree that envelops her. Weather and sun rot her clothes while the two grow further enmeshed, and she utters a noise that sounds like the soft percussion of a hundred starlings taking flight at once. Heike's final thought is of Reiter, of that time in the sunshine, their hands locked together by the edge of the pond, and she imagines Baum with them, the son they never had, flesh and blood and smiling. Before she can smile the thought is gone, and all that remains are two trees forever twisted and entwined, inseparably anchored by a grave buried beneath the tall grass at the edge of the farm.

THE FIFTH STONE

—————————— ✤ ——————————

My first memory is of grasshoppers trapped in my tiny cupped hands. It remains stuck in my head, untethered from time and place, and I recall nothing else but the sensation of their membranous wings fluttering against my skin.

Outside that near void of infancy, my first true memory is of finding the stone. I was at most five years old, and because I fully awoke on discovering it in my family's back yard, the stone became one of my most treasured possessions. It was flecked with glittering minerals between layers of the deepest emerald, and it vibrated as I clutched it, a feeling not dissimilar to those imprisoned grasshoppers. I remember dancing with glee in my little rubber shoes while my oblivious mother stood above, lost in distraction and intense garden-party conversation. Even then I knew better than to tell her what I'd found. Some discoveries are meant to be kept secret from everyone. I took the stone and folded it into my dress for protection until I could find a place where I might study it further. It felt warm against my skin. The stone was the most wondrous thing in the universe, and I knew that I would never find its equal. Until, of course, I did.

The second stone called to me as soon as I spotted it in the dirt during a weekend visit to our Oxtongue Lake cottage, and when I smuggled it back home and compared it to the first, the two sparkled in unison. I kept them beneath my mattress, careful to peek at them only while the house was asleep. When

I discovered the third a year or so later, I had to find a different place to store them. Leaving the three together beneath my bed induced the strangest nightmares.

It was when I found the fourth stone that I experienced my first grand mal seizure. I wasn't older than nine, but already I was straining at the yoke childhood had put on me. While my mother walked along the woodland path in Millbrook Park, I stayed on its edges, existing between trees and steep hills. My mother kept her eye on me, but I did my best to melt into the woods, to become one with the shadows and bark. As soon as she was distracted enough to look away, I stopped to investigate the fauna and take in the sight of Rouge Creek trickling over the fenced-in rocks. I knew the park was nothing like a real forest—especially with the asphalt path leading through its center—but for a short time I was able to pretend. Seed pods and leaves rained down on us like a summer storm.

No one knew how consumed my life was by the stones. In private, I would arrange my collection in various patterns on the bedroom floor, looking for a configuration my intuition suggested was correct. Then, I would delicately commit the shape to paper. I did this in an attempt to understand the stones and their incongruous presence in the world. But also to understand my own feelings of disconnection from those who claimed to love me, and my desperation to be any place that didn't tie me down. Sketching the stones made me as they were—immutable, permanent. But despite my attempts at capturing the stones' mystery, none of the drawings felt accurate. All were approximations—impressions devoid of both power and something else I could not define.

I scoured the sides of the path through Millbrook Park, looking beneath fallen trees and amid flower beds. My mother was distracted with caring for my infant brother, which allowed me to stray farther than I was allowed. The stones I'd found until then had been accidental discoveries, but I was determined to purposely uncover another, and couldn't do so under her suspicious gaze. Time crept on, and when she finally realized I had gone, she frantically called out for me to return. But I didn't. Instead, I hid in the bushes and plotted my next action. It was my first brush with freedom, and I was invigorated. I shifted my weight to find a more comfortable vantage point, and my foot caught something hard. It was as though someone had reached up through the dirt and grabbed hold. I pitched forward before my arms knew enough to protect my face.

I landed hard and it pushed the air out of me, scrambling my thoughts. When the haze cleared, I made sure my mother hadn't witnessed my fall, then looked to see what had caused it. Another stone. It remained in the dirt, half exposed, and was unlike any of those previous. I couldn't describe it; I could hardly look at it—the thing refused to sit still in my hand long enough, vibrating at such an extreme frequency it hummed. As I held the stone, my little nine-year-old hand numb from the vibrations, everything around it vibrated too, accelerating until the two were in synch. Then, the world shook faster, faster, and ripples expanded outward from the stone like reality was the surface of a pond. Light ceased to behave, glowing and pulsing and flashing, and though I remember shocks dance across my limbs and skull, they were so distant I saw them erupting outside the blurry haze. The memory of what transpired next vanished, and I returned to groggy consciousness in my hysterical mother's arms as she sobbed. My brother's tiny lungs commiserated a few feet away.

It took time for my mother to calm down and realize I wasn't in immediate danger. If anything, the only threat I faced was from her constricting hugs. I was terrified of what had happened, the experience of losing control over everything I was. How could I go on when it was clear the barrier that keeps chaos at bay was thinner than an onion's skin? But I kept it hidden, worried she might squeeze me so tight I'd stop breathing.

We were in a cab to the hospital as soon as we emerged from the park, and when we arrived my father was there to retrieve my brother and ensure I was okay. I wasn't—I still felt weak and shaken and disconnected from myself—but I remained quiet and smiled nonetheless, nodding and answering politely, all the while secretly hoping everyone would leave me to my panicked thoughts.

While waiting for the Emergency Room doctor to call us, I remembered the stone I'd found. It still wriggled in my brain and made my shoulder blades and stomach twitch. I was convinced I'd slipped it into my pocket as the seizure struck, and the idea I might still have it made me want to retch. I rose and frantically patted down my pockets, two at a time, as though putting out a fire.

"Elizabeth, sit," my mother ordered, her manic voice wavering. I ignored her and continued searching until I was sure I hadn't pocketed the stone, then I slumped back into the plastic waiting room chair. It was gone, and when I returned home the others would follow.

"You really scared me today, kid. I hope you know that."

"I'm sorry, Mom."

"What were you looking for?"

How could I explain it to her? How could I tell her about the stone and the visions it induced? Especially when it was the reason we were at the hospital?

"I found something in the park. I thought I'd kept it."

She gave me a queer look, then opened her bag and pulled out that terrible vibrating stone. She held it up for me to see. The world dropped away, leaving behind faint chirping.

"You mean this?"

I nodded.

"You were squeezing it in your hand when you—when you got sick. Do you want it?"

I reached out then stopped. The hairs along my arms stood. Quivering found the recesses of my back. A flash of spines, the echo of screeches. What would the stone do to me if I touched it?

A nurse materialized before I found out. She ushered us along. By the time my mother and I were settled and awaiting the doctor, my Emergency Room dance has been forgotten.

The doctor was unconcerned, explaining that sometimes

children simply had seizures. There was no discernible reason, and they outgrew it quickly. Still, she made some recommendations and gave us referrals for more intensive tests. My mother wrestled with me over the following weeks and months to attend them, but at the end of the process not one of the doctors found anything wrong. My family was told to wait and see if the seizures returned. My mother cursed that answer, but it was clear it relieved her. She stopped asking me how I was doing, at least. She also made me promise to tell her if anything like that should happen again. I agreed, continuing to hold secret the three additional seizures I'd already suffered.

They occurred each time I touched the stone. My mother had left it on my study desk as I slept off my adventure, unknowingly providing me with the key to inducing what most worried her. I was filled with dread on seeing it, but was too young to trust my suspicions. It seemed impossible, but I learned quickly that bringing the stones close together was not worth the cost. Once I awoke bleeding from the back of my head, no doubt having slammed it on the ground repeatedly during an episode; another time my lip was bitten almost clean through and had to be blamed on a bicycle accident. The stones were destroying me, each seizure a rope thrown around my neck and staked to the ground. I didn't understand what was happening, but I refused to succumb. Instead, I did what any sane, rational girl would do: I gathered the four stones into an old wool sock and when my parents' attention was elsewhere I found a spot behind our garden shed and buried them. As each shovel of dirt rained down, the pressure on my soul eased.

The fifth stone literally struck me out of the blue. Once I interred that wool sock I left my seizures and childhood behind. Puberty struck soon afterward, changing my body and diverting my thoughts, and my urge to flee my home and what was buried there only grew stronger. I stayed away as much as I could, and when I couldn't I locked myself away from my parents' prying and my brother's incessant neediness. I never thought of myself as unhappy, but being at home, under rule and responsibility, pulled at my being. I wanted to abandon it all and escape.

The fifth stone changed everything. I was walking home from school, books pressed against my burgeoning chest, passing the local baseball diamond. It was early enough in the school year that gym classes were still being held outdoors, yet late enough that I was wearing a sweater and the sky was already painted with shadows. My attention was elsewhere as I daydreamed about how different my life would be once I left for college, and how no force in the universe could ever make me return home. The taste of freedom was so close my mouth watered, and when I closed my eyes to savor it, I was struck. Pain interrupted my thoughts, so sharp I believed my skull had exploded. I buckled in agony, fell to the ground, the sensation eliciting the strangest images in my mind's eye. It was all too fleeting to comprehend, but it lasted long enough to fill me with terror. Harsh chirping echoed and screeched through my head. I writhed on the ground in pain, hand pressed to my throbbing temple, grass staining my new sweater as I sobbed. Someone grabbed me, tried to comfort me and ensure I was all right, but it took an eternity before the pain ebbed and I could pry my eyes open. I lowered my hand from my temple and saw the blood waiting there for me. It ran over my fingers, down my palm, into the cuff of my filthy sweater. It was sickening. I turned into the blinding light silhouetting the face hanging there, eclipsing the world, as he asked if I were all right.

"No, I'm not," I spat. "What happened?"

"I don't know," the boy said. He wore a heather cap, but the rest of his features were concealed in backlit shadow. "You fell down screaming. Then you just started—I don't know. Shaking. Do you need to go to the hospital?"

"I think something hit me," I said. "It was hard." I looked again at the blood on my hand. "Is it bad? It feels bad."

He ran his fingers over my bleeding head, pushing apart either my hair or my flesh. His fingers were rough but warm.

"It's still bleeding. You need to go the hospital. I'll get my

THE FIFTH STONE

car. It's just over there."

He snapped his fingers.

"Did you hear me? You look spaced."

"Did you see what it was?"

He shook his head. The remaining afternoon light illuminated the side of his face. I didn't recognize him, but he smiled and my heart beat with so much wondrous terror I had to turn away. I concentrated on pawing through the grass.

"What are you looking for?"

"Whatever hit me. It's got to be around here somewhere."

I dared a glance at him. His shadow shrugged.

"Why?"

I stopped and looked at my dirty bloodied hands, my stained clothes, my books strewn on the ground. He was right. What was I doing? I didn't know. I just knew I had to do it.

"I won't be able to rest if I don't."

I returned to searching, running my hands through the blades. I sensed him standing behind me, but he didn't leave and I didn't stop no matter how embarrassed I felt. We stayed that way—me pawing the grass like a blind woman, him watching—until I realized I wasn't well. The world was slowly rocking and losing volume. My limbs were getting heavier.

Then, my hand grazed the stone lying in the grass. Those screams I'd cried when it hit me paled compared to the agony of touching it. Every inch of my body twitched alive, and I was engulfed by a seizure unlike any I'd ever experienced. I screamed and screamed and wondered if I'd ever stop screaming.

I was in my house. The edges of my vision sizzled and popped like a stuck film strip. Beyond it, a slowly collapsing star. Everything was rotten and decrepit—cobwebs hung from corners, the floor uneven as dirt pushed through it. There was a horrible pulsing screech, a low frequency that hurt my ears and eyes. I found myself at the foot of an incongruous staircase, and at the top, beyond a slowly twisting corridor, a foreign second floor waited, guarded by a single closed door.

That door, I knew, must never be opened.

I climbed, the staircase twisting with each step. The screeching resumed, long and deep, and the edge of a shadow appeared on the surface of the door beyond. It grew larger. Larger. And whatever cast it followed close behind.

Then the world smelled of dirt.

I opened my eyes and saw blinding pale sky, my limbs heavy, shackled to reality. I tasted dry metal, and every word I tried to speak was random vowels whispered from across the room. There were other noises, but I ignored them, too lost in my skull to make sense of what was happening. When the tumblers in my brain fell into place, I wanted to sit up, terrified and humiliated by what had happened. The boy in the heather cap held me back.

"You're going to the hospital."

And that led to a lifetime of medication. Pills of various sizes, shapes, and colours, all designed to do a single thing: stop the seizures. Epilepsy wasn't the curse it once was, they assured me. I could live a normal life without worry. That was the promise. But a switch had been flipped, and I lived in terror of it. What if the grand mal seizures returned? What if what happened to me on the grass was the first volley in a lifelong war my brain was waging against me? I needed to avoid it at all cost, so I made the bargain with the doctors, with my parents, with myself, and took their pills. Took their counselling and their therapy and everything they prescribed, even as it dismantled and dulled every desire for freedom I once held. Each chained me down one at a time, deadening my dreams and leaving me as everyone wanted me to be: safe and sound and free from suffering. But I got what I wanted; my seizures were gone. And as the years piled on one another, eventually I forgot it had ever been any different.

During those years the boy in the heather cap never left me. The hats changed, the clothes changed, but his smile never did. One day I found myself married to him, another holding the first of our three daughters, and I was never quite certain when each new rope had been tied. By the time those children moved away and left him to me alone, the seizures were so far distant they were forgotten. The pills were merely my pills, and my dreamless nights merely the way I slept. Those years were peaceful, at least. Everything buzzed with ordinariness.

When my husband died, things were not so peaceful. Our daughters were spread across the globe, two unreachable and the third unable to stay past the funeral. I was left to clean our house alone, a single old woman who moved slower than ever, who thought slower than ever, trying to piece together what remained of her life. I was afraid to leave the safety of our home, and yet every room reminded me of him—every chair and plate and pillow and photograph. They once belonged to both of us, and overnight they became solely his. I spent my days going through his belongings again and again, not knowing what else to do. Occasionally, I would stop to smell what was left of him on an old sweater, or touch his jacket and pretend he was still in it. The house was an empty prison without him.

I found something in the bottom drawer of his dresser, pressed against the back and wrapped inside an old handkerchief. I didn't know what it was when I removed the bundle and shook it out. The object fell onto the bed with a dull thud and confronted me—a flat quartz surface, light reflecting oddly. My suffering prevented me from immediately recognizing it. Then, when I did, I was overcome by fear.

He'd kept that fifth stone. The one that had appeared out of the blue, the one without which he and I might never have met. I knew him, his sentimentality—he had kept it because it was the spark of our beginning, and yet when I saw it I also knew it spelled my end. It was a chunk of suppressed nightmare dropped without ceremony into my waking life, and after so many years without suffering dreams of any kind I didn't want it anywhere near me. I left it on the bed and closed the door to the room I'd shared with my husband, doubting I'd ever be brave enough to step past the door again.

Yet I couldn't forget the stone waited for me, as it had

SIMON STRANTZAS

for more than sixty years. My obsession with it grew until all
other thoughts were pushed out of my mind. It didn't take
long before I was forgetting to take my medications, and once I
was off that handful of assorted pills the murky patina cleared
from my eyes and revealed the prison into which I'd let fear
drive me. My dreams flooded back, and in those dreams I was
a child again, unburdened by love's or life's hardships, seated in
my childhood home with the fifth stone in my hand. I placed it
on the ground with the other stones I'd collected—five stones
in a circle, equidistant from one another. I drew invisible lines
between them with my finger, and as I did my dream-self's
eyes grew larger, her mouth wider, and a colossal force pressed
against her. I woke into the dark of the real world. Or what I
thought was the real world. I wasn't all together convinced.

I returned to our old bedroom and stood over the stone.
The house was silent—everything vanished as I gazed deep
into the quartz surface. Could I see ripples emanating from
it? Some strange force pulsing? I extended my shaking hand,
wanting to touch it but afraid. The stones had evoked visions
of a future inevitability I didn't want to admit, and though
it had been decades since I last touched one, its warnings of
something approaching were as vivid as if they'd happened
only minutes before. The visions and dreams, despite being
long abandoned and blocked, were nevertheless trying to
explain something to me, and it had taken me my entire life to
listen. I was being prepared. But for what would only be clear
once I gathered the five stones together.

My daughters had put my husband's Chrysler up for
auction, but it still sat in the garage, waiting for a buyer, and
I still had the key. Getting behind the wheel and out onto the
street was an unexpected challenge—the heather cap atop the
dashboard was a painful reminder of my loss—but once the car
was on the highway a renewed sense of freedom washed over
me. It was fleeting, though, lasting only until I remembered I
was anything but free. I drove as fast as my nerves would allow,
hurtling back to the house I'd once wanted so desperately to
escape, back to where the rest of the stones patiently awaited

my return. On the passenger's seat was a small box weighted with so many questions.

An hour later I was driving down a narrow street I hadn't seen in a lifetime. The car moved slowly over the asphalt and beneath rows of overgrown trees, while the sound of the highway faded into the background. I barely recognized where I was, despite having spent so many years riding my bicycle through the web of neighborhood streets. Like a dream, everything was both familiar and foreign. The bushes and trees were trying to overtake the road and I wondered if the houses I passed had been abandoned. Branches hung low enough to scratch against the car windows and over the hood and trunk, fingernails trying to claw me back. The few street signs that hadn't yet been consumed were inexplicably blacked out. Only my vague childhood memories kept me from getting lost in the labyrinth, steered me through suffocating trees and past blackened signs. Eventually, the branches were forced to surrender to the inevitable and let me pass. My old family home emerged from the foliage and into view.

I took some time to ease out of my husband's car—my muscles aching from sitting for so long. The house watched as I did so, wanting me to look at it, but I refused. I wasn't ready yet to face what was waiting for me. Instead, I walked slowly around the side, opened the small wooden gate, and proceeded into the back yard where our old shed stood.

As impossible as it seemed, the foliage there was more overgrown than what I'd already driven though. I waded into the long grass gone to seed, chirping insects leaping aside as I made my way to the shed. There I eased myself down onto my tired knees, and with only my crooked fingers dug at the dirt. And continued to dig until I found the old wool sock.

I reached down into the hole and pulled it up. The bundle was heavier than I expected, as though the four stones within had swollen over the years, absorbing the thoughts and dreams of those in the vicinity. But I knew that was impossible; it was only an artifact of my newly rediscovered imagination.

Being so close to the stones once again was like a waking

dream, and the world shook and vibrated out of step around me. I carried the sock back to the car and opened the door. On the seat was the fifth stone in its own box, and I felt a pull toward it—all five stones eager to be reunited. I lifted the box from the passenger's seat, and even my proximity to the stone's surface left my fingers numb from shock. I drew back, but forced myself to suffer through the pain long enough to dump the contents of the box into the wool sock. All five stones radiated a fiery heat.

My knees had swollen enough that I had trouble walking, but I managed to reach the front door of the house. It wasn't locked, and when I walked through I realized my once-home had been uninhabited for too many years. Memories of holding my mother's hand, sitting in my father's lap, chasing my brother, all flooded back, and I cried at what had become of them. Everything of my childhood gone to ruin and rot. Why hadn't we sold the house after my mother's death and let some other family try to find the happiness that had evaded us? I couldn't remember the answer, too distraught over the house's state. Or perhaps my memories of the time were too jumbled. All I'd wanted was to escape the prison of that life, and I managed it only under the yoke of medication. I'd traded a cell for a prison, and returning to the house was like stepping behind bars once more.

My old bedroom waited at the top of the stairs. It beckoned me, but I hesitated. Something was wrong, and if I listened, I could hear whatever it was faintly humming in the background. I put my hand on the bannister and the world shifted, vibrated ever so slightly. I watched that second floor and waited for something to happen, for something to appear from around the corner. I waited. And, when nothing came, I made myself climb.

My old legs grew shakier with each step, the world around following suit. The vertigo increased until, out of breath, I reached the second floor and saw the door to my old room. It looked just as I'd remembered it. Just as I'd dreamed it.

The air smelled of ozone. Everything shifted, vibrated.

The stones, too, out of synch with the rest of the world, then slowly catching up. Faster and faster, the vibrations eventually found their balance, started to resonate in harmony. My gut twisted, the blood rushed from my face, my teeth gnashed.

I put my hand against the door to keep either it or myself steady, and the vibrations ran up my arm. There was a noise, a low droning chirp from behind the door that I recognized, and that filled my being with dread. That pressure about which I'd dreamed arrived, pushing down on me as though the walls were closing in, and despite seeing daylight out the landing window I felt submerged in the deepest earth. The air stank of it.

Scratching, pounding, came from my old room. Something was in there, behind the closed door. Something large and powerful and angry. Something penetrating from another place, a weak spot I'd felt throughout my childhood. My nightmares were solid, were real, and they were coming forth. The world rippled from the old sock at my side, concentric circles warping the air around me.

My dreams returned then—images of me sitting before the vibrating door, of me placing the five stones on the ground, equidistant from one another, of me drawing invisible lines from one stone to the next. Then my visions went further, memories of my dreams resurfacing. I saw the door shut with the stones piled against it, saw the determination in my eyes, saw the exhaustion of keeping what was behind that door at bay at all cost.

I looked at the wool sock of stones in my hand, vibrating with potential as the door in front of me shook from the pounding buzz on the other side, and I realized that my entire life had led me there. That I had not found the stones but they had found me. They sought me for this task, to be the one to keep everything at bay, to hold the line between this world and the next, and to do so at all costs. I had been given a burden no one else could bear, and would hold it for the rest of what remained of my life. I was finally awake from my lifetime of dreams—awake and aware of what needed to be done.

I reached into the wool sock and took a stone in my arthritic hand. It jumped, full of charge, and the shocks ran up my arm. I took hold of that stone tight, tighter than I had ever held my husband or my children or my parents or brother. I took hold of that stone and I turned and hurled it at the landing window with all my might. The shattered glass filled the air like stars, and the stone disappeared from view. The pounding at the door beside me grew stronger.

I did the same with the next stone, and the next, each time the pounding, the wailing, the screaming increased, until the door frame buckled and pieces of wood flew and all the stones in the sock were gone, scattered on the ground outside. I collapsed on the floor, unable to hold the inevitable at bay.

I would let it come. I would let it enter this world from wherever, let it do what it wanted. I was not a prisoner, nor born to carry a burden. I would let the world suffer and bleed for a million years as long as I was free.

The door shuddered, broke. From behind it first emerged a long slender leg, covered in spines. One chirp, then another, then a narrow head appeared with eyes as large as my skull, mandibles clenching, opening. It pushed its chitinous body through, and I recognized it. I recognized it from my earliest memory, from before I had any real memories. I recognized it as it looked at me, cocked its inhuman head, and leapt through the broken window into the dying afternoon sky. And behind it another followed. Then another. And another. And then more still. Until the sky was full of them, a plague escaping through a door left unguarded, a plague carried forth into the world on clear membranous wings.

THE TERRIFIC
MR. TOUCAN

———————— ❧ ————————

It's your birthday present. At least, that's what Jeffrey tells you.

"I'm going to take you out, gin you up, probably have my way with you."

You chuckle and you blush because that's what you do, even after thirty years, but you're also happy to be doing anything that will get you out of the house and get your mind off Molly.

"I hope you picked someplace expensive," you say while you pretend-fix your pretend hair-do. "I deserve to be treated right."

"You do indeed," Jeffrey says, then he winks and grabs at your waist to give you one of his bear hugs. You shriek and try not-very-hard to escape his clutches. And you almost feel like you used to.

Thirty years is a long time. After thirty years, you finally feel like you're getting to know someone. Not what they watch on television or what their favourite ice cream is, but on a deeper level. You feel like you're getting to know them almost as well as you know yourself. Those thirty years are a proving ground where you're tested by all the garbage two people can go through. Those first few where you wonder if settling down was a mistake, the hardship of never having enough money, the countless hours of work where you come home too exhausted to say a word to each other. And once

Molly is born you realize all that time you thought you never had was actually right there in front of you, and now that it's completely gone a part of you resents her for it. A part of Jeffrey, too, you suspect, though neither of you will admit it. Which is fine: some things don't get to be spoken out loud. But though the you and the Jeffrey that got married eventually slip away, you realize the you and the Jeffrey that have replaced them are more in tune than ever, and there's no one left who understands you like he does, or him like you. Especially not Molly, who pushed against you with tiny hands when you first tried to feed her and has never stopped pushing. Understanding her will never be less than impossible, which only makes you appreciate Jeffrey more.

So when he tells you to dress up, but not too much, you know exactly what he means, even if he won't tell you where you're going. He keeps his mouth shut the whole way into town. It's like that smile is kept on with screws. There's not a sound from him as he parks the Monte Carlo on Jamieson Street, or as he rushes around the car to help you out. He's mum as you walk the twilight streets, past the straggling commuters finally heading home to their families. You're impressed by his commitment and can't help but imagine all the different places you might end up. Will it be the opera? A fancy dinner at *Le Papillon*? Will you travel by carriage, or be surrounded by friends who are even now tucking themselves into hiding places in anticipation of your surprise? It could be anything—in this moment of nothing, everything is possible, whatever you imagine.

But as you walk further, what you don't imagine is where Jeffrey brings you to a stop—an old schoolhouse set in the town's brick façade. You don't have to, because you know where you are without even looking above the door at the sign that reads Millhaven Theatre. You've been here once before. With Molly. A noise crawls out of your throat, too quiet for Jeffrey to hear.

"This is it," Jeffrey says. "You can open your eyes now."

"My eyes were supposed to be closed?"

"I told you back at the car. I told you this was a surprise."

"You did, but you never said I was supposed to close my eyes."

"How else were you going to be surprised?"

"How did you expect me to walk here with my eyes closed?"

As you playfully banter, a couple dressed in blue walk past, smiling politely but they say nothing to the two of you or to each other. The man is in his seventies and dressed in an old track suit, while the woman with him is half his age and wears a matching scarf. She clings tight to him as though he's about to float away, and you and Jeffrey stop and watch them navigate their way through the door of the Millhaven Theatre without disentangling. You and Jeffrey shrug at one another.

"I still don't know what we're here for."

"You'll find out," he sings.

Jeffrey dashes up the concrete stairs to open the theatre door for you. He's playing at being a gentleman, which irks you and he knows it. With a smile and a wave of his free hand he ushers you in. You smack his face lightly as you go. *Didn't know I was going to do that, did you?* you think, and it's your turn to smile.

There is a bored young man sitting inside a small ticket booth, his sunken eyes drooping as though he's on the edge of sleep. Jeffrey sidles up to him and murmurs. The ticketer's expression doesn't change, and he doesn't look at you, but he takes the money Jeffrey pulls from the old leather wallet Molly bought him a dozen Christmases ago and hands back two paper stubs. Jeffrey trots back over and hands you one, then offers you the crook of his arm. You put your hand inside and he walks you to a pair of large wooden doors with an intricately carved design that's neither remarkable nor offensive. If the circular shapes are meant to represent something it's lost on you both.

"Are you ready for your surprise?" he asks, and when you look at him you see the Jeffrey you first met at the farmer's market beneath the paper Fall Festival banner, and the Jeffrey you stood beside watching Molly run off to her first day of school. There's the Jeffrey from your Spring wedding day, and the Jeffrey in swim trunks from your summers on Bruce Lake. You see all the different Jeffreys you've known, fanned out before you like a spread of shuffled cards, each more knowable than the one before, and you smile again and say, "Sure," because it's all you can manage without choking up.

He pushes open the door with his wide hand and though you don't know what you're expecting, it's not what you get. There is no surprise party or balloons or cake or friends and family you haven't seen in years. You don't see any elephants or clowns or jugglers. You don't even see any expensive jewelry. There's no car or dream home or stack of lottery winnings. There is nothing there that offers any surprises or shocks. It's just a large room filled with clothed tables, most occupied by other couples like the mismatched pair in blue that gave you and Jeffrey that look, and a red-faced man with a broad neck and thick chest who murmurs to his shrinking wife. And to your secret relief there's no Molly, though one of the bored waiters that weaves between the tables reminds you of her, the disdain for his job pinned to his face. Or, at least, that's what you project onto his blank features; it's so hard to be sure what anyone but Jeffrey thinks. In the center of the room stands a large wooden stage. You stumble when you see it—its green and red curtains flecked with crystals—but you keep your discomfort hidden. It's just an accidental reminder of Molly, you think, and nothing more. It looks out of use and no one pays it attention. No one besides a collection of solitary guests seated at its foot, so close they could touch it. They are ignored by everyone including the waiters. Including each other.

Jeffrey looks at his ticket. "I guess that's our table over there," he says, pointing to the left of the stage, maybe halfway between where you are and the curtain. "Number twenty-three," he says aloud and you squeeze his elbow. What else is there to do? The two of you slip between the tables toward the one you've been assigned. When you finally take your seats, Jeffrey lets out a sigh of relief, then pulls close and puts his big warm hand over yours.

"So what do you think?"

"I thought maybe there'd be some surprise guests," you say as you glance at the door behind you. "But honestly I'd rather it just be the two of us out for dinner on my birthday. Surprise parties are never as fun as you think they're going to be. I can only imagine the drama if—well, what I mean is I'm glad it's just us. I like uneventful."

He squeezes your hand once and laughs. "The dinner's not your present," he says while unfolding his napkin. "It's just incidental. We're here to see the show."

You glance at the stage, then glance again to convince yourself it hasn't changed. It still looks unprepared for anything other than a dusting. There are no sets, no lights, no motion nor sign of movement behind the curtain.

"Is Molly—"

"No, no," he says, looking at you anxiously. "It's not— Molly isn't here."

"How was I supposed to know? You haven't told me anything about what to expect."

"That's how surprises work." He smiles. "You're supposed to be tingling with confusion and glee."

"Oh, I'm tingling. Head to toe tingles."

And, still, the stage reminds you of a clock with an unwound spring. Like a guitar left unstrung in the corner of a den. Its potential drained, its energy dissipated. The stage is lifeless.

Birthdays are funny things. You tell each other they're important and deserve celebration, but they're just a day like any other. All they're good for is to remind you how fleeting time is. *First it walks, then it runs.* That's something the first Jeffrey used to say, long before his head turned so round, and you thought then you knew what he meant, but now you don't think you did. You're not sure he did, either. When you look at him, sitting behind his menu, glasses pinching the edge of his nose as he squints, there are creases you've never noticed and his hair is thinner and more silver. You want to reach over and touch him to make sure he's real—that any of this is real. That he and you met; that you've lived a life; that the two of you tried to raise a daughter but messed it up—but for just an instant, he feels impossibly far away. Which doesn't make any sense. How could you know him so well and still be so distant? But you could ask the same of Molly. Molly, who was a baby for less than the bat of your lashes, who found that small piece of you that needed her love, and gave you only rejection. If only you could have found a way to live with it, maybe things would have been different. You don't believe that's true, but a shrinking part of you wants to be wrong.

"May I take your order?"

You turn and the waiter is standing between you and Jeffrey, staring at you both. Guiltily, you pick up the menu and review it. Jeffrey already knows what he wants. He wants the same thing every time, no matter where you go.

"I'll get the steak, medium rare with a side of mashed potatoes. Hold the gravy."

It's an order you could recite for him. The waiter nods and writes the order down. They both turn to you expectantly and you hesitate, long enough for Jeffrey to interrupt.

"Are you having the grilled chicken garden salad?"

"Yes, that's right," you say, as though you'd forgotten until he reminded you. "And I'll have water as well."

"I'll bring a bottle of flat for the table," the waiter mumbles.

Jeffrey interjects again.

"Oh, and can you make sure there's no cheese on her salad?"

He nods, collects the menus, and takes a few steps to the next table. You lean into Jeffrey and ask if you're really that predictable.

"You're still as unpredictable and inscrutable as they come. Don't worry."

You squeeze his arm and he smiles. For a second, you forget all about Molly. For that second, your elation is boundless. But reality returns, as it always does.

"Seriously, though. What are we here to see? At least give me a hint."

Jeffrey smiles, mischievously, and looks at the milling crowd. He checks his watch.

"Unless I miss my guess, you'll be finding out soon enough, so I'm not going to spoil it."

On that cue the music you hadn't noticed playing beneath the room's rhubarb increases in volume—it's 'Piccadilly March', Jeffrey informs you, though it's a bit too jovial a rendition for his tastes—and for the first time the red-with-green-flecks curtains rustle with life. The music swells, the trumpets blare, and into the middle of the stage emerges a heavy-set woman dressed in a dark ill-fitting wool suit with short tails, white-gloved hands clasped behind her back. The woman defiantly marches to the edge of the stage and you can see her make-up is over-done—purple eyeshadow under thick overdrawn arching eyebrows. Her hair looks wet or greasy, pushed back in waves and hanging just above her collar. When she speaks, she sounds like a barker, and you glance at Jeffrey as he nods excitedly.

"Ladies and gentlemen. We are pleased to present to you an evening of wonder and amazement, a night of the impossible becoming possible. Every night is a night of magic, it's true, but this night in particular is different. Tonight, you'll see things that will amaze and haunt and astound you. You'll see things that make you question your assumptions about what is and isn't real. And, best of all, you'll leave understanding that not only does magic exist, but that the world is magic, and that life is the real magic show."

You all clap politely. At least, those around you do. You see that old man in the blue tracksuit trading looks with his wife, and then with the woman on stage. You peek at Jeffrey's reaction; he's smiling buoyantly and clapping uproariously.

"It's a magic show!" he exclaims, as though he's as surprised as you are. Molly's first public performance drew similar reactions from Jeffrey, so it's hard to know how genuine he's being. There's no reason to fool anyone now, least of all Molly, who isn't here, but you still can't be sure until he asks: "Is this the best birthday present ever, or what?" Then, you know, and you nod because you glean how proud he is of where he's taken you, and because you realize you've forgotten all your other reasons. You nod and clap because you both know he's right.

"Our main purveyor of otherworldly mastery, please bring your hands together and welcome, the Terrific Mr. Toucan!" The emcee bows, her greased curls falling forward before a flick of her head tosses them back, and she carefully slinks away into the wing as the main curtains part. A thin unshaven man is revealed, dressed in a wrinkled brown suit, his cuffs reaching an inch too far over his hands, the sleeves of the suit an inch too short. Beside him is a small table on which sits an oversized black stovepipe hat. It's all too on the nose, you think. He bows for the audience; you all clap politely. Except for the row of guests sitting by themselves, waiting for something.

The Terrific Mr. Toucan's feeble voice draws your attention away from your collusive giggling. It starts with a clearing of his throat, a cough both phlegmy and dry, and you can almost hear the sound of his stubble scraping across his skin as he speaks. He's a mumbler, this one, like Molly when she's speaking to you, and the microphone can barely pick him up. He seems oblivious, though. You look at Jeffrey's scowl and recognize his frustration. Mr. Toucan has no stage presence, and you think that's what Jeffrey finds most offensive.

"P-Please observe this hat," he stammers, and perversely you find yourself more interested in what he's about to do. "It's just a—an ordinary hat. Nothing special about it." With jittering hands he tilts the felt hat forward for all to see. Then Mr. Toucan raises his arm, snaps his fingers, and a white-tipped wand springs into existence in mid-air, clearly propelled from some barely-hidden mechanism in his sleeve. Mr. Toucan very nearly doesn't reach it in time, but at the last moment manages to snatch it victoriously from the air. Jeffrey shakes his head, unimpressed, but you find it fascinating, and Mr. Toucan's performance makes you laugh. It's all so absurd.

Mr. Toucan takes a large handkerchief from his jacket pocket and unfolds over the empty hat. After a tap of his newly-caught wand on the upturned brim, he jerks the handkerchief away to reveal the same hat. He reaches inside and removes a small box with a single button on top. The crowd applauds but he quiets them with the raise of his nervous hand, then presses the button with his long index finger. Non-descript European music flows, full of syncopation and horns.

Mr. Toucan's body jerks into motion as though possessed. He moves to the rhythms, his dance so poorly choreographed it can't be by design. Sparks fly from his sleeves like fireworks when he raises his arms, slightly out of sync with the rising tempo. The spectacle is so engrossing you find yourself laughing and clapping along. Jeffrey seems less entertained by Mr. Toucan's shenanigans, but his head bounces in rhythm, and his chuckles come from watching you. After all the years, he only wants you to be happy. You want the same for him. So much so that you'd pretend just to give him this smile.

The reaction of the other couples around you is mixed. Some are as amused by Mr. Toucan as you are, though none are laughing. Most seem unhappy they've spent their money on the show—a tall man with flat unruly hair cut at an odd angle checks his watch and looks toward the kitchen. It occurs to you that you haven't seen your waiter since he took your order. The red-faced man leans over the back of his chair with one arm holding an empty glass. He shakes it absently, as though he hopes the inaudible sound of ice cubes tinkling will summon a refill. He is wholly disinterested in the trick Mr. Toucan has transitioned into. It involves oversized playing cards, and as the magician juggles them a few cards drop to the floor of the stage. A few more wriggle free as he bends to collect the first.

"Do you think it's possible he's this inept?" you ask Jeffrey, just to see if he's thinking what you're thinking.

"It's possible," he says. "It doesn't look like he's doing any of this on purpose."

The notion makes you smile wider. Sometimes chaos can be beautiful.

But while some of the couples aren't laughing due to irritation or disinterest, the inner circle of single patrons aren't laughing due to their study of Mr. Toucan's every move. They stare at his fingers as he fumbles through the deck of cards, manhandles the felt hat, trips over juggling props. They watch as though they expect some divine revelation. That's not what they get.

When the music finally ends, so does Mr. Toucan's awkward dance, and he comes to a stop, out of breath and sweating, long arms slung low at his sides. He looks like he's about to say something to the audience, but instead bows, once to the left, once to the right, holding his hat before him each time as though he expects a line to form to fill it with money.

No one speaks. No one does more than uncomfortably fidget. You now hear the tinkle of ice but you don't take your eyes from the stage, not until the emcee rematerializes from the wing, the soft clap of her large white-gloved hands overpowering everything else in the room. As she takes her position downstage, the curtains with red and green flecks draw to a close behind her, concealing the Terrific Mr. Toucan from view. There is some movement of the curtain once closed, as though behind the scenes bodies are moving against it.

"Our presentation of spectacle and show has reached its inevitable midpoint. We all knew this would come, as it so often does. The top of the roller coaster, the crest of a hill, there is always that moment between what has come and what is to come. It's the moment where the thrill resides. Where the burgeoning unknown inspires. There isn't long to wait now before everything is laid bare. Until then, enjoy your drinks, tip your staff, and make use of all the amenities. Just be sure to hurry back. Once the show resumes, the doors to the theatre will be locked and no one further will be seated."

Chairs are pushed back as people rise around you, blocking your view of the stage long enough that you don't see the emcee leave. Everyone appears confused and irritated, and there's the murmur from some wondering where the waiters are. Or, more exactly, where the food is. The red-faced man authoritatively leads an expedition out of the theatre in search of someone who might hear their complaints. Their partners stay behind and speak only to one another, while many of the remainder filter out to use the facilities. You and Jeffrey stay put, as do the tables of solitary patrons on the cusp of the stage. You ask him how he heard about this show.

"I don't know. How do you hear about anything? People were talking about it somewhere, I guess. Maybe when I was lined up at the deli, or maybe it was at the office. I can't remember anything except about how great it was supposed to be, and I thought, why not? It might be a fun change of pace. Something more than just dinner for your birthday. Something to get you out of the house," he says, though you know he means something else. He looks around at the gathered crowd and frowns. "Of course, dinner might have been the better choice."

"I'm sure there's just a backlog in the kitchen. It hasn't been that long since he took our order." You suddenly realize you have no idea how long it's been.

"You're enjoying the show, though, right? I mean, other than the lack of food? You seem to be."

"Yes, Jeffrey. It's absolutely perfect."

"And you don't mind the magician? He seems like a bit of a putz."

"That's probably my favorite part," you say. "He's trying. It's endearing."

He smiles again—slightly yellowed teeth from his years as a smoker, and his continuing love of coffee. Immediately, you remember how it smells to be in arms, to breathe in the scent of his skin. Like a fire that's burned itself out.

"He reminds me of Molly when she was eight. Do you remember the play she put on for us?"

You flinch before he finishes the sentence.

"It was her first. She was so nervous. Over-dramatic, even

151

then."

"She takes after her old man, I think." His eyes sparkle at you. You shake your head.

"If she had rocks for brains, maybe."

His smile falters, then he looks past you with concern.

"I just wish Molly—" he begins, but you don't listen. You already know all about Molly, and you don't want to be reminded. Not today of all days. You don't want to think about the space she's put between you. Or if maybe it's your fault. You don't even know anymore. You ask yourself why it can't be as easy as it's supposed to be, like when Molly was a baby. When you and Jeffrey would laugh about her at night, when it was only the two of you awake, you with your head on his rising chest, him smelling of cigarettes and engine oil. You could just hear the tiny vibrations deep within him, like the rattle of bare branches before a late autumn shower. But then you remember those days were no better than these are now. Special moments are always gone too fast, and the hard moments always crawl too slow.

Moments like the camping trip to Algonquin when Molly was ten, where black clouds gathered around her and became tempestuous the longer she was cooped up in the car with both of you. That storm swirled in the air around her, thunderous and potent, when you went for a hike, when you took a paddle boat into the lake, when you sat around the campfire and secretly hoped this time she would behave. But when Molly wordlessly turned in too early you looked at Jeffrey who looked and you, and for once you couldn't tell what either of you were thinking.

"This intermission has to be close to ending," Jeffrey says. "This can't be some kitchen backlog. Maybe I should look around. You aren't looking good. You need something to eat." He lays his hands flat on the table, about to push himself to his feet. You put your hand on his quickly, more forcefully than you intend.

"No, it's okay," you say. "I'm fine. Fit as a fiddle. I might even volunteer to be Mr. Toucan's assistant. Can you imagine me up there? Maybe in one of those sequined body suits?"

Jeffrey laughs as you mime presenting your imaginary outfit, and he settles back into his chair. You move your hand to his knee and give it a squeeze. He's right—you're famished—but you don't want him to leave you alone here. You don't want people to look at you the way they look at the people at the front of the stage. You can see it in the eyes of everyone standing, hear it in the half-whispers traded back and forth. You're not sure what it is about them, but their intensity is unsettling everyone. Or maybe it's the hunger. You wish you'd been given that bottle of water, if nothing else. You wish you'd thought to smuggle in something in your purse.

The red-faced man returns with less vigor and fewer members in his entourage. His wife rushes to greet him, and as she reaches out he takes her hands in his own and pulls her away. You're not certain what it means. Other people are so opaque next to Jeffrey. The red-faced man appears out of breath. You feel more than hear the crowd quieting—everyone knows he's about to say something. The only people not paying attention to him are a pair of confused women a few tables away, and of course those seated by the stage. The red-faced man clears his throat. You hold your breath.

But instead of words, there's music. Loud music from behind the red-green-flecked curtain. It's that march again, signaling the intermission is over and the show will soon resume. The red-faced man speaks angrily at his wife as she tries to hug and calm him, but you still can't hear what he's saying, and as the music grows louder, he only grows more belligerent and frustrated. Or maybe it's because no one else seems to care.

The march disassembles the crowd and returns everyone to their assigned tables. Even the red-faced man's face loses some of its crimson as his wife drags him by the arm back to his seat. He doesn't look happy about it, but he doesn't resist.

"I wonder if we should have stood up, stretched our legs," you say, but Jeffrey glances quickly at you with distracted confusion. He'd rather keep his eyes on the stage.

"Maybe. I don't know. It's been a weird show, hasn't it? I'm not really sure what to make of this guy. I feel bad I picked this for your birthday."

"No, don't say that. I've been really enjoying myself. I want to see what happens."

"You've been laughing, which isn't something you do enough. I really like you when you laugh."

You smile at Jeffrey, but you can't really look at him, not when he admits things like that. It makes you uncomfortable and sad.

"I wish I could make your life better, too. I bet you wish sometimes things had turned out different. We made some wrong choices somewhere."

He reaches out and squeezes your hand. The squeeze says you're right, even when his voice tells you you're wrong.

"I wouldn't change a single thing about you."

You don't think that's true.

'The Piccadilly March' doesn't so much fade-out as simply end as soon as everyone is sitting. You take the opportunity to inspect the tables around you. The couple in blue has gone, leaving unused dishes and glassware on their table, and you can see the man with the uneven haircut prattling on to his wife who is barely paying attention. The pair of women at the other table both casually glance at the doors as though eager to leave, and the rest of the tables are full, if not fuller, than they were before the intermission. Or maybe there are fewer tables, except that wouldn't make any sense, would it?

The emcee appears from the wing, adjusting the white glove on each of her large hands. As she approaches her mark, Jeffrey barely whispers, "I think they're about to begin," and you shush him. After a second, he's so studiously transfixed on the emcee he seems to have forgotten he spoke. You fidget with your wedding ring nervously.

"Welcome to the final act of our show. You've watched the Terrific Mr. Toucan warp your understanding of reality, watched as he twisted illusion to suit his whims. The wonderment you feel now is nothing compared to what awaits you behind this curtain. Behold the Terrific Mr. Toucan and pay attention to what he has to share with you tonight. Ignore him at your own peril."

She bows and slips from upstage, back to where she emerged, followed by the drawing curtains. Mr. Toucan is revealed, standing timidly, his large black felt hat still in place beside him, the sheen of flop sweat trickling down his pallid unshaven face even greater. You lean toward Jeffrey to whisper a question, but he's already answering you: "He looks like he's going to be sick."

The stage dims. Mr. Toucan's music box sits alongside his felt hat, but he doesn't look at it. He is concentrating on the floor, terror emanating off him as he struggles to maintain his composure. You think back to Molly and her stage-fright performing that first play for you and Jeffrey when she couldn't speak, couldn't move. When Jeffrey tried to encourage her but only made things worse. You remember Molly's quivering lip, her face twitching as something inside her resolved, hardened, and you remember your own impotence. Or was it something worse? Something you couldn't bear Jeffrey to know even though he knows everything about you? You look at Jeffrey, try to read his face to see if he's remembered, too, but there's no way to know—to really and truly know. Maybe knowing is the real magic trick. Everything else with the cards and the hat and the wand is just a distraction.

Mr. Toucan looks over the audience and even from your seat you can see the palsy in his practiced hands, hear the tremor in his voice.

"Someone please name, name an animal. Any animal."

The audience is hesitant, not sure what he wants. Then a man from somewhere on the other side of the room shouts "toucan", and there is nervous laughter. Mr. Toucan barely smiles as he shakes his head. "Not, not very original, but okay. Now I need everyone in the, in the room to think about a toucan. Really concentrate. Everyone picture the bird in your mind." He closes his eyes and puts his fingers to his temples. "Picture the oversized orange beak, the shock of white feathers on black. Picture, picture the bluish claws wrapped around a perch. Picture its round black eyes as it tilts its head. Imagine it and keep imagining it. Keep imagining it. Don't stop."

Jeffrey's chin rests on his square hands as he watches the stage intently. You look but can't see the image of a South American bird fluttering around in his round head, but you know it's in there. Jeffrey likes to participate; he likes to meet people halfway. The Great Accommodator, that's what you call him.

Mr. Toucan reaches into his oversized hat and pulls out nothing. At least, there's nothing you can see. Only his two fingers—thumb and index finger—pressed together in a pinch. The rest are pointing out. With his other hand he grabs at the empty air below and mimes stretching something out. Then he places a curled thumb and forefinger to his lips and blows. What emerges from behind his palm startles you—a small bulge that swells as he breathes into it, transforming and unfurling from nothingness into something the size of a toucan—its plumage dark, its over-large beak coloured and held at a cocked angle its tiny neck couldn't possibly support. Its wings are unfolded as though the bird is about to take flight.

And then it does. The magician lifts his hand and the still toucan floats into the air and out above the audience. There is some applause, primarily from those solitary patrons in front, but the rest of the crowd doesn't know how to react to the bird-shaped figment crossing the room. They don't understand what they're seeing. Neither do you. The frozen bird tumbles in the air as it rounds the back, then changes direction and begins to return to the stage. As it gets closer to you, Jeffrey leans forward, squinting, and you find yourself silently beckoning it on. But it doesn't make it to your table. A gust or some ripple in the air alters its course, and it tumbles away and back toward Mr. Toucan, who waits with eyes closed and arms and hands outstretched. It's as though he's welcoming back an estranged child.

As the bird-shaped mirage comes within a foot of Mr.

Toucan he returns to life and plucks it from the air. Holding it in one hand, Mr. Toucan raises the shape to his lips and fills his lungs. As he does, the illusion deflates, the apparition vanishing once more into his hands. He then holds those hands in front of him, both palms facing out, to prove there's been no trickery, but all you notice is his skin appears jaundiced. The room is excited, though that excitement is muted by confusion and chatter at the tables. Mr. Toucan barely smiles as he rubs his pale hands together. He does not acknowledge the meagre applause. Rather, his eyes brighten with barely concealed effort, and he calls out a request to the audience for more animals. The suggestions are now plentiful.

"A lion," a woman calls out and Mr. Toucan nods.

"Is there anyone here who, who *doesn't* know what a lion looks like? Anyone at all?" He raises his hand mockingly to shield his eyes as he surveys the crowd; there is the rumble of chuckles.

"Okay, then. I want everyone, everyone to shout out 'lion'."

You're self-conscious, but you do as he asks. Not everyone does. Jeffrey, for instance, only smiles. Mr. Toucan acts unimpressed with the response.

"I asked you all to shout. That wasn't, wasn't a shout. Let's try again." He closes his eyes and cups his ear. You repeat yourself, slightly louder now, along with the crowd. He shakes his head.

"Again."

This time, the noise in the room is trumpetous. Mr. Toucan stumbles, and though you suspect it's part of his routine, you think it's more likely he's actually tripped over his feet.

"Perfect," he says as he rights himself. "Now, concentrate on the image of a lion. Concentrate as though it's the most, the most important thing you've ever done. Picture the lion and don't stop. Ready?"

Everyone nods. Then Mr. Toucan does the same and returns to his felt hat. His hand reaches in and again comes away with nothing. Nothing he stretches then blows into.

And again, that nothing in his hands soon is a blob, and in even less time there's a bubble shaped like a large lion, and it's breaking free of him and slowly floating away. This lion sits on his four paws, majestic mane flowing from a head held high, a snarl forming on the edge of his motionless mouth. While the audience watches its slow tumble around the room—their applause louder this time—you watch Mr. Toucan extend his arms and hands out, his fingers clawing the air. As the lion makes its way to the back of the room Mr. Toucan's face pales and features drop, while his eyes suddenly widen. He proceeds to push, then pull at the air, and the lion obeys, changing direction as though on an invisible wire. As it makes the turn and floats toward your table you and Jeffrey both watch it pass overhead. Jeffrey reacts as most of the audience has, reaching to not quite touch the mirage, but you don't raise your arm. Instead, you gaze at its surface, see the colours slowly change and swirl like the reflections of a soap bubble, though it's in a shape no soap bubble could assume, let alone maintain. The lion passes overhead without bursting, continuing on its way back toward the stage where Mr. Toucan awaits out of breath, and the sheen of sweat on his colourless face makes it all the more exciting to watch.

Then the strangest thing occurs. As the lion clears the last table and closes the distance to Mr. Toucan, the bubble wavers, the shape expands, pushes out as it pulls in, and the colours shift. Mr. Toucan's face contorts, his brow furrows, and in an instant he has grabbed it from the air so forcefully you worry he's about to fall off the stage. But he doesn't. He frantically pulls the lion to his pale bloodless lips and takes it in as though drawing desperate breath. The former-lion shrivels away into nothing in his hands. Into absolute nothing. Mr. Toucan's hands are completely empty. He holds them up for the briefest instant, twisting them front to back, back to front, before he folds over, panting, hands on his quivering knees. The room erupts with momentous applause, and any doubt you had during the first half of the evening that the Terrific Mr. Toucan would fail to live up to his name has vanished and been replaced with awe.

Jeffrey's face clearly announces he agrees with you, you know it that well. But the applause dies down before Mr. Toucan regains his composure, and as it ebbs you notice his knees are still shaking.

"Do you think he's okay?" you whisper. Jeffrey leans forward and shrugs.

There is no other noise in the room but the audience's quiet fidgeting, all of them rapt with attention, waiting to see what Mr. Toucan will do next. Even the abandoned pair of women hold their breath. The silence is so pervasive you worry your ears have failed.

And you can't help it—seeing him standing there on the stage casts you out of the moment, back to your time sitting in other audiences at Jeffrey's insistence, watching Molly as she performed and you cringed. Like now with Mr. Toucan, there were times the world seemed to stop to wait for her to catch up, but when she did her audience's attention had subsequently wandered. You tried to explain what was wrong, but stopped trying once it was clear she refused to listen. Her hatred had tuned you out, and you finally understood the size of the gulf between you. What you didn't understand was how much it would continue to widen.

This is how you know that even if Jeffrey had thrown you a surprise party, Molly wouldn't have come. She would rather do anything else than be forced to be in the same room as you, let alone near a stage. She stopped inviting you to her performances long ago, which was a blessing for you both. Jeffrey frets too, you know, even if he doesn't say it. He doesn't have to. You can see it in his unease when she's around—his muscles tense with expectation, waiting for the imminent outbreak. She says things about you that you couldn't repeat if you wanted to—they're words full of whispered power, terrible words that suggest terrible things. With Molly it's always been as though she's pulling at the end of a lead, trying to go anywhere but where she's supposed to. She's so desperate to throw off the yoke of family—of you, in particular—that you're ready to let her go make the mistakes you know she's making. You can't help someone who doesn't want your help. The only thing you worry about is what will happen when she leaves. Will she vanish from Jeffrey's and your life? It worries you because you don't know how you'll feel, only how you're supposed to feel.

"Magic is all about belief," Mr. Toucan says, and it snaps you from your reverie. He stands with feigned perseverance and fortitude, but you see through the cracks of his determined expression and it worries you for reasons you can't explain.

"All of you, together, believing one thing at one time," he continues, "can make the impossible possible. When you're of one single mind, you can do, can do things you wouldn't dare dream. Let me show you. All I need is one more animal. But, but before you speak, take a breath. Everyone. Take a breath and hold it, and feel the rest of the audience, every other person in the room. Feel their imaginations, feel the animal that takes shape there. And, when you know the right answer, when you *know*, call it out."

It doesn't take long before someone shouts out a name. It happens so fast you don't realize at first that someone is you.

You say *horse* as though it's a question, and hearing the word in the air you feel your face warm. Jeffrey is more tickled than you've ever seen him, which is the only thing that soothes your shame. No one laughs though. And no one contradicts you or tells you you're wrong. If anything, you hear muttered agreement.

"That sounds like the right answer," Mr. Toucan says. "Please concentrate on a horse and don't let anything else, nothing else enter your mind. I mean it. Imagine a horse into life and prepare to be amazed."

Mr. Toucan utters a quiet noise as he dunks his hand into his hat as before. Lips pursed, he blows again into his curved fingers, and another amorphous shape fills his palm then continues to grow. The shape enlarges quicker than he should have air in his lungs to fill—he doesn't stop for breath as it continues to blossom, to reach his size, then larger, while its

160

colours darken. Thin, knotted legs emerge, the rush of long hair, and twisting equine features appear. Gleeful whispers are exchanged by the crowd, and you understand where their excitement comes from. The bubble is a flawless re-creation, and as Mr. Toucan releases it into the air above you the most startling thing occurs. You're not sure who sees it first. It might be you, or it might be Jeffrey, or maybe someone else in the room. All you know for certain is you and Jeffrey turn to each other and you see your confusion and disbelief mirrored on his face. Because what each of you sees, what everyone in the audience eventually sees, is not what anyone other than those at Mr. Toucan's feet expects. That's why they aren't surprised or confused, and their calm might be the only thing that keeps you from losing yours amid everyone else's gasps.

The horse is moving.

At first, it's only a nod of its head, barely enough to set the motion apart from a trick of light or angle. Then, it raises one hoof, followed by the other, and it rears up on its hind legs. Jeffrey, the audience, and you all clap uproariously. It's the most impossible and beautiful thing you've ever seen. Then you wonder if this is Jeffrey's doing. If it's some birthday trick like those he'd play on you before you were married, before Molly, before you knew each other so well inside and out. But it couldn't be Jeffrey. It couldn't be because you'd know, wouldn't you? You'd just be able to look over at him and know what he was up to immediately. And when you look over you *do* know. You know deep within you that this isn't him, that he's as amazed as you are, which means he also can't believe what he's seeing. How could it be real? The emcee's prediction echoes in your head, but you're too transfixed to give it much thought.

A horse. A moving, living horse. An impossible horse. A horse like you'd always dreamed of as a child. A horse like the one you used to imagine your one-day daughter riding once you'd grown old while she'd remained young; the daughter you knew would be your best friend for the rest of your life. The horse in the air whinnies without making a noise, and you remember that unlived life as if it were a dream—no, it's more like this life, this one right here, right now, is the dream, and your unlived life is the one you've left so far behind you only barely recall it. Your dream-daughter laughs as the dream-horse gallops faster and faster, and you stand with one foot on the fence you've built, your dream-husband and you, and watch her. Your hearts fill and overflow with love. Everything you've ever wanted is right there before you, the naïve dreams of childhood realized for an instant. And, just like that, the vision pops, the air rushes in, and the shades lift off your eyes to reveal the worn-out dining room of the Millhaven Theatre, and the stare of a confused Jeffrey as he tries to understand what you're thinking. He seems terrified by his not knowing. You're terrified, too.

There's a shift in the crowd. Something's wrong. The horse is on its haunches, front legs kicking, and you see its face losing cohesion. Like a cloud transforming in a summer sky, the horse's features shift out of sync with one another, pieces drifting away from its symmetry. On stage, Mr. Toucan's eyes are squeezed shut, his hands twisted and yellow as he reaches out for the shape by clawing at the air. His lips move as he strains, but you can't hear what he's saying from across the room. The crowd murmurs, its concentration breaking, and where you were all as one before, now you are a group of separate people, and the horse from your dreams returns, only it's now ridden by Molly, and she's galloping away. Mr. Toucan cries "stop it" over and over, his panic increasing. You survey the room to see how many are drawn to watching him but no one can take their eyes off the once-horse. The long flowing mane has lengthened, and the legs have twisted upon themselves, four becoming three, becoming two. As it reaches the back of the room, it's a jumble of different forms, all fighting for dominance over the shifting figure, and those spectators beneath recoil as it passes overhead, no longer reaching their hands up, no longer wanting to feel or touch it.

Mr. Toucan's suit has darkened with sweat and he's

shouting frantically, demanding everyone focus, focus—as though the trick has gotten away from him and you're all at fault. But that's impossible. It's a magic trick, and he's the magician. It's all choreographed. It has to be, hasn't it? The red-faced man agrees, laughing at the amorphous shape as it takes the final corner and commences its slow return to the stage. But as it moves from the rear of the room toward Mr. Toucan, pieces of it fix into place, no longer mutating above the crowd. The mane becomes a long head of hair, the fused limbs a pair of legs. Bit by bit, the shape is transforming, and you're barely aware of the soft groans coming from the far edge of the room, from where Mr. Toucan stands, fingers palsied, knees shaking. The expression on his face is one of effort and displeasure, perhaps of fear. Whatever the figment has become, Mr. Toucan acts as though he's desperately trying to prevent it. But it continues, a pair of delicate arms sprouting, each ending in a series of perfect digits. It's the face, though, you find disconcerting. The figure is nearly above your table, and you and Jeffrey both watch a woman's features resolve on the bubble's surface.

"Is that—Does that look like—?" Jeffrey asks, but doesn't tell you whom he thinks he sees. Colours in the floating trick continue to shift like a rainbow of oil across the surface of water, but the eyes that have formed now blink, the downturned mouth works its tongue behind thin lips, and the figment's eyes follow Mr. Toucan intently. You look to Jeffrey, look to the fellow with the uneven hair, look to the red-faced man and his wife, and no one seems to understand what's happening either. It's supposed to be a trick, an illusion, but you don't know for certain that's true. And in your head Molly has ridden the dream-horse so far away you can barely see her.

The vision above floats with innate gracefulness toward the wide-eyed Mr. Toucan as though swimming through water. He continues to shout, almost begging, repeatedly telling you all to concentrate, though you're not sure if he's really speaking to himself. Breath rushes in and out between words, and his hands work franticly and violently, stretched away from his body, fingers extending and crossing and curling in some bizarre pattern that seems too practiced to be anything but showmanship. But he doesn't break, not for a second. He continues until the veins on his head are a throbbing map, and the apparition is ten feet from the stage. Then it's seven. Then it's five. The audience holds its collective breath, some shifting uncomfortably, uncertain what will happen when the transformed woman reaches Mr. Toucan. His moans are louder now, so loud, like a trapped animal howling for release. The floating woman is closer still, and her colours swirl, a bubble near bursting but doesn't. Jeffrey seems disturbed, but you can't tell why. You can't tell whom he sees in her oily features. No one can. Especially not Mr. Toucan. And you know this because at the last moment, at the last second when the floating apparition's face is an inch from his, he closes his eyes and opens his mouth to speak, but the figment's hands are already around his head, and her soapy mouth has already covered his and is impossibly swallowing everything. Mr. Toucan's hands dance, but it's different now, automatic, and when his legs crumble the vision does not vanish with a soft pop. Instead, it floats backward a few feet, slowly pivots, and continues its travel. You all watch transfixed as it silently swims through the air above you toward the back of the room, from where it slips through the open door and out into the night.

And it's here you finally turn and look back at the stage, and it's here you find the red-and-green-flecked curtains have been drawn closed.

The lights come up. Everyone remains seated, waiting for the denouement. But nothing happens. No emcee materializes in the wings, no Mr. Toucan steps out from behind the curtain for a bow. No waiters appear with long-overdue meals. Nothing. There is no sound but the coughing and shuffling of the audience.

After a few minutes, the murmuring begins, people asking one another what's going on, as though there are answers they've missed. The red-faced man stands first, his bald head wrinkled, and he coaxes his wife to do the same. He doesn't wait for her to finish putting on her coat before he's dragging her away. Some of the others follow with less severity. The pair of women approach the stage, pull back the heavy curtain as though expecting Mr. Toucan to be lying there, but are unsurprised that he's not. Nothing remains but his upturned stool. Even the large felt hat has gone. The two women glance at one another and wordlessly agree to walk straight out of the theatre.

"What just happened?" you wonder aloud, and stop when you realize you don't just mean with Mr. Toucan. You mean with everything: Toucan, the emcee, the missing audience members. And you think a part of you means with Molly and how she's led you to where you are. You mean with your simpatico with Jeffrey and how you always know what the other is thinking. You mean with all the dreams for your life you once had. How it's possible for anything—for everything—to vanish so completely into thin air. The tables in the audience empty one at a time, people dressing in coats and scarves, fastening buttons and tying sashes. They filter out through the large doors, those same doors that Mr. Toucan's final illusion passed through moments earlier, and like that illusion no one returns. They've already forgotten the magic show. They've left it all behind. They've let the past go.

"We should leave, too," Jeffrey says.

You nod, but do you agree?

Jeffrey helps you into your coat then leads you to the back of the room and out the door. The ticket booth at the front of the Millhaven Theatre is empty, the ticket agent gone, the glass covered in a locked and dented curtain of metal slats. The string of lights outside the theatre have already been turned off, and the streets are darker than you expected, but you think you can use the sidewalk lamps to guide you back to the Monte Carlo.

As you walk, Jeffrey's large arm hugging your shoulders, the two of you don't speak. You don't have to. In thirty years of marriage, of raising Molly, of dealing with everything a pair of people should ever have to deal with, you have had

SIMON STRANTZAS

enough conversations to know how they all will end before
you have them. You already know the befuddlement Jeffrey
feels over what he's seen. You know because you feel it too,
and you know it's a trap. A bottomless pit that you walk along
the lip of, that either of you could fall into if you misstep.
So you don't misstep. You don't let yourself think about that
illusion at all. Instead, you watch the streetlights waver on
the empty street, focus on the feel of Jeffrey's arm as it pulls
you close to protect you from the breeze. You know without a
glance he is looking at the half-moon floating in the sky, and
no matter how hard he tries—how hard you both try—that
untethered brightness reminds you both of Mr. Toucan and
the oily images he conjured from his empty hands.

Maybe it's true that there's plenty of magic everywhere
if you know where to look for it—the magic of falling in love;
the magic of a child becoming an adult—but there's also the
opposite of magic, too. Whatever it is that turns a wheel and
fills someone with hate instead of love, that drives a wedge
between two people who are supposed to love each other. That
kind of magic is just as widespread, perhaps more so. But no
matter how much you know Jeffrey and he knows you, and
despite all the challenges you've faced in a life that transformed
you both into different people, still you found each other and
fell in love. So what if it's only you and him? So what if you're
all you both have left? Isn't that enough? You squeeze his hand
tighter; he squeezes your arm again.

"Did you have a good birthday?"

You close your eyes, push your face into his shoulder, and
murmur.

"I wonder," he says as you bask in his warmth. "How much
of that do you think was rehearsed? I bet those suggestions
from the audience were plants. Co-conspirators. They probably
only said what he wanted them to."

"But what about my horse?"

Your horse. Galloping away.

"Yeah," he says as he slips deeper into thought. "Maybe.
Maybe he improvised it all, but it seems so impossible. I guess

166

that's good magic, though. It keeps you thinking."

"I could use some good thinking. Been doing too much of the bad kind lately." You pause for a minute, but Jeffrey doesn't fill the gap. "I'd like to go back, I think. See the act from the beginning, now that I know the end. Sometimes the beginning makes more sense when you know how it turns out. And you can see how much you missed or didn't understand until it was too late."

"Who knows? I don't think you're supposed to understand it. That where the magic comes from."

"Maybe," you say. "But aren't you curious about what happened?"

He shrugs. "The only thing I'm curious about is where we're going to eat dinner."

You both laugh, and you let him lead you the rest of the way, but the further from the Millhaven Theatre you get, the less sense everything you saw makes, and by the time you reach the car it makes no sense at all. Maybe if you go back you'll sit at the tables at the front of the room with all the other solitary people. That way you can get a better look at whatever it is that Mr. Toucan does. Maybe from that vantage point it will make sense in a way it doesn't now. Because you can't stop thinking about that horse, and the dreams in you it woke before the trick went off the rails. Or supposedly went off the rails, because Jeffrey's right: who knows? Tricks are really lies, and magic's job is to fool you, to pretend the things you want most are true. To let you believe for an hour that the rules don't apply, and you go along with it because a world where the impossible is possible is more appealing than one in which it's not.

Jeffrey opens the Monte Carlo's door for you and waits until you're settled before dashing around to the other side. While you wait for him you blink, but it takes forever, and part of you is surprised that by the time you open your eyes again the world hasn't changed. The car around you is still the car, the man sitting beside you is still your husband, and no time has passed. But you know it has. It always does. The only question is how much and how fast.

You find yourself thinking about that horse from your dreams, and the sight of Molly riding away on it. You watch its muscular legs propel it down a wooded path as she rides into the long shadows cast by the trees. Rides until she's no more than a speck in your eye. Rides until she's even less than that.

ALEXANDRA LOST

─────────────── ❧ ───────────────

The sunlight through the windshield bounced and refracted, filling Alexandra Leaving's eyes with wriggling stars. Leonard drove his Chevrolet across upstate New York with his foot pressed firmly to the floor, and though she pleaded with him to slow down, he met her protests with further, more dangerous weaving. She eventually stopped asking, and instead kept her eyes focused on the map.

"How much longer do you figure before we reach the coast?" he said.

She checked the clock.

"It was supposed to be about ten hours from Buffalo, but we hit that traffic so now I have no idea."

The map in her hands was the most important thing she owned. She clung to it: her tether as she drifted out into the unknown. She would not use a GPS—technology could not be trusted to tell her where she was. Only a paper map made sense, something on which she could chart their route, drawing for hours before they left. Every hour on the page marked; she knew where they were supposed to be each step of the way. Her father had become lost when she was seven; lost and never found. She was terrified the same might happen to her. Having their journey carefully plotted made her feel safer. But she hadn't anticipated how fast Leonard would drive, and how that speed would compromise the work she'd done. "We'll get there faster," he assured her, but it was impossible—they didn't have a clear idea where they were. If they missed the ramp to the next highway, she worried they would never realize it and simply drive on forever.

"There's an end to the highway," Leonard said, reading her thoughts. "As long as we keep driving we'll get there. At the end of every highway there's an ocean waiting to be found."

She smiled, anxious. For a moment, she forgot how much of a mistake she'd made. For a moment, she remembered why she'd let Leonard take her so far from home. She did it for him. To prove that despite the anxieties and worries that clouded her head, she was good enough for him—even if she didn't believe it. When he realized she had never seen the ocean, he spontaneously decided he had to take her, and she pretended she was spontaneous enough to go.

"I read this article about a couple who just flew off to Europe for few months without packing anything but their phones and a charger," she said, explaining all the research she'd done before they left. She saw his lip quiver, but she wasn't sure of the cause. "They bought new toothbrushes wherever they went, washed their clothes in strangers' houses, and just met as many people as they could. It was like there was this whole world of people working together to help them get by. It was surprising."

"Surprising, how?"

"I don't know," she said. She ran her hand over her shorts to dry it. "I guess I asked myself if I'd do the same—if I'd help a stranger like that."

"I think you probably would."

She didn't say anything. She wanted to believe he was right even if it sounded unlikely. But more importantly, she wanted him to continue believing that sort of thing about her. It was important he not know what kind of things dwelt within her head. He wouldn't understand. No one had ever really understood. Not her father when he was around, and certainly not her mother once he was gone. "My little lost girl" was what he'd called her as he held her tight in his arms. They sat in their warm backyard as the sun set earlier each summer day. "My little lost girl," he said, and squeezed her the way no one had squeezed her since. And she didn't know what he meant, not until he was gone. Then she knew the feeling well.

She looked out the window at the passing scenery. She and Leonard had not spoken in some time, and she liked the quiet rhythm of the wheels on the road. Between the Chevrolet and the horizon the grass dipped and sloped upward, and tiny farms dotted the distant landscape. Farther still lay a series of hills obscuring what lay beyond. All she knew of that land was it was occupied by giants. Wind turbines, more than a dozen in a row and sprouting upward, blades moving in slow endless circles. They stood so far away that Alexandra could not fully grasp their enormity.

"You can tell how big they are by their spin," Leonard said. "If they were closer, the blades would be moving a lot slower. Those turbines are huge—you just can't tell how huge things are from so far away."

"I can *feel* how huge they are, though, if that makes any sense. They make my head loopy."

They almost missed the ramp onto the interstate. Unending miles of highway banked with forest, giant trees too thick to see between, covered in oranges and reds and golds like a burning sunset. Alexandra felt insignificant beside them, no better than the insects crushed against the Chevrolet's windshield. When those trunks petered out, she saw, in the distance, the glint of cars moving away.

Her map—she needed to consult her map.

There, the forest was demarcated with a faint brown line, and almost upon it the blue ink of her pen where she'd traced their route onward. She looked from the map, afraid it was too late, and saw the green sign on the shoulder pass in an instant, hanging branches covering its warning. The ramp was imminent.

"Here. You want this exit here!"

"What?" Leonard slurred as though awoken from a dream. Alexandra watched the exiting lanes rush toward them. Panic seized her.

"This is it! This is the ramp. Take it. Take it. Take it."

Leonard snapped awake, pulled the wheel hard after the marked lanes had already split. A symphony of horns trailed, and the Chevrolet shook from the forces pulling it in multiple directions. Alexandra was flung aside as the car wrenched itself into the proper lane, and as Leonard tried to straighten its path, the tail began to wag. He spun the wheel all the way to the left, then again all the way to the right, trying to keep the car from skidding as the horns blared louder. Back and forth, back and forth, the tail swung until finally, with only a minor tremor, he regained control over the car. He accelerated away from the complaining motorists.

Once safely out of danger, Leonard turned with another grin.

"I hope we didn't go the wrong way," he said.

Alexandra did not understand Leonard's obsession with the ocean. He hadn't been born on a coast; he had lived in the same small dry town as Alexandra long before she met him. The ocean never arose during their courtship's early months, and why would it? It was not typical dinner conversation. And yet, he seemed aghast when she revealed in passing that she had never seen the ocean herself. His dumb silence eventually gave way to incredulity, and it was from that point his dreams became consumed with taking her there.

"Wait until you see it," he promised. "It's so immense you'll feel completely insignificant."

The idea terrified her.

Water was never something Alexandra was comfortable around. Small amounts of it for cooking and bathing didn't bother her, but once the bodies became larger—fountains, pools, lakes—her anxiety increased. It wasn't a phobia—she did not fear water like some feared snakes or spiders—but instead it seemed to whisper to her whenever she was close. The words were too quiet to make out, but they left her with an unfathomable urge to submit herself to it. To walk bare-footed into the waves and let them consume her. Mind. Body. Soul. The water unnerved her because the water wanted her submission, wanted her to lose herself to its power, and the sensation that swirled in her head was as suffocating as any drowning.

They pulled off the interstate for dinner at a small unnamed restaurant, dark branches draping over its burnt-out sign. Alexandra folded her map carefully and placed it in her bag where it would be safe at hand. Leonard watched her, the hint of amusement twitching in his lips, but said nothing. When she stepped from the car Alexandra realized the parking lot was nearly empty, and inside the restaurant, it seemed no more than three of its dark wooden booths were occupied. The rest had places set and menus out, prepared for occupation by guests who might never arrive. When the teenage hostess finally greeted Alexandra and Leonard, her hair tied in a tight bun against the back of her head, Leonard immediately asked where all the customers were. The girl shrugged as she marked their table off her list.

"I guess not as many families are travelling right now since it's so close to school being back."

Leonard nodded, satisfied, but the hostess didn't wait long enough to see it.

She sat them by the window. Alexandra saw the western sky and the sun change colour like autumn leaves.

"I still can't believe you've never been to the ocean," Leonard said over his menu, not lifting his eyes from the rows of barbecued meat and pasta. "You've never felt the urge? Not even once?"

She shook her head.

"It's never really been a priority, I guess. I've never been much of a traveller."

"Wow, that's amazing. I feel like I'd be happy if all I did was travel. You know: get on a plane and hop from one place to another—like that couple in the story you told me about earlier. Maybe stick around for a few days. When I was just out of school, I took a trip around Europe. It was fantastic!"

She nodded, not sure how to explain that she'd never felt the same drive. The idea left her queasy. Already, she felt so lost, so untethered, that the only way she could hang on was to surround herself with the familiar, the comfortable. At home, she knew where her favorite restaurants were, where to get the clothes she liked. At home, she knew how far it was to the office and how long it took her to get back in the evening. At home, she was safe, and the constant gnawing fear that seemed so much worse at night, in the dark, behind her closed eyes—that fear that she was anything but safe, adrift in the void of the unfathomable universe—was a muted shout from deep within. The terrors squirmed inside of her, but she was able to keep them contained.

Leonard couldn't understand. He clearly *enjoyed* the sensation.

"What's great about Europe is how old everything is." He looked at her, but his eyes saw something more. "We don't have that same sense of history here. You walk around a European city, you *feel* part of how ancient everything is. It's all stood for so long you begin to wonder if it was there before there were people to see it. The old world is so close at hand, yet it's so distant and unknowable. You walk by buildings with the most beautiful and ornate carvings—even those half in ruin—and they seem so impossible. Yet, there they stand, and *have* stood through riots, revolts, and marches; mankind has done so many things by uniting into a single force, both for good and evil. It's amazing to be in touch with all of that."

"I've always thought about going," Alexandra lied, "but I've just never done it. Maybe one day."

"We should totally go. I'd love to show you around. I think you'd really get a kick out of it."

She smiled. Then the waitress arrived with their drinks.

✄

"Are you sure this is right?"

They'd driven for an hour after leaving the restaurant, and in that time traffic had thinned and the dark orange sun had reached the horizon. The encroaching dusk only heightened her panicked anxiety.

"I don't know," she said. "We're still in upstate New York, but I can't figure out where. Nothing matches the map." Worries swam in her head in frenzy, and she couldn't stop herself from feeling she'd made a horrendous mistake in her calculation, and her precious map was wrong. If that were true, she truly was adrift, and the feeling of the earth widening around her made her limbs stiffen, her breath wheeze. If Leonard feared the same, his face did not betray it, covered as it was by deepening shadows.

"Maybe it's time to pull over for the night. We can't be that far from the coast—maybe a few hours? Let's stop at a motel and get a new start tomorrow when we have light."

It took another twenty minutes to find a motel, and by that time the highway was so dark the motel's glowing red sign shone brighter than the moon. Leonard pulled into the parking lot, and helped Alexandra out of the car. After travelling for so long, she felt unsteady, as though her body was still hurtling forward along the highway, and it took a few steps before she saw the world through human eyes again.

The man behind the counter couldn't have been more than eighteen, his face spotted and blotched, his curly hair shaved near the temples. He was courteous, but he was bored and tired and went through the motions because he had to. Even when, for her peace of mind if nothing else, Alexandra asked him to show her where on the map the hotel was, he did so with a vague point, and wouldn't be pressed to do more. He seemed more interested in whatever he'd been doing as they arrived, and when she looked over the reception desk partition while he entered Leonard's name into the computer, she saw textbooks lying spine-flat beside the phone. The titles were upside down, but the pictures looked like star charts.

"So you *do* know something about maps. Are you studying astronomy?"

He didn't bother looking away from the computer screen. He simply and unceremoniously slid his open notebook to cover the page. She looked at Leonard, who shrugged nervously but said nothing to the boy. Alexandra hated herself for backing down. She even thanked him when he gave them the key.

Later, in the motel room, she remained fuming at the small wooden desk, trying to retrace the route on her map. All the lines looked the same to her, all the roads feeding into the highway like rivulets. Leonard dismissed her unhappiness.

"He was probably worried you were from head office or something, checking to make sure he was doing paid work and not school work."

"I don't know," she said, looking from her map while he unbuttoned his shirt. "It didn't *feel* like that's what he was worried about."

"Well, what else could it be?"

She didn't know. And, she supposed Leonard was right. It didn't matter. "All that matters is that we're here, together," he said. He ran his fingers through her hair and she put down her pen and looked at him. She touched the side of his warm face, felt the stubble scratch her fingers. He took her hand.

The room was small. The only other furniture was the uncomfortable queen-sized bed, and its springs creaked with each small movement. Leonard suggested they move the blankets to the floor, where it was quieter, and it was while lying there that he moved his hand under the front of her nightshirt and placed it on her bare breast. He then lifted himself onto his other arm and placed his mouth over hers.

He tasted of salt, but mixed with the sweetness of his saliva Alexandra didn't mind. His tongue found hers, invading her mouth tentatively, and the flesh was rough and soft and made the hairs along the back of her neck stand. Her mind drifted for a moment, swaying as though in a dream, and she

ALEXANDRA LOST

had to focus herself to remain in the present with Leonard and not recede into her crowded thoughts.

Leonard's face twisted as he pushed into her, as though willing himself to occupy the same physical space, to join with her on a quantum level. Yet though she bit her lip and arched her back, and though her flesh warmed to the point of fire, she felt herself being pulled away all the same, cast backward into her mind, a powerless witness to events unfolding. Leonard's breath hitched, his brow knitted, he cried some unintelligible word, and she felt the warmth of him flooding into her, coursing through her body like a violent tide, reaching each extremity. Her fingers vibrated, her scalp raised. Leonard continued thrusting afterward, but she couldn't tell for how long while lost in her muddled head. When he finally rolled off, out of breath, she had returned to the surface of her thoughts, and felt aching sadness, but she did her best to throttle it as he perched his head on his bent arm and brushed the hair from her face with the other. He said it was so he could see her better, but she saw nothing in the dark.

"Are you enjoying the trip so far?"

"I think so," she said. "I like that we're doing it together. I don't think I could have done it alone."

It wasn't until she spoke the words that she realized how true they were. Her father's leaving had done more to keep her tied down than anything else, and she had succumbed until she was no different than those giant shadows of slow-spinning blades she and Leonard had seen pinned to the horizon, in motion yet unmoving. They were the reason she let Leonard take her away from where it was safe. If she didn't try to rebel against the sickness she felt the farther from home she travelled, he would surely be the next person lost to her. So she followed him into the unknown, with only her thin overdrawn map as protection, and did her best to endure.

Leonard stroked her hair as the two lay in the dark of the motel room. He whispered to her encouragingly, trying to ease her terror, and she struggled to concentrate on what he said and not get lost in her own anxieties.

"I keep thinking about how much you're going to love the ocean. You'll absolutely freak when you see it—especially if we take a boat out to watch the whales. I went once before with a—well, she was a girl I knew. It was a few years ago. Anyway, going out on the ocean is a trip, pure and simple." He paused, uncertain he should continue, giving her a chance to ask about who that other woman was. She wondered how many women he'd taken there, how many before her had there been. But Alexandra was succumbing to the warmth of his touch, and his droning voice. She didn't want to disturb it by speaking.

"Even if you don't see any whales, you see all sorts of other crazy things. When I was out there, I just happened to be on the boat with a marine biologist, and she pretty much became the *de facto* tour guide for us. There was this school of fish... Have you ever seen a huge school of fish before? Maybe on television? It was larger than that. It was massive. All those sleek black bodies slicing through the water, all moving as one." He moved his hand away as if to illustrate the size, but even if it weren't too dark to see, Alexandra did not open her eyes. "They say the reason a school of fish can react so quickly is because they act together, each fish part of a single super-mind. They're much more of a hive than bees are, I think. The school stretched out so far I couldn't see its edges, as though they encompassed the sea—millions of lithe bodies becoming one giant creature beneath the waves—all sharing a single thought, all using a single voice. It was so beautiful. I really hope we get to do that—go out on the water. You have no idea what it's like!"

Leonard's disembodied voice continued whispering nonsense to her in the dark. It was warm and comforting, so she let him ramble on as the day's journey finally found her.

In her dreams, she and Leonard drove the length of an extended highway bridge, flanked on both sides by endless water. The wheels hummed as they passed over the asphalt, so filling the car with volume she heard nothing else. Not the radio, not Leonard beside her, not the black shapes that crested the water's turbulent surface before submerging once more. She heard nothing but the teeth-gnashing drone. Even her shouts were inaudible over the noise. Lost and panicked, she felt they'd been driving that road forever. They were moving too fast, and when she looked down she saw her own foot pressing the pedal to the floor of the car. Reflexively, she lifted it, and the throbbing in her head intensified in response. The only way to quell her nausea was to press the pedal harder, move faster, burn along the solitary bridge. She looked beside her but the passenger seat was empty; she alone was driving. She alone was crying. And she drove. And drove. And drove.

And she did not wake well-rested. She felt drained; her swollen, tired eyes nearly impossible to open. At some point before morning Alexandra had moved into the bed, dragging a single blanket with her, and from beneath it she watched Leonard perform his morning rituals. She rolled her sour tongue and wished she had some water, though the notion of drinking anything made her ill.

"Good morning," Leonard said. "I'm pretty much ready if you want to hop in the shower now."

"I think I might lie here a bit longer. I'm not ready to get up yet."

"Er… okay," he said. "But we've got to check out, so don't leave it too long."

"Why? I thought we had until eleven."

He stopped his preparations to look at her. "What time do you think it is?"

She rolled over and checked the display on her cell phone. The digits didn't immediately make sense. How could it be nearly half-past ten?

"Why did you let me sleep so long?"

"Let you? How was I supposed to stop you? You wouldn't budge this morning. That must have been some dream."

Fragments surfaced in her memory, flashes of that

179

expansive body, the foreboding of what lay ahead. She felt restless and agitated, possessed by a tension nearly at its limit.

"Yeah, it was pretty crazy," she said, then stretched her arms as far as she could and sat up. The discomfort in her head worsened. "Ugh. I feel horrible."

"Take your shower. You'll feel better once we eat."

She rubbed her palms against her face, doubtful.

✂

Out the Chevrolet's window the trees had returned, though they kept a cautious distance from the highway. Leaves slipped off in the breeze in a steady stream, golds and scarlets in long spiraling chains through the air. Alexandra and Leonard continued eastward, and with each mile travelled the tether connecting Alexandra to her home in the dry country stretched thinner and thinner. Staring out the window, trying to keep her eyes open while her skull tightened, she felt something like a soft pop, and her vision filled with light. Somewhere ahead, somewhere distant, somewhere future, a soft gentle roar echoed. The waves, the surf, the vastness. Leonard was right. There was power in the ocean. She heard its whisper for the first time, urging her onward. Fingers wriggling inside her head.

✂

"How long before we get there?" she asked. Her condition hadn't improved since waking, but the discomfort had become a dull ache behind her eyes. Her mouth parched, head throbbing, she did her best to hide it from Leonard.

"Only a few hours. Maybe two? You're the one with the map."

She nodded and looked down at it, but the brightness of the sun flared, and no matter how she squinted she couldn't see the lines she had drawn. Everything was escaping, fluttering into the aether, and no matter how desperately she tried to catch it all and draw it back it merely slithered through her fingers.

"I know you have everything plotted out," Leonard said, nodding his head toward her without taking his eyes from the road or the cars he weaved through, "but it's amazing how much has come back to me. I remember that hill over there—" He pointed to the left at a large incline, the peak of which was a new horizon across the cloudless sky; "—and how giant shadows moved across it. This place, where we are right at this second, is so beyond real that I can barely process it. Some people say there are extra senses? This must be what they're talking about. Because I can sense how much we belong together, on this journey, right now."

Alexandra nodded, though she barely understood him as he continued. The pain rattling in her skull intensified. But instead of dulling and distancing her from reality, it drew the world into sharper focus. The rush of the ocean a hundred miles away echoed in her crowded head, quelling her lifelong displacement and isolation. The car travelled quicker toward the coast, quicker than she'd thought possible, and while Leonard spoke Alexandra's eyes returned to the over-bright map crumpled in her hands that was coming into focus. The worn folds condensed the lines she had plotted, shortening the distance between where her and Leonard's trip had begun and their final destination. The truth of the journey slipped into focus, and Alexandra finally understood. Eased of the nag of dislocation, the knowledge of where she was—of *when* she was—became clear. And it felt *good* to finally understand. Beneath the discomfort of her throbbing head she wondered if that was how the rest of the world felt. Present. Aware.

Cars whizzed past as the Chevrolet raced across the highway, barely slowing for the austere toll booths. Leonard's face was serene in the bathing sunlight, while Alexandra's was covered by jittering hands working her throbbing temples. When the pain became too unbearable, Alexandra asked if they could pull into a rest stop so she could use the washroom, and there she splashed water on her face and took some chalky tablets, but the endeavor did nothing. She remained in excruciating pain, and yet was terrified Leonard might stop if he learned the truth. The risk was nearly incalculable, so instead, with the taste of bland chalk still on her tongue, she smiled and told him everything was fine. But even as she did she barely saw his face behind the stars that had gathered in her vision. His muted voice asked her twice if she was okay, and Alexandra responded with forced casualness. She hoped she didn't look as pale as her reflection in the washroom mirror had suggested, or speak with the slur she certainly heard. But if Leonard noticed either, he was too polite to say, and they were soon back in the car speeding toward the ocean.

The highway signs increased with the amount of traffic, forcing Alexandra and Leonard to slow down, but it was clear they were closing in on the coast. Commuters clogged the lanes beneath a sun risen to near its height, and the heat in the car steadily increased. Leonard seemed unbothered, but Alexandra had to remove her jacket and cardigan in an effort to cool down. The spasms in her head multiplied.

"The earliest we can check into the hotel is three o'clock, so we might as well go to the ocean first. There a little town off the water called Bearskin Point that would be perfect. It's where I caught the whale-watching boat, so we can find out when that runs as well."

Alexandra's headache knotted itself, but she kept her face calm. "Sure," she said. It was all she could manage without betraying distress.

※

After a time, Leonard stopped asking questions as he navigated the merging highways to Bearskin Point. Alexandra looked down at her map through squinting eyes as the lines contorted and skewed. Each time she thought the car was off-course, a landmark passed suggesting the opposite. She asked Leonard how he knew where he was going.

"I don't. I'm just following the signs." But even with the throb in her head, she knew there were no such signs. The map had been important until then, the foundation on which she'd been able to survive for so long. But the ocean, too, called to her, its quiet voice growing, and she didn't know which she could trust.

Leonard drove on with unerring confidence, at once quieter and more intense. Alexandra's face was turned out the side window, watching passing cars drag boats away from closed summer homes, her face grimaced in pain. She had travelled too far from home, her tether stretched near its breaking point, and as Leonard drove faster that tether continued to stretch thinner still.

She asked herself why she didn't speak up, why she suffered quietly. Racing thoughts screamed something was wrong, but they were buried deep in a tangle of pain, slipping away with every second the Chevrolet closed in on the vast ocean. She had spent so many years—too many years—cooped in her small dry town, never moving beyond its imaginary walls, a bird in a cage. It was only as she approached the Atlantic and felt the difference in the air, the openness in the contrasted sky, that she began to suspect there were bars.

She had never felt so unbound, and it was terrifying. And yet, for all her freedom, she felt anything but lost. Her map was clenched to her chest, a symbol of her clarity; her life *was* the map, laid out in an exact path, the end-point of its journey set. The inevitability was itself a structure to which she was bound and soothed, and she felt no more in control of it than a bottle in the surf.

The transition from highway to street was seamless, and from there to side road even more so. Leonard guided the car through turns and stop signs without once stepping on the brakes. The tires squealed with each jerk of the wheel, and the momentum reignited Alexandra's disguised pains, but she

SIMON STRANTZAS

bore through them. Despite the pull back to where she had come from, back to where her father had stroked her hair one last time before becoming lost for good, she was convinced that her freedom lay in seeing the ocean, that it was only in that sight, witnessed until then solely in dreams, that would ultimately and finally find herself. Leonard had to be right. Once she was able to stand in the water and look eastward toward where the sun emerged, she would finally stop running away from the world, and stop being afraid of running toward something better. On facing that immensity, her longing pains would reach their end.

Bearskin Point appeared no different than any small town she had seen, but Alexandra's head swam so that she no longer trusted her vision. Behind the white and grey façades, she saw a large shape loom, its wide wings stretched outward, but in an instant the shape dispersed, the clouds that comprised it pushed apart by warm winds.

Leonard drove the car slowly along the short road to Bearskin Point, passing small stores with local crafts and paintings displayed in the dark store front windows, the warped glass reflecting strange shapes and colours moving. No one walked the abandoned road, and Alexandra wondered if she and Leonard were the only travellers left in the world. A sharp pain punctuated the thought—a charge through her head that Alexandra was unable to contain. The smallest moan emerged.

"Not much farther," Leonard said.

Bearskin Point was a small circular outcropping into the ocean. Despite her draw toward it, Alexandra travelled the remainder with eyes closed, struggling to contain her encroaching delirium. Her tether was stretched to a thin gossamer thread, and she felt every tug on it, every twang. With clenched, bloodless fingers around the car door handle, beads of sweat slipped down her neck, steamed off her chest. That thread was so taut, so painful, that it blocked the vision from her eyes. Blind, her body felt it continuous motion, falling into the depths of nothing, fading from a spiraling world of

184

teeming shadows.

"We're here!"

Leonard's voice jarred her awake. She opened her eyes, though initially wasn't certain she had.

She stepped out of the car onto her shaking legs. Leonard rushed to help, but she remained upright, never prying her eyes from what was laid out before her. All pain and discomfort forgotten.

"It's..." She couldn't think of words to follow.

The surface of the water stretched outward, encompassing the horizon. There was nothing else; only a line that met the clouded sky. It seemed unreal, the dark contrast of elements separated by that thin sliver; it went on and on forever. And, yet, there was something else out there, something more, moving toward them. She could not see it, but it was coming. Something large.

"Leonard, can you—" she looked at the wasteland of rocks between her and the water. "Will you help me down to the beach? I don't think I can do it alone."

"Yes," he said, and held out his hand.

They took the first step onto the rocks together, then one at a time as he led her down to the ocean's edge. With each successive step, she looked at the water's calm surface, knowing what was out there was ever closer.

"Careful you don't get your foot trapped," Leonard said. "These rocks can be dangerous."

"Okay," she said.

It took ten minutes to reach the edge of the water, and when Alexandra's foot first sank into the wet sand an electric jolt travelled through her. The air smelled as it did after a thunderstorm, wet and cold, and the standing hairs sent shivers over her arms. All sound ceased; she simply existed, as much a part of that place as were the rocks and sand and air. As much as the water and everything moving under its surface. She was at one with everything as she had never been before. Not in her own home, not in the arms of her father, not beneath any lover or among any friends. She struggled for a word that described it all, but as soon as she had it, it was gone, swimming away.

She released Leonard's hand and stepped forward, each foot leaving a fading print in the wet sand. She stepped to the lapping edge of the ocean and then continued onward—the water rising first to her ankle, then to her knee, then halfway up her thigh. She stood alone, watching the endless horizon, waiting for what was to come.

It did not take long.

She doubled over, unable to keep upright as waves of excruciating pain travelled from the frigid water around her legs. Leonard stood behind her—somewhere on the land or perhaps holding her, she couldn't be sure—and she tried to scream but no words emerged. Or, if they did, they were inaudible over the rushing sound of the surf churning beneath her. It was as though she were being lanced by a burning metal rod forced though her skull one inch at a time, burning hotter the further it travelled. Her head was thick with pressure, and behind her tightly squeezed lids stars refracted and filled her vision. There were shapes in the endless field, enormous masses that moved in the distance, eldritch things that watched from the depths of a between-space she only now saw was connected to the ocean, the primal force of the drowning earth. And behind them all she saw *him* on the horizon, elephantine arms reaching out to draw her in close. Alexandra forced her eyes open, unable to bear any more, and the tears rushed forward, falling into the water. There, in the waves, each transformed into a silvery-sleek creature that darted away. More tears fell, more creatures darted, as though a tear between worlds had opened behind her eyes, and through it fell children of another place, all of whom streamed toward the great thing that approached from out in the distant depths, something no doubt older than the earth, older than even those ancient things behind her watering eyes. They swam forward in the churning ocean and she didn't know why, didn't know what it all meant, didn't know where Leonard was or how many times he'd been there before, or when she had been impregnated with the horror. So many questions, burning inside her cracking head, so many tears falling she could not stop, and she prayed the pain would end and that she could once more be blind to what she was a portal for. But she knew it would not happen; it was too late. Whatever was inside her, whatever emerged from the beyond, would not stop until she was consumed, transformed from flesh and blood back to the essential salts that had formed her, left to mix and dilute, returning home at last to find herself within the great ocean of tears beneath which some unfathomable future approached.

ALL REALITY
BLOSSOMS IN FLAMES

1. GALA

It took no more than five minutes at the fundraising gala for Mae Olsen's swelling feet to transform her new shoes into a pair of iron maidens, and she contemplated turning around and walking back out the door before it was too late. But it already was; Oscar Rowing had noticed her, and he was waving her over to join the small coterie of AGO benefactors he'd assembled.

"Olsen, I was just telling the Ramseys and—Mr. Graves, is it?"

"Please," he said. "Call me Halton."

"I was just telling the Ramseys and Halton Graves about *Le Manteau*, and all the repair work we had to do to Aldus Roget's masterpiece."

"Um... yes. That's right. I—we spent a month of late nights fixing it. Actually, we just finished the work about an hour ago."

Each word out of her mouth made her cringe. They all seemed so wrong and in the wrong order. Oscar Rowing watched her with an expression that edged the line of disapproval.

"You have to tell us what happened," Mrs. Ramsey said, her eyes so wide they threatened to steal attention from the diamond broach pinned to her chest. Mae was unsure how candid she should be. Oscar remained as always inscrutable.

"Well," she hesitated. "It was the fault of Enfants Terrible. They're a group of failed artists or something who've spent the last year staging protests about the commercialization of art. They were behind those paint balloons at the Chinook Statuary a few months ago. I suspect they feel damaging important pieces of artwork like Roget's will make some grand statement." Mae glanced at their faces, disappointed that none registered any particular concern. "The museum ended up determining our night security guard, Kenny, was responsible because he sneaked out for a smoke instead of checking on the Lismer Wing. Of course, he was fired the next day. I don't think he took it well."

"Well, I think you folks are all miracle workers," Mrs. Ramsey said. Her plump fingers held the stem of her glass delicately as she swirled her wine in a hypnotizing motion. "When I heard about what happened I think my heart stopped."

"I'm just glad you could save the painting," said her heavy-lidded husband. Mae noticed a chuckle spill from between Halton Graves's thin lips. He was tall and lean, and his sports jacket appeared long enough out of style that it might have actually come back around. His face was the sort of leather one only finds in the Mediterranean. And he was watching her. Mae blushed.

Oscar cut in. "We have a crack team at the AGO. Simply the best. We're very proud of them all. Why Olsen here is so good she's almost an artist herself!"

"Almost," Mae said with as much of pleasantry as she could muster, while unable to prevent her thoughts from travelling back to her small apartment and the half-finished still life on her easel; and then to Milk, the coffee house on College Street, where her two pieces hung beside dusty and yellow price tags. The Ramseys laughed politely, not understanding the joke, but for Mae the insult, even inadvertent, was painful. At least Halton Graves had lost interest, distracted by *Le Manteau*, his glass's rim pressed to his lips. He looked at the painting hanging across the room, Mae understood, because he was supposed to, but she doubted he could appreciate it. At least, not in the way she could. Mae had spent years studying it in the Lismer Wing, followed by weeks of close scrutinization while performing the repairs after its vandalism. She connected with it as she had never before with a piece of artwork, which was why she'd lobbied against hanging it so soon for the gala. The paint had not even set.

She took a deep breath surreptitiously and reminded herself that her anxiety was unfounded. There would be plenty of time for *Le Manteau* to dry before its eventual return to display in the Lismer Wing. Until then, she could rest knowing there was no permanent damage done. Everything would be okay.

Oscar Rowing's hand on Mae's shoulder woke her from her thoughts. Wordlessly and discreetly, he intimated her presence in his group was no longer necessary.

"If you'll excuse me," she said, "I'm going to the bar. Would anyone care for a drink?"

They smiled but didn't say a word. Halton Graves seemed downright amused. She mused she should maybe bow before she left, but at the last moment guessed it wouldn't be as charming as she imagined. Instead she scanned the gala for the event bar, an oasis lit in the distance.

Her feet throbbed harder, but she did her best to avoid hobbling across the room. She was slightly less successful than she'd hoped. As she flagged the bartender and waited for her few ounces of French Syrah, Mae fantasized about slipping her swollen feet into the pair of sneakers she had beneath her desk upstairs. But she knew she had to remain at the gala and endure, at least until someone from the AGO board made a speech and a pledge drive. As beautiful and mesmerizing at it was, the restoration of *Le Manteau* and other works was not something that could be glossed over. If anything, it would be used as a club to beat more money from those patrons hungry to have a tax-deductible way of shedding excess capital. Mae was an implied part of that plan, and it would be frowned upon if she weren't close at hand to be flaunted should the moment warrant.

But, her feet. Oh, her painful, painful feet.

"You look like you could use some help."

And like that, Halton Graves was standing beside her, mouth like a swing with a broken rope. Was he smiling or laughing at her?

"I'll be okay. I should have broken in these shoes before I wore them. It's the price we pay."

"Sure, but it's up to you if it's one worth paying. Look at *Le Manteau*—" He swept his arm in the direction of the restored painting. "Some would say that everything you've done, everything the museum paid you to fix it was worthwhile in order to preserve our artistic history. But the vandals who marked it up in the first place? They probably wouldn't agree."

"And they're probably crazy," she said. "To ruin something so beautiful for no reason."

He leaned against the bar on his crossed arms. "No one does anything without a reason, especially something so dangerous. For them, I'd bet the cost of preserving the past in such a commercial way is too high. They would probably hate what we're doing now, using art to raise money."

"The irony is we wouldn't be here raising money if not for their vandalism."

He brushed it off. "If it weren't for this, it would be for something else. The museum administration doesn't miss an opportunity to collect money when and where it can." He thought of something and smiled. "Still, you might be right about it being another failed revolution. I find it all pretty fascinating, at any rate. A gin and tonic, please."

Halton Graves's hand wagged past her face to get the bartender's attention. Mae caught a whiff of something damp and musty. When Graves received his drink, he placed a small triangular serviette beneath the glass, and said, "Will you show me *Le Manteau*? I'd like to see all the work you did up close and in detail."

He held out his arm for her and hesitantly she took it. She wasn't sure what else to do. A glance at Oscar's approving smile confirmed she'd chosen wisely.

Le Manteau was a six-foot square canvas on loan to the gallery from the Elias Rasp Collection. It captured Champs-Élysées in the midst of an uncharacteristically harsh winter storm, with nineteenth-century noblemen and women dressed in furs so heavy their faces were obscured. Snow spiralled in vibrant bursts, catching the edges of their overcoats under the coloured gas lamps. On closer inspection of the chaos, their shapes were an inchoate swirl of colours, so abstracted it was as though all natural laws within the painting had broken down, become less concrete, more malleable. A month previous the bottom right corner, just above Roget's signature, had been a spray of silver shellac in the shape of a bisected circle. Now, even Mae couldn't tell there had once been something there.

Graves stood aside Mae, studying the painting intently, his gin and tonic still pinched between his fingers. He was quiet, as though memorizing the gentle dappling of colours that so stood out to Mae, made her fall in love with Roget's masterpiece anew each and every time she saw it. Not many things in the world made her so nervously excited, and much as she expected Halton Graves to, she stood in quiet awe before it.

Which is why she almost didn't react in time when she saw Graves reach his hand out toward the still-wet painting, and why she snatched at his wrist so swiftly that she had no time to reconsider. She flushed with terror and embarrassment when he took his hand back and rubbed his wrist where she'd struck.

"I'm so sorry. I shouldn't have done that," she said, checking behind her to ensure Oscar hadn't witnessed her blunder.

"No, I'm the one who's sorry," he said, clinging to his wrist protectively. Aftershocks continued fluttering through Mae's heart. "It's my fault for being so presumptuous."

"It's just—you can't touch any of the paintings in the

SIMON STRANTZAS

museum. Even if *Le Manteau* weren't still wet, the oils from
your skin would damage it."

"Mea culpa," he said, free hand in the air in implied
surrender. "So, tell me, as the primary saviour for this piece,
what's it like to rescue something? Do you know right when
you see it that it needs your help?"

"What do you mean? How can I tell a painting needs to
be restored?"

He shrugged. "Sure, why not? Like this one: what was it
that told you it needed saving?"

"I'm not sure I understand. It's my job to—"

"Yes, yes, I know that. It was vandalized by Enfants
Terrible. Everybody at this party already knows that." One of
the waiters brought a tray of hors d'oeuvres to him. He looked
at Mae, tilted his head to offer her one, and when she declined
waved the waiter off. "Everyone here knows what they did.
And some think they know why, even if they don't agree with
the justification. What I want to know is something none of
them do. When you, Mae Olsen, looked at this painting—when
you saw it was damaged, defaced—what did you feel? What
said that this painting needed your help?"

"I—I'm not sure I know how to answer that." She thought
for a moment. Stared at the painting. Tried to articulate her
feelings. Halton Graves watched intently. Did he touch his
tongue to his lips? "When I saw *Le Manteau* like that—when I
saw that spray paint on Roget's masterwork, I felt... I felt this
crushing sadness. Do you know what I mean? He put so much
of himself into it. Look at the strokes there near the top; like
flames, each one protruding from the canvas. And the soft
swirls down, imperceptibly differentiating foreground while
leading your eye with subtle distortions of light. The painting
is practically alive and moving, and seeing that ugly mark stole
its life away. It murdered the painting, transformed it into just
a thing. How did I know *Le Manteau* needed saving? I knew
because it didn't scream out for help. I knew that something
was gone, that it was empty. I couldn't bear to see that."

Graves nodded.

194

"Spoken like someone with an artist's eye."

He looked again at *Le Manteau*. Mae looked too.

"And what about you," he asked after a few moments, never turning toward her. "Do you need rescuing?"

"What? I—" she started, but Oscar's cool hand appeared on her shoulder and interrupted her.

"Olsen, I apologize, but I need to introduce you to some people." His thin grey moustache twitched as he spoke. "They've donated a very large sum to the museum, and in return I think they'd like to hear about your restoration efforts with *Le Manteau*."

She hesitated, looked at Halton Graves who gave her a polite smile, but before she could speak Oscar's lifted hand stopped her.

"Please, please, Olsen. We can't keep these folks waiting. I apologize again, Mr. Graves."

"There's no need. None at all."

Mae sheepishly excused herself and followed Oscar across the museum floor where she was introduced, then abandoned, to a small group of investors who had flown in from Trois-Rivières for the event. Their English was not perfect, and in the heightened volume of the venue she couldn't hear a thing they said. All she caught were snippets, enough to gather they were pleased with what she and the AGO team had been able to accomplish in restoring such an important part of the country's heritage. She thanked them again, and explained the circumstances behind the restoration and the difficulties in making the repairs seamless. While she spoke, she glanced back at where she'd left the leathered Halton Graves. He was long gone, and where he once stood were four guests, staring and pointing at the restored *Le Manteau*. Was there something wrong with it? She squinted, and the bottom corner above Roget's signature looked smudged.

"Please excuse me," she managed to say to the confused French Canadians after her story trailed off mid-way through. Mae made her way back across the gala, the pain in her feet forgotten, and with every step she took the crowd around the

Le Manteau grew larger and deeper, their volume blocking her line of sight.

She fought her way through the whispering guests while in the corner of her eye Oscar heatedly argued with a belaboured museum security guard. When Mae reached *Le Manteau*, she saw that all the work she'd done to restore it had been destroyed by another large circle of silver paint. Those careful strokes of colour she put down a few hours earlier were gone, smudged and twirled with silver, until they became something else, something entirely incongruous with the fires of Roget's masterpiece. They looked almost like a galaxy if Mae squinted enough: a spiralling metallic serpent floating above the canvas. The coils shimmered in the gala's candle light, flickering across Mae's dampening eyes.

The rest of the night was a blur of commotion. The head of security was called in to head the search for Halton Graves, but he'd already gone. Blurry video footage of the AGO entrance showed him strolling through the front door as people darted past, then casually turning down the street and out of the camera's view.

An in-depth investigation and assessment was performed over the next few days and Oscar Rowing was brought before the Board to answer how the stranger had managed to con his way past the gala's security checks, and was not only granted access to *Le Manteau*, but also had Rowing act as his personal escort without thorough vetting or questioning. There was no reasonable explanation, and though Mae was confident that he'd fallen for Graves's ruse of importance the same as everyone else, there were others who believed Rowing might be in league with Enfants Terrible, and that the entire incident had been an inside job. Whatever the truth, the news of Rowing's leave of absence spread quickly without clarifying how temporary or indefinite it would be. At least the Board cleared Mae of any blame. She was simply an employee sent to the gala on a whim, a reward for completing an arduous task before the deadline, and though she understood it was best to play the ignorant or dim-witted card she'd been handed, part of her bristled at the idea that it wasn't her integrity that spared her their suspicions. Even so, absolved of blame, Mae got the impression she had attended her last private AGO gala.

While it was true the painting, like each piece in the museum—both on loan and as part of the various collections—was insured, and the AGO would receive enough money to again repair *Le Manteau* and temporarily cover the loss in revenue due to the attacks, the increase in coverage fees and added security for the building meant a tightening of departmental budgets, and in order to maintain a strong public face the pressure to return Roget's masterpiece to the Lismer Wing was even greater than before. As a result, the Board mandated a newer and narrower deadline, and Mae understood the not-so-subtle intonation that Rowing's absence meant there would be no one but her to blame should it not be met. Mae needed to perform a miracle despite her insistence that the job required months longer to do right. Completing the work on their schedule would cost a large number of late nights and early mornings, but none of it would be permanent; the only collateral damage suffered would be the lack of attention paid to the stagnated paintings cluttering her apartment. There, intricate flowers would remain half-petalled, their pistils mere ghosts on the canvas, glimpses of the past bleeding through to the present. The colours should be brighter, more primary, but the longer she kept away from them, the duller they appeared, and the potency she saw in the work dried. After a while, the incomplete versions of the work would simply become the work, their potential squandered, impossible to resurrect. But what choice did she have?

Once *Le Manteau* was uninstalled and delivered to her office, Mae realized all her previous work was unsalvageable. Halton's mixture of aerosols with her still-wet oil paints left an unusable mess, and Mae's first task would have to be the painstaking task of scraping away everything she'd done and returning the painting to its previous state. She tried to keep her frustration tamped down, but could not help but think about all the time wasted and would be further wasted because of Halton Graves. His leathery countenance flashed in her mind as her anger grew, and soon her brushes shook too much to continue working. Retouching something as profoundly affecting as *Le Manteau* required a steady hand to ensure no details were missed or glossed over. It had to be as perfect as it had been before the vandalism, and Mae couldn't do that until her hatred eased and disappointment assumed its place.

It took weeks, and in that time her eyes strained behind the magnifying glass and slow brushes. At times, she couldn't see straight, the world dissected into coloured impressionist blobs that jostled according to an inscrutable ad hoc pattern that left her stomach as uneasy as a wobbling top. She had to lower her eyelids when the world lost cohesion and wait for everything to re-integrate.

✄

There were four wings in the Art Gallery of Ontario, and more than nine thousand works of art collectively stored within them. Calling the place an art museum didn't seem to encapsulate everything about it. Even its Grange District façade was a bizarre Frank Gehry-designed collision of angled concrete and glass, reflecting the intersecting worlds of the artwork within. Sometimes, Mae spent an entire lunch hour in one collection, sidestepping the student artists sketching, tuning out the bored teenagers on field trips, to absorb all the time and precision and thought around her. Her psyche fed on it, digested it into the fuel she needed for her own work. Each canvas, each statue, radiated the energy of creation distilled and concentrated in a single vessel; none more so than *Le Manteau*, which normally hung in a place of pride in the Lismer Wing.

Mae absorbed all she could from the masters in the museum, and when her lunch hour was at its end, she detoured past the African Wing and walked along the Galleria Italia's glassed-in length. Outside, there was a low rumble beneath the world as students walked McCaul Street toward the College of Art and Design, nylon canvas portfolios tucked under their arms, military pants blotched with camouflage and paint. She remembered her own school years with little fondness except for the work, and wondered how many of the unkempt students passing by felt the same weight of their future pressing down. Would any accept a temporary job to make ends meet and get stuck, toiling in anonymity while their peers staged shows in one of the increasing number of small prestige galleries springing up along Queen Street West?

The students rushed as cars passed by in both directions. The street bustled with energy, highlighting the static figure standing on the other side of McCaul. Mae's glance was drawn there by the composition of the world, but she saw nothing noteworthy at first. Just a tall, lean man alone on the sidewalk, dressed in a checkered wool overcoat. An out-of-season tourist, perhaps, looking for the entrance in the sometimes confusing glass and angles of the AGO. But like a slowly developing photograph, the image of the man materialized in her mind's eye, and she turned again and gaped. Halton Graves idly stood there, map in hand, examining the AGO from across the street. He casually took notes before walking another few feet and doing so again. Mae scanned the length of the Galleria in both directions, and in both cases the exits appeared miles away and all the newly added security completely absent. She was alone in the middle of a corridor the length of a city block, too far to do anything but watch as the person everyone had been searching for blithely took notes on the museum he and his co-conspirators had already struck twice. Something bubbled up within her.

But that turmoil stilled when he caught her gaze in the window. He appeared genuinely surprised, dropping the hands that held the map and pencil aloft. He was too far to see clearly, but she thought he might be smiling—or at least wearing that crooked grimace she took for a smile. His hands went to his overcoat pockets, depositing the map in one and the pencil in the other. Then he raised one of his gloved hands and waved at her. Then waved again. He continued until Mae reluctantly returned the gesture, unsure what else to do. She was still alone on the walkway, still a half-block from anything resembling a security guard. Her discomfort increased as Halton Graves jogged across the street, though it was her own heart that raced.

He stood on the sidewalk outside the Galleria Italia, looking at her on the elevated platform. He spoke rapidly but the glass was too thick for him to be heard, and she was too self-conscious to shout back from inside the museum. Instead, she pointed to the end of the galleria where she knew there was an emergency exit not guarded by Security. Graves nodded, smiled crookedly, and set off. Mae hesitated, then strode down the galleria to meet him.

She opened the door intending to step out, but Halton Graves immediately filled the frame. Caught off guard, she retreated and let him in. Graves was dishevelled, with patches of hair standing askew and his checkered overcoat streaked with salt and grime. But his eyes were still lit, and when they looked into her own her tongue became a prune.

"I'm glad I ran into you, Mae. I hope you can forgive me for disappearing from the gala. I suddenly felt very unwelcome."

"I'd say so," she said, indignant because she knew she ought to be. "You caused a lot of damage."

"Oh, I'm sure the museum will survive the embarrassment. Nothing permanent was done."

"This time."

"Well, we've only been at this a little while, after all. Give Enfants Terrible some time." He smiled at her and she couldn't tell if he was being serious.

"Time to do what? What's your goal here?"

He was about to speak, when they both heard voices close by. Visitors to the museum moving from one wing to the other. He stepped closer to her in the doorway to keep out of sight. She shrank into the shadows.

"I don't think we can talk about this here," he whispered, watching the passing tourists. She nodded, struck dumb. "I need you to come with me. Will you come with me?"

She nodded again. Why couldn't she speak?

There was no time to retrieve her jacket, or make any preparations for leaving the museum. There wasn't much thought at all other than to follow Halton Graves as he led her outside, back onto McCaul Street, and north toward Dundas Avenue. Mae kept her face turned away from the windows of the AGO, worried someone might recognize her. A voice in her head screamed that she should not leave with him, that she should turn back and report Halton Graves for the criminal he was. Reason after reason to flee presented themselves in Mae's thoughts, but no matter how many she counted, her legs would not stop chasing after him.

At the corner of Dundas, he cast a lazy glance to ensure no one was watching, then motioned Mae onward with a nod, directing her into a narrow alley discreeted behind a row of Chinese restaurants. She hesitated, wondering again what she was doing, but went forward anyway. Halton Graves followed close behind.

Mae tensed. His footsteps clapped softly against broken asphalt as they trailed her. To the right was a chain-link fence, separating the lot from another, the six-inch tall concrete barrier not enough. The alley smelled of fish and other cast-offs from the rusted dumpsters. She didn't know where Halton Graves was taking her—to some secret club behind an unmarked back door? To the place he would murder her and leave her body for the rats to discover? She slowed, nervous, and jumped when Halton Graves caught up and pinched her elbow gently.

"Not much further ahead."

She wanted to speak, but her dry throat prevented it, and by the time she could he had already pulled ahead. Mae considered turning around while she was still able and escaping from Graves and whatever awaited her at the end of the malodorous alley. But to her surprise she didn't. Her curiosity was too great.

Twenty-five feet farther in, the alley opened into a small

square. In its middle a grate was set into the ground, and everywhere else was a network of fire escapes and papered-over windows. Halton Graves placed one foot firmly on each side of the inset grate, pulled each leg of his trousers up an inch, then bent down and grabbed hold of the bars. They trembled as he lifted, making an aching wrench as the shifted grate revealed a narrow set of stairs descending into the dark.

"If you're ready to make a real difference," he said as he rested the cover on the ground. "Then you'll need to climb down. I'll be right behind you."

Mae swallowed the ball of nervous energy that had amassed in her throat.

"And if I'm *not* ready?"

"If you're not, you go back. You go on. Just like everybody else. Maybe someday you'll even forgive yourself. But you won't be an artist, because real art is about taking risks. Without risks, the art inside of you will eventually wither."

Mae looked at the tall man in the dirty checkered overcoat and ruffled hair. Looked at his creased leather skin, his simmering eyes. She then looked down at the hole in the ground, at the dirty concrete stairs that, one by one, led into darkness. And then she looked into herself and asked what she was doing, and if she'd utterly lost her mind.

And when she was done looking at all these things, she descended the concrete steps. Halton Graves followed close, and when she looked back at him, above her on the stairs, he had the grate resting on his shoulders and was lowering it back into place an inch at a time, sealing her off from everything.

2. LUMIÈRE

The first thing Mae encountered in the darkness at the bottom of the stairs was the odour. It was sickening, the smell of stagnant water and concrete, and she raised her hand to cover her nose and mouth. "Where are we?" she asked. Her voice twanged with echo.

"We're in the storm drain runoff channels."

Mae nodded, distracted by the sound of rodents scurrying in the distance. Halton Graves touched her arm. Her flesh pulsed.

"Don't worry," he said, flipping the switch on the small flashlight he pulled out of his overcoat pocket, illuminating a circle of cold sharp blue. "It's absolutely safe. Follow me."

He shone the light ahead of him and walked into the dark channel. Mae took one last look at the shafts of sunlight spilling down from the stairwell, and regretfully chased after him.

"Are you sure this isn't dangerous?" she said. Her shoes clacked against the concrete. The sound ricocheted around them.

"Completely. I've walked this stretch hundreds of times. Maybe thousands. And I've almost never had an accident."

"Almost?" she repeated, and he turned to look at her. There was little light thrown back on him, but what there was lit his crooked smile.

"I should probably apologize to you. After all you did to fix that Roget painting, I should have left it alone."

"Yes. You should have," she said. "You nearly ruined it."

"But it's so crass. It needed a good ruining, I think," he said, then smirked again as though his joke were the funniest ever spoken. "But you managed to fix it again, yes?"

"I will. And it will be as close to the original state as possible." She wanted him to be impressed, all the while hating herself for it.

"Good. It *should* go back up. Maybe it will help you make more money for art's corporate gatekeepers. Maybe earn someone a nice bonus. Now, stay close. Our destination is just up here."

The channel they'd been walking down continued ahead, splitting off into a junction while another intersected it on the left. Halton Graves shined his flashlight about ten feet into the new channel.

"We've arrived," he said.

"But—but there's nothing here. There's just a wall."

"Exactly," he said. "Nothing at all to see here or draw the wrong someone's attention."

Halton Graves smiled, half-crazed, and Mae doubted again the wisdom in following the criminal. He took a step toward her and snatched her wrist before she could step back.

"Here," he said, and pressed the flashlight into her hand before she could struggle. "Shine it on the wall."

Mae was unhappy, but did as she was asked.

Halton Graves went back to the wall. He removed his gloves one at a time and put them in his pockets, then waved Mae closer. When she was as near as she dared he put his hands on the wall again and pushed. It slid easily, and travelled down the channel until he could move it to the side and reveal the dim corridor behind it, lit with tiny hanging bulbs. He waved her in.

"Welcome to the Path," he said.

Mae had heard of the place, but no one had reported setting foot there in so long she didn't believe it was real. It had been an urban legend, like reptiles in the sewers, because that's what it sounded like. Sandwiched between the office buildings that dotted the city and the subway system that spread like a web to support it, the Path was supposedly once a maze of interconnected corridors and storefronts designed to move those who worked above and those who travelled below from one building to the next without them having to face the elements or outside world. Over time it had become something else: a secret passage that the city had mysteriously closed, then sealed and hid as though it had never existed. The whole notion was preposterous. And yet she found herself standing in a narrow corridor, the remains of small shops and businesses lining it on either side. The air smelled better than in the runoff channel, though it was still stale and sweet. Halton Graves pushed the fake wall back into place, sealing off the corridor behind them, then took his flashlight back from Mae and switched it off.

"The wall's pretty ingenious. It's real concrete, so it sounds authentic to anyone tapping on it, but everything is on a counterweighted system. You have to know the right place to push. Try the wrong spot and it won't budge at all. It keeps the entrance disguised and prevents patrolling maintenance crews from finding us."

"Sounds elaborate," Mae said. Graves smiled at her.

"Let's keep going," he said.

They continued along the narrow corridor, following the thin strands of hanging lights. The tiny bulbs reflected off the windows of the abandoned stores, and those store windows reflected one another, until they multiplied and compounded into a darkness filled with stars. It was like walking into the night sky.

"It's just in here," he said, reaching across the corridor to a boarded-over travel agency, the only place the bulbs did not reflect. Beneath the sign that read *Lumière Travel* was a door, and Graves opened it and let light spill across Mae's feet. He held it open as he ushered her inside.

The old office had proper hanging bulbs and enough of them that a flashlight wasn't needed. Inside, all the abandoned furniture had been pushed to the edges of the room, and the centre was taken up by a long table covered in stacks of paper and maps. There were clusters of orange extension cords lying across the floor to power the lights, as well as a small refrigerator, microwave, and a handful of humming air purifiers. There were also charts and articles hanging everywhere, and along the back wall at least a dozen canister tanks, but Mae saw none of this on entering. Instead, she was drawn to the beautiful young woman with the pronounced nose seated at the table, long legs stretched out and crossed at the ankle, and the two men opposite her: one bearded in an oversized tee-shirt covered in what looked like dried clay; the other looking twice as old and ruddy with days of unkempt stubble and wearing a brimless hat. The latter two were hunched over the same map and pieces of electronics. All three looked at Mae like a pack of wild dogs. She tried not to move. Or show fear.

"These are Enfants Terrible," Graves said. "Or, at least the regulars. We have a few more independent agent members as well. Meet Vienna, Wynn, and Albert. Not their real names, of course."

"Halton, who is this?" The older man, Albert, was unamused, his voice hinting at anger, his blotchy face and bulbous nose hinting at something else, something Mae thought she could smell from across the table despite the damp odour of concrete that lingered. As Albert spoke, Wynn slowly folded the map they'd been looking at before she and Graves entered.

"This is Mae. She's the one I told you about from the gala."

"The restorer from the museum?" Vienna said. Her spread of freckles made her look genuinely shocked. "Why would you bring her here?"

"We agreed we needed someone to replace Kenny."

"Isn't this a whatdoyoucall it? A violation of our protocol, or something?" Wynn asked, though he seemed more interested in collecting the spool of wiring and circuit boards from the table.

"I'm aware," Graves responded. "We wrote those protocols together." He removed his overcoat and threw it over an unused chair. A cloud of dust billowed. "In fact, I think the protocols for new recruits was my idea."

"Then you should know how serious we're supposed to take them," Albert interjected. "Who vetted this person?"

It was all too much for Mae. Too overwhelming.

"This was a mistake. I'm sorry, I should leave. I shouldn't even be here," Mae said. The other woman, Vienna, raised her arms and her eyebrows with an impatient sigh. Graves stood between them.

"No, you aren't leaving. Give me your hands."

"What?" She looked to the others. They only glared.

"Your hands. Give them to me."

"I—" she said, then held her shivering hands out in defeat. He took them into his own. His flesh was cool.

"Now, look into my eyes. Look straight into them."

Mae did. They were like burning clouds. Her face flushed, and the embarrassment only made it worse.

"There," he said, squeezing her hands lightly. "I've vetted her. It's fine."

Vienna's legs crossed and uncrossed. Albert huffed. Wynn muttered something about danger as he closed his tool box.

Graves pulled out a chair for Mae to sit on. As she did, she pretended she hadn't noticed the others dragging their work away from her line of sight. The abandoned office looked lived-in, and she wondered how long they'd been cooped-up underground. At least the lights were bright—it let her get a good look at the shelves weighted with paint cans and the various tools and loose instruments relegated to the far corners. Everything an art terrorist would need, she told herself.

"Why am I here?"

The four Enfants Terrible exchanged looks. Only Graves spoke.

"You're here because you can help us. Because you *want* to help us. I knew it as soon as we met at the gala."

"You did?"

He nodded. "You respect authority, but you're not a victim of it. You aren't bound by conventions because they're conventions. I could tell your internal compass was figuratively pointed to true north."

Mae found that description unrecognizable. What she saw in her reflection was a small person ground in the gears of the world machine; one who had refused promotions at her job for fear they would prevent her from doing what she was already too exhausted at the end of her work day to do. A person whose time with a brush in hand was growing so infrequent soon she'd have to think of herself as someone who *used* to paint. Mae spent her waking days doing what she could to help preserve what little beauty there was against time's inevitable entropy, but she knew in the end chaos would win out and everything would fall apart. But she liked his description of her better. It sounded less dire.

"I don't understand what you think I'm going to do. You're all criminals. So much of my life lately has been spent trying to fix everything you're trying to destroy."

"Destroy?" Albert slammed his palm on the table. Everything rattled. "Do you even understand what art is? How can you have no idea what we're doing here?"

"Why don't you explain it to me?"

"It would be easier explaining it to a rock."

"Now, Albert, maybe you should slow down—"

"Don't give me that, Halton. She's a brush-monkey. She probably got her start painting copies of *The Starry Night* to sell on the waterfront. There's no proof she knows anything more than how to mix paints. It's already pretty clear she'll call the cops as soon as she leaves here. The last thing we need is her giving them any idea what we're planning next."

"I have no idea what you're planning next. But if I did, you better believe I'd be telling the police the first chance I got. You need to be stopped."

"See? This is on you, Halton." He thrust his finger like a sword. "If we get caught because of her, it's going to be your fault." Mae watched as the corner of Graves's mouth dropped, or the other corner lifted, into that crooked smile.

"This whole thing is my fault, Albert. If it wasn't for me Vienna would still be in the University Centre, hanging her paintings where no one could see them, and Wynn would be still wandering aimlessly. And you? You'd probably be in a ditch somewhere, looking for meaning. I showed you the entrance to the Path. I got us into City Hall and got us the maps."

"Sure," Wynn interjected. "And we were the ones who stuck our necks out for you when the police were asking questions. We were the ones helping you in London and Hamilton and all the rest. There's a circle of trust and you broke it."

"I haven't done anything close to that. I've helped guarantee Enfants Terrible's survival. If you've lost faith in the cause, you aren't forced to be part of it. Go on, go home.

Leave the revolution to the believers."

Albert's ruddiness deepened as blood rushed to his face. He trembled, ever so slightly; Mae worried his heart would stop right in front of her. She had no idea what to do.

But the pressure in Albert deflated with only a long sigh, and he folded back into his seat, then reached into his jacket and pulled out a small flask. As soon as he unscrewed the cap, the room smelled sweet and hollow. No one spoke. The air purifiers' hum made the air leaden.

Finally, Mae could no longer take it.

"You broke into City Hall?"

"Technically," Graves said.

"We got in through the Path," Vienna interrupted. "But it's not like there were any guards around. We had the run of the place for hours."

"Where were the guards?"

She shrugged.

"They were supposed to be there. They all punched in. We never saw one, though. When Wynn found the Planning Office open and we saw the maps, we knew right away what they were. We grabbed copies and walked right out the front door. It was almost too easy. Like in a dream."

"No," Wynn said. "It wasn't like in a dream. In a dream it would have all been more complicated. That kind of dumb only happens in life."

"It was a long time ago, Mae. But knowing the city and its forgotten places has served us well."

"To do what? Vandalize? That's the big plan Albert was talking about? It sounds like you're the ones who don't understand art."

"It's not vandalism," Graves countered. "It's bigger than that. Bigger than us all. Art is more than just what's hanging in the museums or the galleries. It's a part of everything, the lifeblood that runs through the world. Through us all. Art is what connects us to one another. It's the closest thing to magic we have left and it should be alive and take risks. Art should never be shown off in a gala. It should be displayed where it might be ripped down or shut up at any moment. That's the sort of revolution we want. We want art to be whispered about, not talked about. The only way to make art dangerous is to *be* dangerous."

"And that's why you're holed up in this underground travel agency? To be dangerous?"

"You'd be surprised," Graves said.

"I doubt it. How dangerous can you be? You can't even get the name of your stupid group right."

Mae was not feeling herself. The anger over what she was witnessing grated on her, and the white noise of the air purifiers wasn't helping. She did not like being heckled and questioned about her loyalty to art, not when she sacrificed so much of her life to it. Who were these Enfants Terrible? What had they done other than try to tear down art under the guise of protecting it? What would the world be like if they succeeded in their lunacy? So much would be lost.

The rumble of the subway ran through the floor and up her legs while the four self-styled revolutionaries stared at her. It was bulbous-nosed Albert who spoke first.

"Still convinced she's the right fit, Halton?"

"More than ever."

Mae's face burned, but she didn't turn away. Instead she looked at the frowning Albert as he shook his head, then pulled his flask out again. Vienna and Wynn remained silent. Graves's lopsided smile remained a cipher.

"Come on, Mae," Graves finally spoke, retrieving his coat from the chair. "Let me lead you out of this dungeon. I think the fumes are getting to everyone."

Mae nodded and stood. No one else said a word. No one else looked at her as Halton Graves led her to the door. They showed no interest in seeing her off at all.

"Don't mind them. They're good people and devoted to the cause. Sometimes that devotion makes them forget the social niceties."

When they reached the fake wall, Graves pulled it open slowly, peering through the crack until he was certain the coast was clear, then stepped aside to let Mae pass. She hesitated, looking back over her shoulder at the Path. There was some noise echoing from its depths, a scurrying behind the string of lights that fell back and behind the turns of the corridors.

"How long have you been hiding down here?" she wondered.

"I don't know if I would phrase it quite like that," Graves said. "But we've been down here for some time. We've moved from store to store, looking for all the amenities we need, and to make sure we don't get too complacent, but it's always somewhere along the Path."

"And you've never come close to being caught?"

Graves cocked his smile.

"No one comes in here. No one knows how. Other than the rats, and they only show up when the subway shakes them out of the walls. We have the place to ourselves. It's once we leave that things get dangerous, so if you don't mind..."

He held out his hand to usher her past him, back into the runoff channel so he could close the entrance behind them. As soon as the fake wall was in place the corridor turned impenetrably black. The smell hit her right away and she raised her arm to cover her mouth. Graves turned on his flashlight. Something scurried in the dark.

"Why did you bring me down here, Mr. Graves?"

"Halton, please."

"Why did you bring me down here, *Halton?*"

"You're something different, Mae. At least, different from *them*—the people you work with. You understand there's more to all this. I was at Milk a few days ago and saw your paintings."

"What? You can't—"

"I wanted to see what you could do outside the confines of reproducing someone else's work. I wanted a clearer idea of the real you. It's the only way to understand someone, I think—look at what they create when they're given a chance. Your work told me a lot. How old are they? What I mean is: did you paint them before or after working at the AGO?"

"After I started there," she said. She was uncomfortable talking about this with him. Her artwork had been so secret from so many for so long she almost forgot how to interact with people about it. "All the before work is gone by now."

"I suspected as much. I don't know if you can see it, but there's a gentle appearance of effortlessness to you that's pretty remarkable. Even the glazes give the appearance of being thrown together and landing perfectly by happy accident. It's remarkable. I knew when I first met you that you were special, and destined for something bigger. I want to help you achieve that. I want you to leave your mark."

"By ruining things that are valuable and sacred?"

"No," he shook his head. "We want nothing of the kind. But we *do* want you to do something. It's nothing dangerous, and no one will get hurt. We aren't bad people, Mae, you have to see that. We just want to wake up the world."

"That's great," she said, the flattened words muffled by her sleeve. There was the hint of wavering sunlight up ahead.

"Do you know who I saw when we were first introduced at the gala? Someone thrust into extraordinary circumstances, with the pressure of an entire promotional complex weighed upon her. Someone who nevertheless rose with aplomb to the challenges presented. I saw someone whose' love for creation propelled her head-first through all the barriers in her way, and who found love deep in art itself. That's someone who understands Enfants Terrible, someone who wants to bring those same barriers down for others. We can do it together, Mae. We can show the world the truest art is the art of rebellion. We just need your help to do it. The only question left is, will you?"

They reached the stairwell leading back up to the real world, the world she'd left behind fewer than two hours before. She hadn't even stepped out of the runoff corridor and already Mae knew that once she did, everything that had just occurred would become like a dream, and her regular life would take hold once again. She wasn't sure if she wanted that. Part of her wanted to stay in the dark forever.

212

Graves climbed the stairs into the light. When he reached the top he pushed the grate to the side far enough that Mae could slip past. Then he offered his hand to help her. She did not take it.

"You still haven't told me what you want me to do," she said, ascending the stairs.

"It's nothing," Graves said. "At ten o'clock, Thursday night, open the door we used today in the Galleria."

"That's it?"

"That's it. Ten on the nose."

She climbed back onto the street, temporarily blinded by the afternoon sunlight. When her eyes adjusted to the brightness, she found Graves had gone and the iron grate was closed. The alley looked different from how she remembered, as though she'd resurfaced in a different place altogether, one made to mimic the first, albeit imperfectly. Mae walked back to the street, ignoring the tension in every brick of every building that walled the alley, the cumulative effect of everything about to explode at any moment. She hurried toward the opening along the broken uneven asphalt, and when she finally spilled out onto McCaul, she found nothing had changed. Students still wandered, cars still drove by, and the world itself went on as though ignorant of the grand secrets lying below its surface.

The walk back to work was terrible. Not only was Mae not dressed for the hike, but with each step she took she wrestled with how to justify being absent for most of the afternoon. She couldn't admit where she'd been—she could barely admit it to herself. And yet when she arrived at the AGO she found no one cared. No one had even noticed she'd been gone, or if they had they assumed she'd been in another meeting about the absent Oscar Rowing, or doing more research on the *Le Manteau* restoration. Either way, no one commented or was concerned, which relieved Mae's anxiety, but also highlighted what Halton Graves had implied: her coworkers and peers had become so divorced from life that they had already atrophied. Mae didn't want the same to happen to her. She wanted to notice things, to live and breathe the world. Desire to break her stagnation bolted through her, a crackling energy threatening to explode; it was all she could do to wrangle her overflowing and colliding thoughts. She buzzed as she left for the day, and it did not stop while taking the subway, nor while eating dinner. In bed, the room continued to shake around her even as she forced herself to remain still, breathe slowly, and wait for sleep to come. When it did, it was fitful, and the next morning she rose filled with exhaustion and dread. If she could have laid back down and slept through the rest of her life, she might have.

But coffee perked her, breakfast energized her, and memories of what was to come solidified in her mind. She remembered the imploring eyes of Graves, the exhaustion of Albert, and the determination in the faces of Wynn and Vienna. They wanted what all good Dadaists wanted: to effect change to the world through art by any means necessary. She understood that, just as Graves had expected she would. There was so much that needed changing, and if the price of that was temporary damage to art's shared history, then maybe, just maybe, it was worth it. So far, as Graves reminded her, they'd done nothing irreparable to any piece of art, and even if they had, so much was digitized and recorded that perhaps a few sacrifices could be made. It wouldn't be the first time the arms were broken off the Venus de Milo, or the beard broken off of Tutankhamen's tomb. It wouldn't be the last time artwork was lost or destroyed by a careless old Spanish woman touching up her church's 19th century fresco of Christ. It wasn't that Mae thought these events were caused by similar pseudo-Dadaists, all thinking as Enfants Terrible were, but would it be such a stretch of the imagination if they were? If the need to remind the world that art was about transgressing the establishment, not joining it, had always been there, and always would be? And, if that were the case, wasn't her helping Enfants Terrible necessary, and an important part in assuring life's continued momentum?

She found herself in her apartment at night, contemplating

her half-finished canvases, wondering how she could continue working on them when, despite what Halton Graves had told her, they were all failures of effect. So trite, with such boringly bourgeois iconography that simply looking at them left her angered and despaired. It was abundantly clear that her careful brush strokes belied her lack of originality—witness the muted colours, the safe patterns—and it took a great force of will not to prime over everything and start again

Why was she like this, she wondered. So crippled with self-doubt and loathing. Enfants Terrible were not trapped by their inconsequentiality, and as a result were making a difference where all Mae could do was follow the same script she always had, the same script as everyone else, day in and day out, from the cradle to the grave. Boring and predictable. Safe and easy. She had assembled a life without challenge, and took no risks that weren't thrust upon her. It shouldn't be good enough. She should want more, no matter how much it frightened her to strive for it.

Enfants Terrible had what she should want, which is why it wasn't strange that, conversely, they should want her. Or, if not all of them, then Halton Graves. He unquestioningly believed she would understand the truth and act on it. His trust in her about something so vast and important was unprecedented, and sitting there on her bed, staring at the patchwork painting drying on its easel, she wondered if it was the greatest mistake he'd ever made, or the greatest chance she'd ever been given.

At first the weight of doing anything that might damage a piece of artwork was too much to bear. But as she thought about it, considered about how Graves and his movement rekindled something inside her that she'd forgotten, she wanted more. She wanted to be part of art in ways she'd never experienced or imagined.

The days between seeing Halton Graves and opening the door as instructed were interminable. Every moment at her desk was filled with a quiet anxiety and desperation. Had she not had *Le Manteau* to work on, she might have found herself going mad. As it was, the anticipation of her approaching task made it hard to concentrate on anything else. When Lynda from the museum's volunteer staff tried to tell her about the latest vandalism to affect *Overground*, a boutique gallery on the fringes of Queen Village, it was all Mae could do to contain her pride. She wondered who it had been. Had Vienna slipped in? Maybe Wynn had broken the windows? Who removed a handcrafted porcelain matryoshka doll and left the word CAPITALISTS painted across the windows? These were mysteries to which she didn't want the answers. All she knew was their missions had garnered the media's attention, which meant the time for parlour tricks was ending. The next time Enfants Terrible made the news, it would change everything.

And if she needed further evidence, on her way to the AGO Thursday morning she noticed two peculiar things that would not have stood out had she not been hyperaware that the world was transforming. The first was a glimpse of a lanky bearded man in his twenties, dressed in too short trousers and a heavy ski jacket. He was disappearing around one of Gehry's acute corners, and though Mae didn't get a good look at him, he bore a resemblance to Wynn, whom she presumed was taking measure of the building and its exits. The second thing was less obvious, which made it more likely to be an indicator of Enfants Terrible's presence. She noticed by chance a small sticker pasted to one of the telephone poles outside the museum. Though all the posts up and down the street were covered in billets of different sizes and shapes, this one was simply a reproduction of a photograph. There were no numbers, no text, nothing to indicate it was anything more than a snapshot of flowers blooming on a summer's day. The sort of thing someone might post on the eve of winter to remind passers-by that there was an end to everything. The photography on the billet however had a large cross hacked into it with a rusted blade, and what might have been something beautiful had been cruelly defaced, all in the name of art.

There was no denying it. Art's freedom was its power. She

glanced at her watch. Only twelve more hours to go before she needed to be at the glass door to usher in whatever future awaited.

When Mae removed her magnifier visor later to check the clock, it read half-past nine, and she was seeing double after staring so long at *Le Manteau*. She pushed away from her desk, raised the visor onto her forehead, and rubbed her eyes hard enough that the world decayed into coloured fractals. It was impossible to concentrate on what she was doing. Not with the rattling alarm clock that had seemingly replaced her heart. She checked the clock again to find a minute more had passed. The multitude of thoughts racing through her head collided with and spilled into one another. She forced herself to remember how to breathe, and when to do so, to keep from hyperventilating. Perhaps if she moved she might burn away her excess nervosity.

Pacing was easier when she was alone. Those moments before everyone arrived in the morning and those after they'd left at night were the only ones in which she could relax. With quiet came calm; with calm, focus. Except Mae felt neither while waiting for ten o'clock to arrive. What she felt was exhilarated. Once Graves and Enfants Terrible were in the AGO, she didn't know what they'd do. But their impassioned strike in the name of art put them in league with other pseudo-Dadaists like Duchamp or Banksy. Why wouldn't she want to be associated with that? Why wouldn't she want to be part of something bigger than herself? She glanced at the clock. It was time.

Mae surveyed the hallway before stepping from the office. Most of the lights had been turned down, leaving only enough illumination for the cleaners and the night-owl staff. She passed a huddled trio of young administrators who didn't speak to her, only stared wide-eyed as though they'd been caught. *Act normal*, she silently reminded herself. *Act normal.* Even though she had forgotten how to walk naturally, her knees struggling to balance her weight, she repeated the mantra until she passed the trio. They resumed their whispering once she was farther down the hall.

Without the chaos of the full staff moving through the building, the offices were an enambered landscape, as if the Galleria had been replaced by a life-sized painting. But there was something else in the stillness; a vibration beneath that she could sense without being able to see. Mae's pace slowed to a stop and she waited. She could feel it building, a slow pressure that gradually increased until the Galleria began to shake like an egg on the point of fracture. Mae reached out to steady herself, and as her fingers touched the wall the sensation dissipated, its momentum gone, leaving Mae wobbling and confused about what was real. Had she hallucinated the quake, or had it actually happened? Her head was still swimming, yet she tried to remain undeterred and push on.

She encountered no one else in the halls of the AGO, and when she reached the door Halton Graves had asked her to open, it was with only a minute to spare. Blood pounded in her ears, and she closed her eyes and willed it to stop. What the hell was she doing, she asked as cold realization flooded into her. It was crazy. The whole thing was crazy. She suddenly wasn't certain she hadn't hallucinated meeting Halton Graves as well, let alone following him into a storm drain, then subsequently through a secret tunnel. It was ludicrous. And yet there was proof. If it wasn't real, then nothing was. Just a communal dream where there were no rules and nothing was impossible. But life was clearly not that, so the impossible could only be impossible, and Enfants Terribles's secret tunnel really was a secret tunnel.

The pounding in Mae's ears continued, growing louder. She opened her eyes to check the time and was startled to see a lithe hand rapping on the door's glass. Was it Vienna? The hand rapped again, the sound echoing in Mae's head. Her watch read ten o'clock, but it felt much later. She wanted a better look out the window to see Vienna standing there, but could not bring herself to move. All she could do was stare at the disembodied hand as it rapped, the urgency increasing threateningly.

Minutes passed but the most Mae could bring herself to do was stare at the door's lock bar, knowing she had only to push it but finding herself unable to do so. There was a red sign hanging above, one she had never seen before. In engraved silver letters it warned not to prop the door open. Part of her suspected it was written specifically for her, specifically for this moment. The knocking had become more violent, more desperate, and Mae found herself stepping back, pulling away. There was a ghost of herself that pushed forward, laid its fingers on the cold metal bar, and the feel of that phantom chill was enough to make Mae clasp her ears and flee down the hall away from the incessant echo of knuckles on glass.

3. LISMER

Waking the next morning was difficult. It had taken so long to fall asleep that in desperation she swallowed a sleeping pill near 2:00 a.m., but all it managed to do was strand her in an unyielding hypnagogia where she floated for hours until the sun pried her eyes apart. Mae rose tired and drugged, hallucinating being out of bed three times before managing to actually do it. She struggled to remain upright as she staggered to the bathroom, where she rinsed out her mouth and brushed down her tangled hair and tried to ignore the sickness brewing in her stomach. It was only then she inspected her face in the mirror and realized the person staring back wasn't one she recognized. That particular Mae appeared twenty years too old, with grey streaks at her temples that contaminated the curls of her rusted copper hair. She pressed the bags under her eyes, hoping in vain they'd retreat permanently into her face. When they didn't, her slumped shoulders could no longer bear the weight of her exhaustion.

The evening's events had humiliated her, as did how close

she'd come to making a catastrophic mistake. The memory clung to her like a tactile film, despite how hard it was to believe. But that was unsurprising—disbelief was the body's way of distancing itself from trauma. Yet under the pulsating shower head, when her thoughts were most unbidden, that distance shrank, and Mae berated herself for ever considering opening the door and letting Enfants Terrible into the museum. It would have been cataclysmic, and she had come too close to allowing it to happen. Even eight hours later and many miles away, amid the raging hiss of water on the shower's glass, she was still haunted by that dreadful rapping echo.

It would be so much easier to hide beneath her bed covers until the world faded away, but she knew if she fled it would mean spiralling into the void. She had to return to the AGO and pretend all was well; resume the restoration of *Le Manteau* and attempt to mend Enfants Terrible's damage to return it to its inspirational glory. Then, when she returned home, she would open her paints and start a new piece of her own; a different piece, a better piece than those left unfinished. She would put brush to canvas and produce something so wholly and uniquely hers that it wouldn't matter if anyone ever saw it. She might not even show it to anyone. The dream of having her own work hanging among those framed Reubens and Westenhimers in the Lismer Wing was no longer important. Frankly, it was all bullshit. What mattered was she was creating for herself and only herself. She was going to do what she wanted, and take as much time as she needed to do so. Enfants Terrible would not steal art from her with their terrorism, no more than they could steal it from the world. Their thinking was flawed, and Mae understood what she hadn't understood before—that art was stronger than all of them. That *she* was stronger than all of them.

In a haze of motivation, Mae strode across Dundas and down McCaul, and did not slow her pace until she saw the circle of people gathered outside the AGO. There were police cars cordoning off the street, their coloured lights swirling in the air like fireflies, and when she reached the periphery of the line they held she saw groups of people she knew, employees of the museum mixed with some faculty from the College of Art and Design. Coworkers were clustered, whispering among themselves, while faces she'd never seen before were twisted onto people jogging in both directions. There was shouting from the officers, and a mounting sensation that everything had gone horribly wrong. The bottom of Mae's stomach fell, and she knew she had to leave, that she wasn't safe, but couldn't think of where to go.

"Mae!"

The commotion of the crowd's gossip and the engines of the white and yellow security teams did not disguise the sound of her name. She had to resist the instinct to bolt into the throng of spectators—frantically pushing her way through would only draw unwanted attention and suspicion.

"Mae, come over!"

A hand waved above the heads of the crowd. No one else seemed to notice her, but she worked her way forward carefully nevertheless, praying silently as she approached. At least the phantom rapping had disappeared, swallowed by the noise outside the AGO and the erratic beat of her own heart. As the crowd thinned, she saw the small group of her coworkers huddled against the cold. Each of them scrutinized her, and the urge to flee strengthened. It took everything she had to feign normalcy.

"Oh my God, did you hear what happened?" asked Lynda, the rosy-faced volunteer who had summoned her. She wore purple mittens and a triangular winter hat with wool braids.

"No, I just got here."

"I can't believe it. Oh my God, I can't. Who would do this?"

Everyone in the circle stared at their feet. A pock-marked man from the Accounting Department two floors down shook his head.

"There are surveillance cameras everywhere. No way one of them didn't catch something."

He looked at Mae after he'd said it, as though he knew

what she'd almost done and was waiting for the right moment to share. But despite her paranoia, rationally she knew it wasn't true. How could it be? And she hadn't done anything, anyway. She hadn't opened the Galleria door, hadn't let anyone into the AGO through it or any other entrance. She was innocent of everything except coming back from lunch late, and it didn't matter how much it felt like all the damage could be traced along a branch of lines back to her and to her meeting with Enfants Terrible; none of it was her fault. The overwhelming sense of guilt she suffered about her trip underground was as much of a mystery to her as it should have been to everyone else.

Amar, one of the junior restorers, shivering in his grey smock streaked with two handprint-shaped stains, held ink-blue fingers to his head as he muttered, "I can't believe this is happening. I can't believe it."

"But what happened?" Mae asked, then closed her eyes for a moment.

"It was a complete massacre. So many pieces are damaged or missing," the accountant said. "The police won't let us near yet. We saw some exhibit works being moved earlier, but they were all under sheets."

"I heard someone crying about the museum, but I don't know who it was," Amar said, sniffling from the cold or his own tears. "It must be horrible. Horrible. Who would do this? Who would damage such wonderful work?"

"We all know who," the accountant said. "Those Enfants terrorists. They have no shame, no decency, no respect. What's an 'art terrorist' anyway? Just someone who wants to get on the news. I hope they catch these animals and burn them. No, you know what? Burning's too good. Let them rot in jail for all the damage they've done."

Mae repeated *they don't suspect you* over and over again in her thoughts. It was becoming harder to concentrate as her anxiety recursively built.

"Do you know anything about them?" the accountant asked, and Mae blanched. Before she could stammer an answer,

Lynda responded.

"I don't know any more than what I've read in the papers. But I don't think they've ever done something like this before. I mean, I heard from Shanice that the police closed the museum to the public for the rest of the day; no one but staff is getting in. And that the Lismer Wing is going to be shut down for probably another month while everything gets repaired and redesigned. Oh my God, Mae, you don't even know, right? What they did with *Le Manteau*?"

"What do you mean? What about it?"

Lynda looked to the other faces in confusion.

"It's gone. You know that, right? They took it. Oh my God, they took it right out of the Restoration Department like they knew it was there, and maybe took some other things, as well. No one knows yet for sure."

It didn't make any sense. Mae must not have heard her right.

"They're probably going to have to triple your team," the accountant said. "By the sounds of it, those Enfants Terrible really shitted the place up. I wouldn't be surprised if some of the exhibits were lost for good. "

"You can't put a price on that," Amar said.

"We don't have to," he replied. "That's what insurance appraisements are for. We'll get ours; you better believe it."

The hours waiting in the cold outdoors were nothing compared to the chill inside Mae as she slowly realized what she would face when the police reopened the AGO. They began by permitting the staff to enter a few at a time, and when it was Mae's turn she passed through the ad hoc checkpoint in a daze, producing her badge while her mind was focused on what she did not want to find when she reached her office.

She hurried past shell-shocked coworkers in an effort to affirm her dread. As she approached the Restoration Department the odd shape of the door frame telegraphed a warning that she struggled to accept. The frame was broken in two pieces above the jamb, and when she stepped through it she found her brushes and tools littered the floor. But the sight of the empty easel on the other side of the room was devastating. *Le Manteau* was gone.

Le Manteau was gone.

Mae bent, weak and numb, and retrieved her scattered belongings. Her body felt a hundred miles away and out of reach. Everything trembled.

For a while, she considered with no small hope that she'd imagined the whole thing. It had happened before: a half-remembered dream that had seemed so real it was taken for granted. Once she believed she'd been written a letter by a former professor explaining he had taken a position at the Louvre and needed her there, only to find later that morning the letter he'd sent was not where she remembered storing it. She searched for the better part of an hour before she recalled that Professor LeCroix had passed away two years earlier, and that she in fact had no memory of actually receiving the letter. It nevertheless took time for Mae to reconcile the real with that disreality. With this memory in mind, Mae shut her eyes and tried to force herself to wake up, praying she'd find herself still in bed. Instead, she found the broken door and the gaping hole where once there had been a lock, and she knew it was all real.

Days passed and Mae still hadn't seen more of the Lismer Wing beyond the taped off entrance and closed signs. Security guards stood watch as plain-clothed police officers ducked in and out beneath the protective plastic curtain, obscuring anything more than the edges of the paint-stained floor. Beyond the barrier waited Mae's bench, her lunchtime seat from where she once gazed into the swirls of *Le Manteau* and imagined she was actually peering through a window to witness the real world beneath reality's dull veneer. She wanted to believe Roget's masterpiece still hung in front of that bench behind the plastic tarps just waiting to reveal further truths in its brushstrokes, but it was gone, hoarded away in Enfants Terrible's underground bunker alongside the rest of the artwork the collective had stolen during their ongoing campaign.

What she did eventually see emerging from the wing were a number of the damaged pieces carried by gloved museum staff. Paint was splashed across three of the Byatts, and a hole was punched through a large Gerstein, but those were likely the least compromised works assessed. The more time-consuming pieces would be held back so her department could concentrate on them later.

With *Le Manteau* lost, and sculptures and artifacts broken, the damage done was on so massive a scale that there was no way Mae and her existing team could handle it. The task would take too many years to complete. The Board had little choice but to hire as many bodies as possible from anywhere it could. Mae didn't know how they managed it, but within a few weeks her team had almost tripled in size, with new restorers inserted into any open office space regardless of whether or not there was sufficient room to work. Yet as with any speed hiring spree, the quality of restorers varied greatly in talent and motivation. Of the lot, Mae counted no more than three who could be relied upon to do more than suck money from the museum. Conditions grew so loud and cramped that Mae's already heightened anxiety and depression over *Le Manteau*'s theft became nearly impossible to manage. She tried headphones to block out as much of the noise as possible, but even they could not exclude the low rumbling of voices that shook the floor and weighed on her like an iron grate.

And, worse, Oscar Rowing returned to oversee the newly expanded team. Mae had settled on believing what everyone else believed—that he was gone for good—but wherever they temporarily moved him, it appeared just as simple to move him back, and he reappeared with a triumph in his step that announced he wasn't going to lose his second chance by being soft. Within days he was closely monitoring those under him, second-guessing everything they did and where they were going, until it became clear to Mae that there was a hunt on for whoever had helped Enfants Terrible gain access to the AGO to commit their crime. Rowing said as much as he walked through the department, scrutinizing everyone. Each time he approached, Mae panicked, and no matter how many times she reminded herself she'd done nothing wrong, still she worried that a day of reckoning was close.

She wished she'd never let herself get involved with Enfants Terrible and their twisted beliefs. It was unlike her to be wooed by such theatrics and zealotry, or to fall in step with dangerous plans so foolishly. Why had she followed Graves when only a few weeks later he seemed less of a person and more of an abstract collection of features—a set of lidded eyes, a crooked smile, a sonorous voice and easy gait? From the distance of time, they added up to nothing that should have affected or distracted her. And yet, when in his presence, everything seemed unreal, and every word he spoke mesmerized her. There was something about Halton Graves she had no name for, but it nearly lost her everything just as she'd already lost *Le Manteau*.

If only she could have saved the painting. She knew he had it stored away somewhere underground in the Path but couldn't tell anyone without implicating herself. To speak would be to put her head in a noose, and with Rowing growing desperate to nab a culprit she worried he'd pull the rope first and ask questions after she swung. She briefly considered running away, but escape was impossible for a multitude of reasons; the most pressing being the news that Oscar Rowing had begun interviewing those employees who had been in the museum the night of the vandalism.

It took careful manipulation, but after discovering Lynda had endured one of Rowing's earliest investigations, Mae did her best to pry as much information as she could from the volunteer, but the answers she received were frustratingly vague and unuseful, and did nothing to alleviate her anguish over her own eventual questioning.

"I don't know what they were looking for, but I wasn't in there long," Lynda said. "They asked me what I was doing here so late and who saw me and who I saw. All that seemed to be enough."

"Who did you say you saw?"

She shrugged. "Oh my God, who remembers?"

Mae wanted to thank her, but her heart was so far into her throat she couldn't speak.

It was impossible to sort through the stew of emotions Mae lived with while walking through the AGO. There was the guilt and the fear over what had happened despite her playing no actual role in it beyond casual observer—an accomplice only in her lies of omission; there was her sorrow and pain over the loss of Roget's *Le Manteau,* a piece of work that she had imbued with all her desire to become a recognized artist, and whose loss felt in an inexplicable way like the loss of her own dreams; and there was the anger. There was always the anger. And it was directed primarily at Halton Graves, with herself running a close second.

The anger was what made it hardest for her to move through her day as though nothing were wrong. Everyone at the AGO was upset over the vandalism to some degree, and she hid behind that explanation when she found herself unable to bear being inside her cramped office with so many unfamiliar people and so much noise. But sometimes the anger became too much to bear, and she had to pace through the hallways to burn it off before it consumed her. Mae repeatedly reminded herself that there was nothing to worry about, that the best thing to do was forget that night, forget *Le Manteau,* forget Graves. The worry would destroy her if she couldn't let it go. And yet Halton Graves had already ruined her life—he and his team of miscreants and criminals, leaving her with nothing but regret over all the things she'd never done. She stormed through the back passages of the AGO, her anger, instead of dissipating, growing into fits of blind fury. So blind, in fact, she did not notice Oscar Rowing's inevitable approach when it came from the opposite direction. Not until he held out his hand to stop her.

Mae uttered a short cry, shocked by his manifestation and by the flood of dread that crashed against her. He hadn't changed physically since leaving, but nevertheless he now seemed towering, his imposing face betraying both perturbance and unease. When he spoke, however, neither surfaced. Like his smile, his voice was artificial and rote.

"Olsen. I've been looking for you."

"You have?" It took a tremendous amount of willpower to remain static and affect nothing was wrong, even when she was convinced her face said otherwise.

"I haven't seen much of you lately. Not since the gala."

She swallowed. Nodded.

"I guess you were away for a while," she said.

"Yes, I guess I was. And there's been a lot of excitement since then. I thought maybe you and I could talk about it if you had some time."

"Time?" Mae repeated, scrambling for a response. She did not want to talk about the *excitement*—she did not want to talk to Oscar Rowing about anything at all. She only wanted to escape the madhouse she'd locked herself into. But Rowing wasn't so easily dissuaded.

"I think you could help me a lot, Olsen. For instance, you and that Halton Graves seemed close at the gala. It made me wonder how long you two have known each other."

"That was the first night we met," she said.

"That's clearly not true; even if he hadn't asked for you that night by name, I would have seen it in the way the two of you isolated yourselves. It didn't surprise me at the time— you're bound to make a lot of contacts in this line of work. But there was something with this one, and I'm sorry I didn't get more of a chance to speak with your friend."

It was the way he pronounced *friend* that was most disturbing.

"I don't know what to say, Oscar. I'd never met that man before in my life. After you introduced him to me, we only spoke for a few minutes before he was gone."

Oscar Rowing nodded, but his squint did not reassure Mae. His eyes burned through her, and she struggled to remind herself of her innocence. But his stare made her uneasy, and her fear that her discomfort might look like guilt made her more uneasy still. A building anxiety that required intense concentration to diffuse.

"Well, Olsen?"

He'd asked another question that in her panic she'd missed.

"Pardon?"

"I asked if you've seen him since the gala."

"Who?"

But it was obvious. Behind Rowing, two police officers crossed the hall. They were mid-conversation, but at the last moment one turned and glanced at Mae.

"Yes, of course, Halton. I mean, no, I haven't seen him, but yes, I know who you mean. No, though, to answer your question. No."

"Really?" His reaction amplified her worry. "I want you to be absolutely sure before you answer this question, Olsen. It's very important you do."

Mae swallowed. Just a hundred feet or so ahead was the exit—so close, and yet so out of reach. If only she'd left a minute sooner. If only she'd gone home that night of the break-in. If only—

"Olsen?"

"No, I haven't seen him. I mean, yes, I saw him once, accidentally, but I wasn't involved in anything. Oscar, I just want to go home. It's been a long week and I'm tired and could use some sleep. Can we do this tomorrow?"

"Of course," he said, but instead of backing away he put his hand gently on her shoulder, pinning her in place, then lightly squeezed. "But I want to show you something first." With his other hand, he reached into the breast pocket of his striped blazer and pulled out a small folded piece of paper. He presented it to Mae. She looked down at it and felt absolute dread overcome her. She wanted to throw it away and run as fast and as far as she could. To another city, to another country. Anywhere but there. Instead, she unfolded the piece of paper and asked herself how life had led her to where she was. She'd always tried so hard and cared so much. She wondered if that had been her downfall.

"I've always liked you, Olsen, and you know how highly I think of your work, but I think you'll agree that we need to talk right now. Maybe it's better if you come up to my office, and we can go over again what happened last night."

Mae nodded, but she continued to stare at the photograph he'd given her. It was a security camera print-out of her in the Galleria Italia doorway a few weeks earlier, Halton Graves standing over her in the shadows.

✄

The long, glacial walk to Oscar Rowing's office was more excruciating than she'd ever imagined, and when she reached it two plain-clothed investigators were waiting as though they'd known she was on her way. Joining them was Veronica from Human Resources, whose face retained its normal disgusted frown and whose eyes did not look up when Mae and Rowing entered.

The next three hours entailed Mae unburdening herself of everything that had happened—her accidental meeting with Halton Graves; the entranceway in the alley behind Dundas; Albert, Vienna, and Wynn, whose names were fake; Halton's subsequent request she open the door for whomever had been sent the night of the vandalism—and answering a series of increasingly pugilistic questions posed with the intent of breaking her story, or at least causing her to slip and admit she'd been involved. But despite the confusion their cross-examination caused, Mae stuck to what she'd said because it was the truth, and it was everything she knew or had done. Everything, except how close she'd actually come to opening the Galleria door. Even in her tired and anxious state, she knew that would likely be the difference between going home and being an accessory to a crime.

But despite her honesty, they still treated her as though she were a criminal. Veronica never once looked at Mae through the process, instead choosing to stare stone-faced at the small stack of papers on Rowing's desk, or whisper to him with unbridled disapproval. Meanwhile, the plain-clothed officers spoke without introducing themselves, and when their questions were exhausted and their poorly-hidden suspicions that she knew more than she was saying were aired, they did not bother trying to correct that oversight. Still, she detected an ember of excitement in their movements once she'd described to the best of her recollection where Enfants Terrible were hiding and how to find them. The two men noted this information greedily, with the clear intention of acting on it as soon as enough officers could be gathered to raid the Path. If nothing else, she suspected that revelation was the tipping point that allowed her to remain unincarcerated for the time being.

Oscar Rowing, however, seemed less enthused. Every word of her story, from meeting Halton Graves to her hiding her knowledge of the attack before it occurred, seemed to hurt him on a fundamental level. His face crushed by inches and fell, and before she could finish answering everything put to her he had picked up his telephone and requested Security pack her desk and escort her out of the building. Not only was her time at the AGO over, but she would likely never get another job in her field again. There was nothing more for Mae to say or do but apologize for the thousandth time, but knowing it would do no good she stood instead, wiped her eyes, and let two Security guards she had never met usher her through the AGO's back passages. Coworkers emerged from their offices as she slunk by, her embarrassing box of garbage in her hands, but no one looked her in the eye. Not Lynda or Amar or any of the rest. Mae had become nothing; a no one. No more deserving of sympathy or pity than the monsters that had ruined so much of the museum's artwork. She wanted to stop and shake them, tell them what happened at the AGO was only the first volley in a war against the concept of art, but she knew no one would hear her. She had become as invisible and as dumb as a ghost.

4. MILK

The safety and security of Mae's bed kept her hidden beneath its covers for weeks. The days were a blend of wine and whiskey and anything else she could find in her apartment that might dull the understanding that it was all ruined; everything she'd worked so hard for, gone in a single regrettable instant because of one mistake too many. Days blurred past as she sank further, the bottle's clarity replacing her own, questioning what she had done that was so horrible the universe would plot against her. But even in her stupor she knew the blame belonged to Halton Graves and his band of vandalizing and thieving criminals. Their spree continued unabated as her life slipped down the neck of a bottle. All she had ever wanted was to sit before Roget's *Le Manteau* and get lost in its swirls, but not only had Enfants Terrible taken the painting away from her, they cut off her connection to *all* the paintings in the gallery. She was barred from returning to her only refuge, and in her more lucid moments she wished with shaking jaw and clenched fists that they would one day get what was coming to them. That one day the universe would punish Enfants Terrible as it was punishing her.

But as essential as alcohol was in cleansing her palate of what she'd almost done and the ensuing consequences, her cupboards and shelves were not endlessly stocked; eventually she reached the last of her reserves and the bottom of her soul. From there, she had no choice but to climb back out of her depression an inch at a time.

The haze of drink finally met its match in the setting sun of day, and Mae gnashed her teeth and drank water to dull the pain. She was cross-legged in front of the painting she'd been working on so slowly for so long—the sketched flower beneath, the half-painted petals over top that erupted from the stamen in oranges and yellows and reds like an autumn fire. And, at the centre, the smallest beetle imaginable, swollen with potential as it consumed the heart of the plant. Mae stared at the insect, willed it to move, to swallow the canvas it was painted on, then spiral outward farther and farther until it swallowed the easel, the floor, the bed, and finally her. She wanted the painted beetle to destroy the world. But it refused, instead remaining motionless, a fixed thing of paint and varnish, while Mae continued to hurl her ineffectual fantasies upon it.

Nevertheless, the painting had potential. Something could be made of it. But everything that occurred to Mae was so much smaller than she dreamed, so much less than she wanted. Back in school, Professor LeCroix tried to convince her that brushwork was like sculpting from stone. "The canvas contains multitudes," he lectured with an upturned nose and hare-lip. "Each of your strokes carves away a sliver of the unnecessary nothingness of a blank canvas until you unveil the hidden truth." His face twitched with pride, but he was wrong about stones and he was wrong about canvas. Her charcoal or chalk or brushes did not carve away the unnecessary; they carved away the possibility. Every mark on the canvas meant a hundred million paintings vanished, and each successive stroke limited things further still. It was devastating how much was lost, and Mae did not fail to see how it paralleled her own life. So much of herself had been stripped away over time, her own potential mined and discarded until only an empty husk remained, a shell in need of some purpose. Maybe that's why she fell for Halton Graves's deceits. Maybe she believed in him because she needed to believe in something to fill the hole. But it was a lie like everything else—her job at the museum, everyone who was supposed to care about her but who hadn't called since she'd lost her job. She was unmoored and adrift, and even the act of painting wasn't enough to anchor her. She was treading water, but it wouldn't be long before she grew tired and drowned.

Mae turned on the television to distract herself from her spiralling thoughts, and from the bottle's easy answers. No one from the AGO had kept her updated on the investigation of the break-in—anyone that could have wanted nothing to do with her—but she had been able to glean bits of information from the nightly news, hints that there were developments unfurling. She hoped something she had told the police had been useful—seeing Graves in handcuffs would make her feel better both about what had occurred and what might happen to her. But where the televised news normally provided a level of relief with its staid sets and teleprompted routines, she instead found herself discomforted by what she saw when she tuned in. Immediately, her head simultaneously shrank and expanded as the effect of her hangover took hold again. On screen, there was little preamble from the anchor, though he now appeared somewhat distressed. He leaned against the news desk, the room behind him dark while the light above too bright, blowing out the colours onscreen. Sweat beaded on his brow, and his hands twisted themselves as he spoke to the camera. Each word that fell from his mouth was garbled gibberish delivered as though underwater, and despite how Mae played with the volume, she could not clear it. The anchor spoke, looking more and more pained, glancing around him for longer and longer periods as his profuse sweat collected. Shadows rippled across his forehead while he persevered, and Mae understood too slowly that it wasn't the sweat causing the movement. Instead, the surface of his balding skull bulged and buckled, his skin the rubbery meniscus on some dense boiling liquid. The anchor rubbed his forehead as Mae ran her hands over her slick face and wished for someone nearby to confirm what she was seeing, what she was feeling, but her apartment was full only of empty furniture—furniture that, too, was bubbling, shapes pushing against the upholstered and wooden surfaces, each item close to bursting. A blanket of unbearable tension weighed down on her, and yet Mae found herself becoming lightheaded as everything around her inched closer and closer to coming apart. It would take only one little prick to open the world. Just one tiny hole in the onion skin surface that barely contained the building pressure and turmoil. Once it opened, nothing would be left.

The anchor's voice startled her awake. Returned to his brightly lit desk, he sat smiling, delivering the final piece of the news broadcast. The words he spoke were still incomprehensible, but Mae realized it was because the volume was too low, and she was feeling too sick. If only she had an ice pack or even a bag of frozen peas to wick away the pain, but her freezer held nothing but a half-loaf of dried bread. She saw the screen flicker from across the room, the image of the anchor replaced by that of the Police Department Superintendent who was speaking into a bank of microphones at a press event. The officer was leaning forward so he could be heard.

Mae's attention was held by the images that flashed across her television. A group of officers and reporters milling around the run-off channel entrance Halton Graves had revealed to her a lifetime ago, the grating open and the alley taped off. The footage was followed by that of dark passages and a sea of flashlight beams bouncing in the dark. Those small circles lit up with different colours as they grazed the walls, flashing in the blackness and mirroring the sparks behind her closed eyes. Mae's head throbbed as she absorbed it, wondering what might appear from around the multitude of dark corners. But nothing did. Instead, the screen changed again to the site of a recent occupation now vacant: the Lumière Travel agency in which she'd met Albert, Vienna, and Wynn, but since then lights had been torn down, the tanks against the far wall knocked over, and wires or cobwebs knocked loose from the ceiling. Lumière Travel was emptied of everything else but the cardboard boxes and loose papers that littered its floor.

Mae needed to breathe. She wandered the streets in a daze until the chill set in and she realized that somehow she'd stumbled her way by muscle memory and habit back to the familiar sights of the Grange District. A few blocks away was the angled peak of the AGO, cresting beyond the tightly-packed rows of buildings like a mountain top, and the sight of its glass panels shimmering in the sun drained her blood and stalled her pace. Yet it wasn't the museum that inspired so much dread her skin crawled to escape but the familiar narrow alley tucked behind the row of Chinese restaurants a short distance away. And even then it wasn't the alley itself that filled her with worry—an alley littered with broken asphalt and the smell of rotting fish; an alley that opened up onto an iron grate set in the ground; an alley now as taped off and as guarded by milling police officers as the AGO's Lismer Wing—but instead the surprising claim that alley still held on her.

As she approached it her stride grew shorter. She didn't know if she could face seeing the alley's entrance. And yet she couldn't deny it. Would it be possible to slip past the officers? Find her way through the grate and through the run-off channel into the Path? If she did, would she find Graves down there with Vienna, Albert, and Wynn, all four of them plotting their next big mission? And if she found them, what would she do? As much as they were to blame for the destruction of her life, a part of her could not deny the despair that followed knowing Enfants Terrible had gone somewhere she might never find them. Her connection to that electricity had been severed along with the likelihood of seeing Halton Graves again. She didn't understand any of it and perhaps never would.

The ground shook as though about to split open, and Mae saw a yellow cement truck slowly making its way down McCaul Street. She watched as it was ushered into the alley by the officers and listened to the shouts from city workers dressed in fluorescent orange vests, barely audible over the rumble, as they appeared from either side of the slowly rotating tank. The sudden realization of what was happening hit Mae hard, and she gasped. They were going to seal the entrance to the runoff channel. They were going to seal the entrance to the Path. Mae found herself rooted, staring at the alley that beckoned her, wrestling with what to do.

And then Halton Graves walked past, and the world cracked open.

Only, it wasn't really Graves. The man was too tall, too

blonde, with a flop of hair that bounced with each step he took. But his coat was checkered with a similar pattern to the one Graves wore, and his gait matched Graves's same loping stride that for a brief moment Mae made the mistake, and the fear that plunged through her was enough to make her reconsider her plan. She did not want anything to do with Graves or his agents, and the idea that she might have, even accidentally, left her feeling weak and vulnerable. Her knees threatened to fail. Whatever she felt since her termination from the museum, from the job she'd had for years, from being so close to both sites that accented her monumental failings, she could no longer let it control her life. She needed to make a change.

What she needed was a place of safety. A place no one from her lives might know her, but where she wouldn't be alone.

Milk was as close as she could get.

✼

The coffee house was only two blocks away on College Street; two blocks in the opposite direction of the AGO and of that guarded alley, which made them all the more appealing. When Mae reached Milk, she collapsed into one of the hardbacked seats without removing her coat.

There wasn't much to the place that drew people in, which was what Mae preferred. The University campus was only a short distance further east, but far enough that those students who ventured outside the perimeter were looking for something more exotic, or at least more comfortable. With its mediocre coffee and day-old pastries, Milk did not offer an attractive destination. All it had going for it were its large bay windows that faced out onto College Street, and its location near the mid-point between the University and the College of Art and Design. Two of Mae's paintings hung on its walls, and had hung there long enough that all their neighbours had vanished and been replaced for one reason or another.

Mae looked at her dusty pieces displayed above the head of an oblivious student and wished the canvases were bolder. Or at least bold enough to draw notice among the dozen or so others that filled the walls. Instead, her paintings looked like something one might buy on any street corner. They were all and only veneer.

But as she stared, she wondered if they might not be something more, too. Veneer or not, they were hers, and proved she was capable of more than people expected. Like Professor LeCroix might have said: she contained multitudes, and perhaps embracing that was the secret to life after her failure at the AGO. The world made a little more sense every time she finished a painting—seemed that much more ordered and understandable. Her art cleared away the fog that clouded her mind, and she believed it could be more—she believed *she* could be more—if only she gave herself the chance.

"Are these yours?"

It was a woman's voice; smooth, with the lilt of Northern accent. Mae turned to the beautiful face with freckles clustered on the apple of each cheek. It was familiar, yet out of context Mae could not place it. The hook of her pronounced heavy-tipped nose was what triggered the connection in Mae's memory.

"How did you find me?" Mae asked.

Vienna took the bag from her shoulder and sat down, uninvited. Her lithe arm swept stray crumbs off the table.

"It was pretty easy. Halton told us once you worked at the AGO as a restorer, and that you had some paintings in a coffee shop on College Street. It didn't take much to find out your name and Twitter did the rest. Someone spotted your paintings here and let me know."

"What? What do you mean? You asked *publicly* about me?" She stood up, rubbed her face. "The police already think I had something to do with all this. They're going to be sure now!"

"It's okay, calm down," Vienna said, putting her rosied hand out. "No one is going to make the connection. I was very careful."

"How can you say that? You just told me you went on Twitter and now everyone who knows you knows the truth."

"Sit down, please," she whispered. Mae obeyed, not knowing what else to do. Her heart was beating so fast the world wavered before her eyes with a rumble. "You remember that my name isn't Vienna, right? It's one of Halton's stupid code names. No one who knows 'Vienna' is on my Twitter feed. As far as they can tell, I'm a student asking about a local artist. That's it. It's all safe. You don't have to worry."

"But the police—"

"If they knew anything, we'd *all* be locked up by now. Halton has done a lot of massively bone-headed things, but he knows how to keep under the radar. He only let himself get noticed at your gala because he wanted to. Because he wanted to make contact with you. Of course, he didn't expect you to narc us all out to the cops, but that's okay. I forgive you."

If Vienna was baiting her, Mae refused to bite.

"Why would he want to make contact with me?"

"Your old guard, Kenny, mentioned you. That's why we targeted *Le Manteau* that first time. To get your attention."

"That makes no sense. None of this does," Mae said. "Why are you telling me this? Why are you here?"

Vienna's smile turned plastic and Mae glanced to find the waitress approaching. Vienna stuck two fingers in the air and ordered them each a Guatemalan coffee.

"My treat," she said.

"I don't want your treats. I want to know what you want with me."

"All I want to do is apologize for how I treated you—how we *all* treated you—when Halton introduced us. We were having some trust issues, and you were an easy target. We shouldn't have done it. So, I'm sorry. I really want to make it up to you. Let me help you."

"Haven't you done enough? Talking to you and your friends has already cost me my job and it might end up costing me my freedom. I should call the police right now. Tell them you're here."

Vienna grimaced. Exhaled very long and slow.

"Mae, you probably won't believe this, but I had nothing to do with getting you fired. I certainly wasn't part of any plan to cause you grief. That's not what Enfants Terrible is supposed to be about. I mean, yes, we caused some damage, but it was always small and repairable. Nothing as criminal as what happened at the AGO."

"But I saw you! I saw Wynn skulking around outside, and I saw you knocking on the door. And I knew both of you were coming because Halton told me to expect it. I saw you through the glass door."

Vienna was about to say something before the waitress interrupted with the two coffees. When she left, Vienna leaned close and spoke in a near-whisper. She smelled like rosewater.

"Yes, Wynn and I were there, and we saw you, too. We saw you not open the door. So, we left. We left and I texted Halton and told him we weren't getting in, and I was glad. That was it. You believe me, don't you? I would never do something so heinous. I'm a good person."

"Then how did they get inside? If you didn't find a way, then what happened?"

"I wouldn't know," she said. "But I bet you Halton does. I don't know if he had a hand in it and didn't tell me, or if there's something else going on, but he always seems to know more than he talks about. Honestly, sometimes I think it's all an act—like he does shit and keeps quiet when it comes up to hold something over the rest of us, or maybe he has nothing to do with anything but likes to pretend he does. Halton desperately wants for everyone to look at him like he's this big radical, but... I don't know. I used to be utterly convinced everything he did was right, but lately I'm starting to wonder if he has any idea what he's doing at all."

Mae shook her head.

"I've felt it, I guess," she said. "The first time I saw that stupid smirk I forgot myself."

Vienna looked down at her coffee; tucked her hair behind her ear. She didn't look up.

"I was just a second-year art student when I met him. It was at one of those Riverdale pop-up galleries that are gone now. I didn't really know what I was doing there; I felt like an imposter. Then he rolled in the door as though it was *his* gallery and walked right up to my painting. He'd seen it from the street, he said, and when he glanced through the window and noticed the expression on my face he knew he had to come in. I still don't know what that even meant. But he pointed to my still-life and told me something he'd noticed. Not just in my painting, but he made me feel as though it was just in my painting. He said if you look at all the artwork people have ever created and study the fruit in them, you can see changes over time. Yes, that's right. *The fruit.* Peaches start small and over time they swell. Oranges, too. Melons get thicker, riper, and strawberries larger. He said he saw the same thing in my painting, and that he could think of a hundred different reasons for it to be the case, but there was only one that he believed: that real artists dream bigger than the world, and they in turn shape the world. He told me my painting was proof I was a real artist. He said he could see that from the street." Vienna eyes flicked up once, quickly, to meet Mae's before returning to the coffee. "I think, after that moment, I would have done anything for him."

Mae swallowed.

"You love him."

The air sucked out of Vienna as she sat straight, her eyes wide, bow lips parted. Then she swung her head side to side, looking to see if anyone heard, though no one could have.

"I mean—"

"It sounds like you love him."

As Vienna stammered for a response, Mae felt a rising anxiety and a pressure that tightened her head and distorted her vision. It was as though she were seeing the world through a warped lens.

"I don't know anymore. I used to think I loved him; then I thought I loved only his mission. But now? Now I feel lost and abandoned. I guess that's natural, considering I have no idea where he is."

"He's gone?"

"He's disbanded the group. The mission's on hold. Whatever happened at the AGO has turned the heat up too much, so Enfants Terrible has gone into hiding. And since Halton was so insistent we not share any personal information about each other no one even knows who he really is or how to find him. Essentially, I'm done. Cut off. Adrift."

"What about all the agents Halton said you had?"

"There weren't that many more to begin with—just enough who wanted to do something different, but not enough to believe in the cause. I saw one guy on the subway a week or so back, but thankfully he didn't notice me. Or, if he did, he was smart enough to keep his distance. I wanted to help fix the world, and I used to think Halton Graves was the one to do it, but it's become pretty obvious I was wrong. I think I'll go back to school. I can afford it and I don't know what else to do."

She took another sip from her coffee, looking to Mae like a wilted flower, crumpled into herself. How weird was it, Mae thought, that she wanted to paint her? But the moment vanished as Vienna snapped up straight and then to her feet.

"I'm sorry. I don't know what came over me. It's been a crazy and confusing few weeks. I shouldn't be saying any of this to you."

"No, it's okay. I understand. The thing in your life that defined you is gone and you don't know how to fill the void. Believe me, that might be the one thing I get right now."

Vienna looked at Mae with weariness and embarrassment.

"You know," Mae continued, "it's probably a good thing they're sealing off the entrance you were all using to the Path. Maybe it will give you some sense of closure on this whole thing."

Vienna's brow furrowed.

"They're trying to seal it off?"

"I saw it before I came here. There was a cement truck and

a lot of noise. The police were everywhere. I was—I couldn't get anywhere near it."

"Well, I didn't know that," she said, "but it doesn't surprise or worry me. We've achieved one of Halton's goals and have become Enemy Number One. That means the message is going to reach more people now. I almost feel bad about everything hidden down there."

Mae felt niggling unease.

"What do you mean?"

"The paintings. The artwork. All the pieces Halton and the rest of us took. That's where we left it."

"What? No. That's impossible. How could they be down there? The police. They went down. They found Lumière Travel. I saw it on the news."

Vienna shook her head.

"No, it's all there. We'd have been told by one of Graves's sources if they found anything. I think even *you* would have heard about it somehow. No, I'm sure it's all where we left it; hidden, just in case someone found us. Halton, Wynn, even Albert... we didn't want to risk something happening."

A sudden realization. "Wait. *Le Manteau*? That's down there, too?"

Vienna shrugged. "Probably. If Halton took it, that's what he would have done with it."

It was Mae's turn to stand.

"We have to tell someone. We can't let it all be sealed away."

Vienna waved off the idea. "I'm done worrying about it."

"We can't—I mean, the cement trucks... they're there now. They've probably already started! But, but if we say anything—Oh God, if we say anything or do anything, we'll go to jail. Forever. We can't show our faces near there, but if we don't..."

Mae was pacing and the other patrons of Milk were eyeing her. They knew something was going on, and if she kept babbling, they'd figure out what and everything would get more difficult. Vienna took her hand. It was softer than

Mae expected.

"Sit down and be quiet for a minute. Listen, I'm done with this. I'm done with Halton and all the rest. I don't know. I just don't believe in him anymore. I don't believe in what he says about art being liberated. There's something definitely wrong, but I don't want to throw my life away on his crazy plans. I wish I could say I know Wynn or Albert will go get that missing artwork, but last time I spoke to them it didn't sound likely. They'd lost faith in him, too. I think Albert crawled into a bottle a long time ago and isn't in any shape to do much. And if no one is around to tell Wynn what to do, he won't do a thing. So there's no one left. The paintings, all that artwork, will stay buried until someone finds it or remembers it's there."

"But you can't leave it. You can't. Aren't you the one who said art shouldn't be imprisoned? If we don't rescue everything, what was the point of all this? What have you been risking your future for? What did I throw mine away for?"

Vienna shrugged.

"I told you, Mae: I don't care anymore. I want to go back to my old life. Go back to school. I'm done."

The two women sat across from each other, not speaking. Vienna clutched the strap of her bag while behind her Mae's paintings were a taunting backdrop. They seemed to swell as Mae fretted, their surfaces becoming uneven. The way the light hit the piece furthest from the door made it appear as though the canvas had been torn. Her thoughts were invaded by *Le Manteau* and what its loss would mean for the world. Would mean for her. Mae hesitated, not wanting to say the inevitable, but knowing she had no choice. Vienna seemed to be waiting to hear the words.

"How?" she started. "How can I get them back?"

The briefest half-smile tugged at Vienna's lips as she pretended to think.

"There might be a way," she said. "Maybe."

Vienna lifted her bag and rummaged through it before

withdrawing a sheet of folded paper the size of a folio, tinted the lightest mimeograph blue. She placed it on the table between them, then looked straight into Mae's eyes. She slid the paper over.

"Take a look at this."

The paper unfolded and unfolded until it covered the table. A mass of lines both dotted and dashed ran in every direction, with scribbled notes and doodles written by at least four different sets of hands. Mae had no idea what she was looking at until she saw the street names on the axes and understood. Vienna waited until Mae finished comprehending the task before her.

"What you said before about our faces is true, but the police don't need to see anybody's face. The reason we stole these maps from City Hall was because it let us travel everywhere underground. There are entrances to the storm system all over, not just the one they're sealing off behind the Chinese restaurants. This map of the different ways into run-off channels will get you into the Path, and I've marked how to get to the artwork we hid there."

"And you just happened to have this with you?"

Vienna smiled. Shrugged.

Mae looked the map over. There was an entrance off of Adelaide Street, which would allow her to approach the Path from a different direction from where the police and city crews were working. That would help her avoid being discovered.

"What do I do once I find everything?"

Vienna shrugged again, then drained her cup of Guatemalan coffee.

5. LOWER OSGOODE

Reaching the alley on Adelaide Street was easy. The map outlined where Mae should search, and once she snuck behind the pawn shops and discount rug wholesalers she found another grate much like the one on Dundas, set under a small brick alcove at the base of the row's furthest corner. Staring down through its iron bars filled Mae with a sense of terrible longing for the past, as though the woman who had last peered through a grate into Graves's pleading eyes was a different person altogether, a person with whom Mae shared memories but not understanding. It was impossible to know what that woman had thought—she was too different from the Mae that replaced her. The only aspect they shared was a desperation to see *Le Manteau* free and in one piece, and the only way that might happen was if Mae did something she would never have imagined being able to do. But everything about herself since meeting Graves and Vienna and the rest of Enfants Terrible had been a revelation, and if she could continue on after so much had been taken from her then perhaps she had transformed far more than she realized.

The grate did not lift easily for her, but Mae was able to slide it a few inches, then a few inches more, until she'd cracked enough of an opening to squeeze through. She attempted to drag the grate back over the opening to hide what she'd done, but she lacked both leverage and strength. After a few minutes of sweating, she gave up, counting on the short walls of the alcove to disguise it was not in place, and reminding herself that she'd need the grate out of the way for her eventual escape. Mae wiped her brow, then her hand on the side of her leg. On her way from Milk she'd stopped to buy a new flashlight and a chalk stick to help her on her hunt. Mae was determined to retrieve *Le Manteau* and anything else she could carry from the hidden spot Vienna had marked on the map. It was better that than risk them being lost forever. She would return everything she could to the AGO where she knew the artworks would get the attention and restoration they required. She needed to do something to repair the destabilization Enfants Terrible had caused, even if it meant those pieces would fall back under the control of the very people from whom Halton Graves and his cohorts had been trying to hide them.

In the dark of the runoff channel, Mae turned on the flashlight. The beam shone bright across the concrete like a needle through the dark. She pointed the light at Vienna's map to orientate herself before taking her stick of chalk and drawing an arrow on the wall that pointed back to the stairs, followed by the number *one*. If she became lost, the arrows would be her trail out.

The smell of the storm channel was worse than she remembered. She covered her nose and mouth and shone the flashlight ahead of where she was going. Her footsteps echoed like a snare off the concrete walls no matter how softly she walked. No one else should have been down there, but Mae didn't want to take the chance the police had returned to search for more evidence. For a moment, she imagined what might happen were she discovered and decided it was best to not know. She wanted to believe the police would listen to her explanation, but she suspected otherwise.

The corridor was long and featureless, and without anyone accompanying her the spotlight-led hike took on its own monotony. The same walls passed over and over, lit for a few moments before disappearing in the dark's wake. The only sounds were her twanging steps, hypnotic and outside of time. She periodically stopped to confer with the map Vienna had given her but it quickly proved useless. It was impossible to know how far she'd travelled; after a few minutes, she remembered nothing but mile after mile of dark tunnel. No other sound or movement.

Yet, as she proceeded further into the dark, she worried that the monotony was only a trick put in place by Enfants Terrible. That somehow they'd designed the storm channel themselves, and instead of a corridor that led straight to the Path's entrance it was a slowly constricting spiral using *Le Manteau* as bait. What might be at the centre was a thought Mae could not let herself have, though she felt something bordering the dark that swarmed beyond the furthest reaches of her flashlight. Mae forced herself to keep the light pointed at the ground, pushing the circle out only so far. But every footstep threatened to be the one that dropped the curtain of darkness and revealed what that something was. Mae took smaller, less confident steps while her small flashlight tried to carve some circle of day out of the night. The voice in the back of her head, the one that had warned her not to follow Vienna's map, not to listen to Enfants Terrible, the one that had told her to remain at home instead of trying to find *Le Manteau* and all that was hidden—that voice had given up, as though accepting that outside itself, in the dark, something terrible awaited, and there was no choice left but for Mae to give herself over to it.

Mae stopped walking, sweat trickling down her neck. The dark was getting to her, making her doubt reality, and she had to tamp it down before her imagination triggered something. Already, the walls of the corridor felt tighter, and the fingers of claustrophobia tickled at the edges of her mind. She had to maintain control. The entrance Graves had shown her had to be close. It had to be. She reached into her pocket for the stick of chalk to draw another numbered arrow on the wall and when she lifted the flashlight to the concrete she was startled to find someone else had been there before her.

She'd seen graffiti before, but nothing so elaborate and primitive at once. A large animal on all fours, like a bear or an ox, stood ankle-deep in the runoff water, and from its back emerged something Mae took to be a kind of cat, pulling free from the larger beast like an insect moulting. From the back of the cat, another animal Mae could not identify, emerged in much the same way. Over and over again, smaller animal from larger, like matryoshka dolls, each successive beast painted more vibrantly and bizarrely than the last. They became less and less identifiable the further the link was from the primary beast, a recursive repetition that filled the wall with coloured lines crossing and intersecting, weaving a pattern of bodies uniformly punctuated by pairs of silver eyes. Those orbs glowed in the reflection of the flashlight, seeming to hover above the concrete. Mae brought her light closer to inspect the graffiti, and was startled to discover the figures hadn't been done in spray paint but oils, their rough strokes embossed on the runoff's walls. The painting shouldn't have been down there beneath the city streets, lost in a gallery of darkness. She stepped back, and the beam of light widened, the motion causing the illusion of movement in the painted limbs. The silver eyes rotated as though adjusting position, and she swung her flashlight down the corridor quickly to be sure nothing was on its way to greet her. She did not find the lack of results reassuring.

Keep moving forward. That's what she had to do. Just put everything else out of her mind and keep moving forward. She drew a numbered arrow hastily beside the painting on the cleanest piece of concrete she could find and started again, her pace faster to distance herself from the shuffling echo trailing close behind.

In her haste she almost passed the junction. It emerged from the shadows unexpectedly, disguised until the last moment by a thick curtain of dark. Water underfoot kicked up with her sudden stop, and she shone the flashlight into the narrow channel at where Graves's false wall should have stood. Instead, what she found was the wall had been moved aside, the bulbs strung overhead no longer powered even dimly, instead giving way only to more dark. The sight unnerved her, and she halted before crossing the threshold into the Path, no longer certain what she expected to find. Would it be the police? Enfants Terrible? Something else? Water dripped and splashed in the runoff corridor's echoes, then a rustle. Mae flashed her light back the way she'd come and found nothing. The walls of the corridor she passed through however lit up with the golds and oranges from a massive painting she was too close to comprehend. The image wavered, the edges rippling as though on fire. She wondered how she had missed seeing it during her approach. The painting bubbled and cracked—first its wavering centre bulged slightly, then further as though something were trying to push through. Her free hand rose, shaking as it reached to touch the coloured membrane that held whatever it was at bay. But Mae knew the battle was already lost, that the painting was about to crumble and reveal something she did not want to see. Mae instead shone the flashlight away and reminded herself that the dark played tricks. The dark played tricks. And the stench of stagnant water was no help. Her clothes were damp, her skin coated with a slick film.

She soldiered forward into the narrow Path. It was more confined than she remembered, and she fought the claustrophobic panic wanting to overtake her. It was hard to believe Graves had abandoned his underground bunker, especially when there were so many corridors in the byzantine Path where he could hide. He had mentioned spending months walking them using his stolen maps, which she assumed would make it easier for him to evade the police. So why would he disband Enfants Terrible and vanish? Part of Mae didn't believe it. She followed her memory and Vienna's map toward the abandoned Lumière Travel, and carefully monitored each grimy window for a glimpse of anything that suggested she wasn't alone. But there was no sign of life in the subterranean corridors and abandoned shops. The rumble of the subway train rushing underfoot travelled up her legs; the vibration gently swinging the powered off lights above her.

Enfants Terrible may have gone, but they'd left their mark. The news reports hadn't revealed the great lengths to which someone had gone to paint the surfaces of the Path. Mae slowed to shine her flashlight on the patterns overlapping and interleaving in post-impressionistic haze above her. It had to have taken months to complete, and even then it seemed impossible to create something so delicate on concrete in the dark. Had the corridors already been painted when Halton brought her to meet Vienna, Wynn, and Albert, and she'd been too distracted to notice? Mae reached out her hand to touch the paint. It was hardened and fully polymerized. She shook her head. That was impossible; there was no way it could already be set.

The chalk in her pocket continued to aid Mae in tracking her movements through the Path. She still found herself disoriented twice, forced to double back and take a different route to find Lumière Travel. Each time she did she made sure to correct the arrows that marked her way further into the bramble of stale and damp corridors.

It was just as Mae became convinced Vienna and Enfants Terrible had tricked her that the flashlight's beam found a reflection she recognized. Or, rather, a lack of reflection, as the boarded windows of Lumière Travel revealed themselves again as a void in a series of reflections. The door had been knocked off its hinges, allowing shadows to fill the agency. Mae carefully stepped through the broken frame, letting the circle of her flashlight guide her a few feet at a time. The walls had been stripped of the maps and charts that had once hung there, and the heaters and purifiers, too, were gone, removed along with their orange extension cables. Within the flashlight's lit circle she saw the after-image of Enfants Terrible sitting at what remained of their long table, bickering and arguing, and behind that after-image the reality bathed in harsh LED light—overturned boxes and scattered paper, boot prints and crushed plaster. Mae walked to the back of the room, careful to step over the debris across her path, moving the broken chairs and knocked-over shelves. With each step the dust rose to flutter against the light like moths, and she waved it away as best as she could. But it was impossible not to inhale, and when she did her bellowing sneeze was momentous. It took three sneezes for her nose to settle down, and by then her eyes were full of spots and tears.

The instructions Vienna had given her to find the stashed artwork were so straightforward Mae could hardly believe they were still undiscovered, but despite the news footage and the clutter of the agency office, no one appeared to have stumbled upon them. At the back of Lumière Travel were the canisters Vienna had described, standing amid dust that floated like snowflakes. Some had been knocked over in the earlier chaos, and the total number was fewer than Mae had been led to believe, but they were where Vienna promised, and when Mae shone her flashlight at the wall behind them she could see the faintest of seams. It was only once she ran her fingers along the tiny gaps and felt the sharp edges pinch her skin that she admitted Vienna had not been lying. And it was only when she found the inlaid hinges and the divot of a handle that she dared accept she was about to rescue *Le Manteau*.

Her trembling hands made it difficult when she positioned the flashlight on the floor a few feet away. Mae picked up the canisters one by one, heaving them across the room. As each was cleared and the surreptitiously disguised door uncovered, Mae breathed heavier, imagining what artistic wonders might be within reach. *Le Manteau* wasn't the only piece Enfants Terrible had stolen during their crusade to tear down the hypocrisy of the art world. There was no telling how much artwork they'd had access to, how many paintings and sculptures thought lost that were in fact safe and secure. But Mae cared only about one, and it was close. So very close. Vibrations ran down her arms as she moved the last of the canisters and retrieved her flashlight. *Le Manteau* awaited her rescue. She traced out the edges of the door with her fingertips, and when she found the inset handle she took hold and pulled. The door snapped open.

The circle of light was the first thing through. Mae lifted her flashlight and peered inside. The beam travelled the floor, finding empty tubes and cans of paint. There were splatters everywhere, but in the harsh light they were dark blotches like rot in the concrete. Discarded brushes were scattered on the floor, pitched aside haphazardly as though useless, the tail of their impact like a dark skid. As she pushed the circle of light further into the room, it kept going, going, farther than she expected, until it hit a bare wall. Mae leaned further in, moving her flashlight along the concrete, slowly and carefully at the outset, then faster and with abandon as the growing cold spot in her stomach spread. The room was empty. There were no missing paintings or sculptures. No stolen pottery or statues or sketches. And there was no *Le Manteau*. If it had ever been there, it was gone, taking with it Mae's hopes, and the one thing that could have consoled her.

The wheezing in her lungs was more pronounced, the blood pumped madly in her ears; Mae took a seat on one of the broken chairs pushed against the wall. It was all gone. Enfants Terrible were gone, her job at the AGO gone, *Le Manteau* gone. There was nothing left of her. It had been all taken away and destroyed. Even her own dreams had stalled. Two completed but ineffectual paintings sitting neutered in Milk, the third half-completed for so long she knew she'd never touch it again, no matter how many times she stared at it every night. She was in her mid-forties and a failure. She'd achieved nothing, reached none of her goals, achieved none of her dreams. Instead, she was stuck in the dust of the underground, hollowed out, waiting for an answer from the world that wasn't coming because, really, what was the world going to say? It wasn't going to apologize. It wasn't going to tell her everything was going to be fine. Because it wasn't. She knew that, and the world no longer cared enough to lie. Graves and his team wanted to give art back to the people, let it inspire them with hope. The irony was it was what killed those same things in Mae. She would have been happier if she'd never discovered it. Mae laughed. But it was mirthless.

Something fell in the corridors of the Path. A clatter from one of the disused stores, maybe the police doing a last check of the site before the concrete started pouring. Mae grabbed everything she came with, held the flashlight high, and rushed out of the store and back into the Path, aiming her flashlight beam in the direction of the last chalk arrow leading her out.

The numbers were further apart than she'd remembered, and it took some time to find where she'd left them. In reverse the landmarks no longer looked the same, and the arrows had been too hastily drawn to relay much certainty. Checking Vienna's map did no good—almost nothing matched her notes, and when it did it was often in contradiction to the other sets of handwriting scribbled along the margins. Mae's progress back was slow, but she felt confident the direction was right. She could smell the bitter air of the runoff channel carrying toward her, and was sure she saw a familiar corner ahead. But there was no corner. Just an unexpected fork in the corridor.

It was a cold realization and it took her a moment to recover.

SIMON STRANTZAS

How could she not have better marked her route? Did she not notice there were two paths when walking toward Lumière Travel? No, she was sure there had never been a branch, but in the dull light that certainty wavered, and everything blended together as her anxiety grew. Further noises echoed in the corridors, but she was unsure of their direction. They surrounded her, rattling the small lights hanging overhead, but it might as easily have been a passing train, even if she hadn't felt its rumble in the soles of her feet.

All Mae wanted was to find that fake door back to the runoff channel, and in turn the grate on Adelaide Street, but nothing was where it was supposed to be. She'd drawn thirty-seven arrows. She knew that as well as she knew anything, but though she found the thirty-seventh, then the thirty-sixth, next she found only the thirty-third, followed by the thirtieth, then subsequently the thirty-fourth. And, after that, nothing.

Despite her planning, she was lost. Panic twisted inside her and she struggled to tamp it down before she lost her head. Surely if she retraced her steps back to Lumière Travel and started again she could find where she went off course. The arrows and numbers... they would show the way. They would have to show the way.

She focused her attention on the flashlight's beam as it ran up and down the corridor walls, reflecting the glass from the abandoned storefronts. Behind those windows, clothes from decades earlier were carpeted with dust, making them uniformly grey and nondescript. None provided any sort of landmark to guide her.

When her flashlight unexpectedly found a chalk arrow on a wall, the sense of relief was overwhelming. In close proximity was number twenty-six which reassured her there was some escape, even if the number was faded and the arrow above it headless. She knew she'd drawn both, but in her haste did she forget to complete them? She held the flashlight closer and thought she saw scratches at one of the arrow's ends but she couldn't be sure. She only knew it was a shaft of chalk on a wall that failed in its one purpose: to indicate if she was travelling to freedom or deeper into the Path's labyrinth. But it was something. An indicator she was on the right track, at least. There were only two possible directions to go, and each would have to eventually lead to another number that would tell her if she should continue forward or double-back. There was still doubt, but it would paralyze her if she considered it, so she made a conscious effort not to.

Holding the flashlight to her watch showed she'd been trying to escape the Path for over two hours, which was nearly twice as long as it had taken her to get from the Adelaide Street grate to Lumière Travel. She was in trouble. Her phone was useless, and another set of arrows and numbers failed to materialize. None of the stores looked familiar, and the graffiti she'd seen sporadically painted had vanished. Vienna's map was a nonsense tangle of colours. If the abstract lines had made sense to Mae before, she didn't know how. Trying to return to Lumière Travel was no longer an option: she would never find her way back. The attempt would only condemn her to walk in continuous circles. All she had to cling to was the notion that the Path ran beneath different downtown buildings, so if Mae continued long enough, she might find some way out. An egress through an unused door into a sub-basement. Anything that she might escape through. But her hope was dwindling.

When the claustrophobic walls of the Path suddenly ended, Mae retreated in terror back to the safety of the corridor. After so long enclosed, the open space didn't feel right. She shone the flashlight ahead and tried to make sense of what it revealed. The light ran along the floor and walls in circles until Mae understood where the corridor ended and what the open space was: the abandoned courtyard for the underground mall. And, in the middle, encircled by a ring of stores, was a large opening in the floor.

Bordered by a waist-high glass partition, the hole emitted the noise of machinery grinding with periodic flashes of light that illuminated the Path's low ceiling. It was the subway. It had to be the subway. Mae approached the glass border and looked over the side into the hole. There was nothing there but further darkness, the sort her flashlight wouldn't penetrate, but she heard that mechanical clacking, albeit louder, and smelled the unmistakable scents of ozone and engine grease. The flashlight flew around the lip of the observation level, back and forth without caution, and when that revealed nothing in the narrow dark Mae put one hand on the railing and followed it until she found what she knew had to be there. A seized escalator that descended into the dark. But it was also hope. What was the point of having corridors like the Path under the city if commuters couldn't reach them? Especially when the subway itself was already running beneath? There had to be a way for passengers to move from one to the other, and when she unfolded Vienna's map and inspected its chaos she found exactly what she expected—a station on the line that she'd never seen because it was likely shut down and removed from the official maps once the Path was closed off. But it was on Vienna's map. Mae wanted to kiss the ground. A subway tunnel would mean escape—whether by emergency exit or another station. There was a way out. Mae teared up. There was a way out.

Mae shone the flashlight ahead of her as she descended the stopped escalator one step at a time, ignoring the way everything beyond her lit circle dropped away into the abyss. She couldn't see the bottom, but she kept one hand on the rubber railing and trusted the stairs would lead her safely to the floor beneath and a way out. Light continued to flicker from beneath, but it was only after she'd taken a few dozen steps that she was sure it was real and not her eyes seeing sparks in the nothingness. Her heart pounded against her chest with anticipation—she'd impossibly managed to escape the police and being trapped alive underground. The only thing she hadn't managed was rescuing *Le Manteau* from wherever Graves had stashed it, but she couldn't let herself worry about it. Not until she was above ground.

When the distance between steps suddenly shrank, she knew she was near the end of the seized staircase. But still that last footfall startled her. Despite her hope that the haze of light would intensify once she came closer to the subway station, everything was as dark as before. Her flashlight found a set of turnstiles though, and an empty ticket booth whose glass was either fractured or covered in spider webs. On the painted brick wall behind the booth the station's name, Lower Osgoode, was stencilled, though like her arrows the letters had faded and cracked over time. Her breath echoed in her ears with a tininess and there was something in the air, an odour too familiar to be real.

It was only when Mae raised her flashlight and looked above that she realized she was right. The smell of linseed oil. The walls and ceiling were covered with the largest painting Mae had ever seen. At first she thought it was a *Le Manteau* reproduced on a massive scale—the expressionistic brush strokes with a similar sense of weightlessness and gathering like fireflies swarming in fractal patterns. But she could only take in a small circle at a time, and where she expected those strokes to form a silhouette, there was a torrential rainstorm, and where she expected a distant cityscape, she found the colours of a sunset. The strangest part was her inability to determine what the painting was at all. She swung the lit circle over the walls and ceiling, but whatever was illuminated was too small to be clear, and never seemed to match with anything else she'd seen. It was formless to the point that she wondered if there was any form at all.

Who would have had time for such a massive project? And more importantly, why? Why create something forever buried and locked away in the dark? There was no way a single person did it, but why would a team come down, especially when they'd need lights and scaffolding to complete the job? It didn't make sense. Mae's flashlight showed the floor was covered in drippings, but even that was bizarre. There should have been bare spots where the scaffolding was setup, and there were none. Just paint everywhere on every surface.

Then the paint shifted. She didn't believe it was anything more than the echo of a stray shadow flickering, but her body

SIMON STRANTZAS

understood. It held her breath, made her step back. The paint moved under the glare of the flashlight, only slightly at first, but then unmistakably. Mae took another step back, retreating to where she'd come from, only the escalator she'd descended was no longer there. And with it the turnstiles and ticket booth. Panic rose as she confronted the impossible. It was all gone. Only the endless paint-spattered floor stretching out around her remained.

Mae forgot how to scream. Her circle of light was so small, and the solid black so vast and pressing—it was as though she were at the ocean's nadir, shining the thinnest of slivers into its depths. And she was sinking further.

Time lost its relevance. Inside that construct, there was nothing more than that moment. She clung to the ground, terrified she would be pulled from it, the only anchor she had, and drawn into the void of madness. Mae put her hands over her eyes, tried to tell herself she had inhaled toxic fumes or simply lost her sanity. Anything to convince herself that none of what she was experiencing was real. But she didn't believe it. She didn't believe any of it.

Paint floated in the air. All around her in the darkness colours appeared, coalescing into a giant mosaic, an impressionistic world in brush-strokes unlike the world she knew, and yet so clearly the world that was. The swirling eddies took the shapes of people, the inanimate approximating life. They moved in mockery, breaking as they paced around where Mae stood gobsmacked. No, she realized: not a mockery. They were life come undone. They were the turnstiles and escalators and ticket booths. They were the tunnels and travel agencies and galleries. They were the thread being pulled and everything coming apart, degrading into strokes of paint in the swirling chaos. Free in their formlessness. As terror rolled through her head her eyes played tricks on her, colours fading in from the dark. Not lights—they were not lights— but colours nonetheless. They slowly appeared around Mae: ambers and aubergines; verdant greens and violets; surfacing on the blank canvas. Mae became hypnotized by them, her

258

panic snuffed as her mind surrendered wholly. The colours dawned, and as they became more pronounced, they mixed, formed patterns, shapes. The light from her flashlight became a series of squiggling eels that spilled from the lens toward the wall. Then the flashlight, too, became nothing more than a box. And then paint. Then separated and became less than paint. Became only colours of paint. And the colours broke down further, became something beyond colour. Became the idea of colour. But still it wasn't done. The swirl of disintegration cascaded around her until Mae felt it take her as well, and she realized she'd already long since come apart and lost her cohesion, her being. She became less solid, but rather than flee, she embraced it. There was a peace there she'd always been searching for, an understanding of the truth. In the nothing she'd found it.

And then the world split open and Mae's head followed.

6. REVEL

Winter had never been Halton Grave's favourite season. He preferred the summer, when the women strutted down Bay Street on their lunch breaks while he watched from behind a pair of dark sunglasses. He'd loved it ever since he was a boy. He still missed how the days seemed to stretch for weeks, and the world was so full of unhindered possibilities floating on the warm air. But summer was an old memory as he trudged through the slush, his hands so deep in his checkered coat's pockets that he risked dragging them on the icy sidewalk, all in a futile effort to track down and reform Enfants Terrible.

He was convinced the police had moved on to other cases after Kenny had confessed to breaking into the AGO and causing all that destruction. By way of proof, the former security guard offered up *Le Manteau* and admitted to having worked with Enfants Terrible at one point, but declared with no small paranoia he'd been ousted for a variety of invented reasons. It was perhaps the worst thing that could have happened. Halton had been happy to take credit for the vandalism when all the forces of the city were after him and Enfants Terrible—after all, they'd received headlines and their message was being loudly broadcast in articles and blogs. But once Kenny's admission came to light all attention shifted from Halton's message of artistic corruption to the ugly gossip of Enfants Terrible's internal workings and Kenny's delusions. The traitor's face had become the face of the movement, splashed across front pages and subjected to in-depth editorials, the ex-employee of two organizations who'd been looking for crazed vengeance. What should have been Halton's greatest achievement was ruined, and being in hiding there was nothing he could do to dispute it. That was why it was urgent he reform Enfants Terrible and return to creating a stir. It had absolutely nothing to do with the dwindling state of his monetary reserves.

Halton hadn't seen Wynn, Albert, or Vienna in months, not since he made the mistake of bringing that woman from the AGO down to Lumière Travel. He'd been so sure he could trust her—she was so small and unassuming, in her button-down cardigans and her big dreams of being an artist, that he was certain it wouldn't take much to get her on his side. He'd always been good at being convincing—all it took sometimes was listening with interest to what someone had to say. Mae Olsen most especially. It was by knowing her dreams that he understood how she could help him achieve his. She was another person who wanted what she didn't think she deserved. Halton recognized the look because he saw it everywhere, in the eyes of everyone—fear of taking what they believed life owed them. Vienna had been a student working on her Bachelor's when Halton found her, and within only a few weeks she was out of school and supporting the cause. With Wynn and Albert, it had been even easier. If only Kenny hadn't lost his job at the museum, if only Halton hadn't grown cocky and decided he could ignore Albert and find their next inside agent on his own, he wouldn't have had to spend the previous months lying low, and he certainly wouldn't have lost all the artwork he'd rescued as the police cleared the Path looking for Enfants Terrible. It was a horrible time, and an even worse set-back, but now that the investigation had finally eased, he was determined to regroup and rebuild.

It took some effort, but he finally had a lead on where to find Vienna. She was the key to getting everything back. Wynn was a good set of hands, but not terribly bright, which made for an excellent soldier who was useless in every other way. And Albert had always been less committed to the cause than to the bottle, but at least he knew how to fix things when they broke and could jerry-rig a tap into the grid's power to keep them functioning. What Vienna brought was more useful than any of that: she brought blind devotion to the cause, and a deep trust fund, and without both there was no way Enfants Terrible could wake anyone to the commercialization of art. Or allow Halton to do so in relative comfort. After all, that sort of change wouldn't happen overnight—it was a war that would last his entire lifetime if he played it right.

All he was certain of was that Vienna had returned to school during the intervening months. That had been the plan, at least, should anything go wrong. Vienna would return to school, Wynn to whatever fast-food job would take him, and Albert would likely just retreat into his bottle. Halton made it a point to not learn any more information than those basics in order to preserve the fire wall—he couldn't be compelled to provide information he didn't have—and he insisted the others do the same. Once the group was scattered, it would have been impossible for anyone to connect the pieces. He'd been so proud of himself at the time, but in hindsight the plan had been *too* foolproof, as he'd been reduced to loitering on campus like a creeping stalker, hoping for a chance encounter with Vienna as she travelled between classes. But with thousands of students making that journey once per hour, finding her proved to be increasingly unlikely.

After a few weeks without success, the notion that Vienna had not just left the school but the city for good gnawed at his resolve. He was bereft of ideas, and the odds of him finding another disciple as easily coerced and well-financed as her seemed unlikely. He widened his search, first in the coffee houses off-campus, then any place in the city students might congregate, and with each failure his confidence grew dimmer. Eventually, he barely looked at the foreign faces of the students in the pubs and lounges and billiard halls. And not long after that, he stopped going into those sorts of establishments all together. Instead he walked the streets in the wet cold, wondering how he was going to spread the word without a flock to follow him.

In his darkest hour, he returned to the alleys and runoff channel entrances on his maps, but though Halton was right and the police had gone, the concrete and heavy locks with which they had systematically replaced every grating from every map had not, and no matter how many times Halton shook each one of them, the Path remained permanently inaccessible to him. Locked outside his reach, stranding him with nothing.

He exited the alley, head hung low, and contemplated surrender. Not to the police, but to his lot. The city and its denizens had taken all he had and left him depleted and empty. Halton heard the rumble of a winter storm brewing in the grey sky, and when he looked up he was taken aback by the sight of Vienna striding quickly down the opposite sidewalk as though from out of an implausible dream. She wore a black field coat with a red beret on the back of her head, and carried beneath her arm a long roll of blue paper that Halton recognized at once as one of the now useless stolen maps. He nearly leapt when he saw her, filled with joy that his journey was at an end. All his future plans came flooding back, as though they'd been dammed by his despair, along with his hunger for spreading the word again. Vienna hasn't seen him, and was already too far away to hear his call by the time Halton broke the spell of his stupefaction, but he wasted no time chasing after her.

Halton jogged as fast as he dared on the icy streets, but as the gap between he and Vienna narrowed, he wondered what she was doing with the useless map, and where she was taking it. There had been a plan for everyone to quietly disappear. Carrying one of their most incriminating tools out in the open, even if it could no longer help move through the city freely, was in direct contradiction of that agreement. Was that why she walked with the determination of someone running late? Or was there something else going on? Halton slowed, caught his breath, and let Vienna get far enough ahead that she couldn't spot him if she accidentally glanced back. He wanted to know where she was taking the map. He wanted to know who she was so late to meet.

But as curious as he was, his desire to call off the chase grew with each cold street she led him down, with each snow drift he was forced to circumvent to keep her in sight. His feet grew wetter and colder, but persisted more out of stubbornness than anything else, and eventually he was rewarded by the sight of Vienna entering a small, nondescript coffee house on College Street named Milk. Halton stopped to kneel between two parked cars and watched the front window as she took a seat facing outward, joined shortly afterward by two men. The first he recognized immediately; it was Wynn, and anger flared as he watched the bearded stooge touch Vienna's arm. The second was older, and it wasn't until he turned his head that Halton realized he was a cleaned-up and shaved Albert. He looked healthier than Halton had ever seen him. Happier, too.

It was baffling. Had they all randomly run into each other on the streets somewhere and reconnected? Or had they always known how to contact one another, secretly colluding and dismissing Halton's contingency plans as not worth the effort? He needed to know, especially after spending so long searching for them. The very people he'd brought together in the first place had betrayed and rejected him. It wasn't how things were supposed to go. None of it was right. Anger burned as he stood and headed toward the coffee house.

But before he could cross the street, his march was halted. Another person became visible in the coffee house's window, and it took a moment to recognize it was Mae Olsen. She did not look anything like the buttoned-down AGO employee he'd last met. Instead, her once neat hair was wild and untamed, and her manner was full of unrepentant confidence. There had been flickers of her wilfulness before, but what stood there in the sunlit coffee house behind glass was a different creature altogether. And it made him incredibly uneasy.

She stood over the three as they unrolled the map across the table, and proceeded to point to various sections of it between bouts of mouthed conversation. The three nodded their heads with each word she spoke, and after a few minutes they rolled up the map and all four of them left the coffee house. The entire conversation lasted no longer than ten minutes, and when they departed, they did so one at a time, each heading in a different direction. The last to emerge was Mae, cellular telephone up to her ear, and when she walked, it was directly toward where Halton knelt spying. It was too late for him to move. He'd been caught.

"Hello, Halton," Mae said, slipping the phone into her pocket. "Why didn't you come inside and join us?"

"You knew I was out here?"

"Of course. There's no mistaking those branches. I could have seen those trees from miles away." She stopped and looked up at the sky. "Will you walk with me back to the AGO? We're already starting to lose the light."

He stammered, confused by her strange behaviour, before agreeing. Despite the complicated route Vienna had taken getting to the coffee house, the museum was actually not too far a walk back.

"I thought you were fired from the AGO," he said as the two walked back to the Grange District. Mae's eyes were wide as she scanned everything like a tourist, and when she spoke, it was with a distracted tone that suggested she was barely there. Halton, however, couldn't keep his eyes off of her.

"Once the police arrested Kenny and it was clear Enfants Terrible had either gone into hiding or disbanded, all the museum cared about was getting back to normal. But that meant fixing everything Kenny had damaged, and there aren't enough restoration experts left in the country to do that fast enough. The board couldn't be all that choosey. And I hadn't really done anything wrong as far as they could determine, so they brought me back through a contract position, at least until the clean-up is done. I guess they'll decide what to do with me then. Which is all fine."

"I suppose that means they don't know about today. About your *new* friends..."

"No, I don't think they'd approve of what we're doing." She smiled. It was beguiling. But Halton shook it off.

"What *are* you four doing?"

"That's hard to explain. I'm not sure it would make much sense."

"Try me."

Mae stopped walking again, but instead of looking at the sky she looked at her feet, lifting them one at a time and placing them down carefully. Her body swayed enough that Halton reached out to catch her before she caught herself and continued walking as though nothing had happened.

"I found Vienna first. She was the easiest, and she led me to the others. Once I explained the truth, once I showed it to them, they wanted to help."

"Help do what?"

"You know, you were on the right track when I first met you. I felt it in my bones, even though I refused to admit it. But it was the only reason I ever listened. Art really is the cause of so many of the world's problems. Art has ruined everything. But it's not just commercial art. Your views on what happened are... uninformed is the best way I can put it. Like an ant trying to comprehend the sun. It's too big for you."

He snorted. Shook his head. Smiled crookedly. "Oh, but you do?"

Mae spun and walked backward as she squinted at him, her own face doing a twisted mockery of his smile. It was as unnerving as it was irritating, but he tried to disguise his reaction with indifference. She laughed, then turned back around.

"I went looking for what you hid," she said. "In the Path? After the police were done? I went down there looking for everything you'd stolen. And do you know what I found at the back of that travel agency office you four were using as a headquarters? Behind all those canisters?"

"I can guess," he said.

"If you guessed nothing, you'd be right. But that nothing led me to the old escalator."

It was Halton's turn to stop.

"The what? What are you talking about?"

She nodded knowingly and waited for him to catch up.

"I'm not surprised you don't know. None of the others ever saw it either. Albert used to assure me every time we met that there are no escalators anywhere in the Path—there are none on the maps, and he certainly never came across one or heard anybody else mention they had. He says there *couldn't* be one with the subway running beneath the floor. He says it wouldn't be structurally sound. I guess he'd know; he's a former engineer, after all. But what can I say? It doesn't mean I didn't find one just the same, it doesn't mean it wasn't right there on my map, too. I found the escalator right where the map said it was supposed to be and I took it to the bottom. And that's where I learned and understood what it was, and why no one else had ever found it."

Nothing she said made sense, so how could she be so certain?

"What do you mean?"

She sighed, then pointed ahead. The AGO was up the street, a large crowd gathered around it. Halton had never seen that many people on McCaul before, and as he and Mae approached he noticed everyone had been pushed back from the museum, forced to stand behind an ersatz barrier of police cars. The sky rumbled as though helicopters were circling, but Halton couldn't find any hovering overhead.

"What's going on?"

"I told you I sort of agreed with you—art has ruined everything, and because of it the world is going to destroy itself. It's why I accepted my old job at the AGO. Art has caused too much damage, and we have to act before it's too late to stop. Vienna, Wynn, Albert—they all see it now, they're all part of the solution. I don't think you ever will, though. You're too much like everyone else, stuck in your ways. You need a jolt. This whole world needs a giant jolt."

Halton's heart raced. His face grew cold with sweat.

"What is this?" he asked.

"This? The crowd? I called the AGO and told them about the bomb."

"The *what?*"

"Here's what you need to understand, Halton: this is not the world we are supposed to be living in. This is not the world we were given. I'm not saying this in an Adam-and-Eve sense, but maybe explaining it in those terms might make it easier for you to understand. Let's pretend the world God created for Man, the garden He created where Adam and Eve and all the animals lived in harmony, was not like the world you see now. It was paradise. But I don't mean that there were trees and brooks and all the animals got along and everyone lived in peace. Instead, what I mean by paradise is that there was no difference between reality and dream because none was needed—all creatures lived in a state of flux, with no distinction between the impossible and the possible, the mental and the physical, life and afterlife, fantasy and magic and reality. It makes a lot of sense if you think about it, even scientifically. The vastness of space, the astounding improbability of life evolving on this planet, let alone intelligent life... these are impossible things that could only occur if reality accepted the impossible as an integral part of itself.

"The problem, as always, is us. I've spent a lot of time reading about this since I came back up that escalator. I've read stacks of books and websites, trying to understand what I'd learned. Impossibility is like quantum physics—it's Heisenberg all over again. By witnessing the impossible, by living in a world where there is no reality and anything can happen, each act of trying to understand it, to codify it, naturally changes it. This was fine when the world was covered in animals—well, maybe not fine, but because animals aren't self-aware, the process was eonic. But early man's mind began to grow and expand and as he started to group and categorize the world he froze it one piece at a time. Once he painted his first image on a cave wall, he doomed reality. He fixed a bit of it in place; pinned it and killed it. A line between the real and the unreal began to form, sealing one off from the other, a wall to which we've been adding bricks over thousands of years, unknowingly destroying ourselves. Is it any wonder the world, this garden, has begun to revolt? It's an allergic reaction: the planet, the universe, is trying to wipe us out, destroy these barriers we've erected.

"This is what our new Enfants Terrible is trying to prevent. We're trying to save us all."

Halton took a step back. He couldn't speak.

"You don't see it yet," she said as she checked her watch. "But you will."

On cue, there was a boom from somewhere in the distance. An expanding cloud blossomed above the skyline. The sound of car alarms in the rumbling aftermath. Then, another explosion. And another. Halton looked at Mae, who smiled in awe as plumes of vaporized concrete lift into the air.

"We used those maps you found," she said as panic rose around them. "All the art galleries had to go. All of them."

Another series of explosions in succession. Three buildings destroyed. With each the crowd outside the AGO screamed, ducking from a danger too far away but coming closer.

And then the AGO exploded.

Fire and lights and the Earth trembling. Halton was knocked from his feet by the concussive force, and the streets filled with pulverized stone and ash. People scrambled, trampling anyone who had fallen, and pandemonium surrounded the crater that was once the art museum. All around Halton, pieces of once priceless artifacts rained down on the injured, and where he expected sirens there was only a high-pitched whine. He pushed himself to his knees and saw Mae already standing beside him, flesh torn and bloodied. She held out a trembling hand. Her eyes rheumy with joy.

"Why?" he screamed, though he heard only a muffled version of his own voice.

She pointed at the skyline.

The city was comprised of buildings. One after the other they circled him, and those circles went back as far as he could see. Structures of concrete and steel towering above. Through the dust he saw their shadows, but those shadows jittered behind the veil of debris, and in his delirium it took a moment to understand why. The buildings were transforming. Brick and mortar split apart, and from the parting other buildings emerged, grew into the sky until they too split, birthing more buildings. Towers upon towers upon towers, while strips of asphalt wreathed around them, cars of all shapes travelling the moebius streets, sometimes without wheels yet still moving. The whole skyline opened like a flower in the morning, spreading concrete like petals into the sky. Soon, other buildings were splitting, and from them emerged more of the same. There were tiny, misshapen people in the new windows, some working, some laughing. When they saw one another across the chasms between towers, they danced and waved, and some leapt and glided over to visit those below. Halton watched them float on the thermal winds, not understanding.

"This is only the start," Mae said. "There's so much more to do."

And Halton looked at her, at the blood trickling from the wound at her temple and from one of her nostrils. He wondered if he was having a seizure. But before he could speak her wound became a crack, and the crack inched across her face, under her right eye. She said something to him, but the words were garbled and lost as Halton witnessed the crack spread farther. When it reached her ear, the entire quadrant, eye and all, gently swung outward, and from the gap tendrils spilled out, thickened, sprouted tiny pink flowers as they continued

SIMON STRANTZAS

to grow and branch. Halton looked into Mae's remaining eye, but she was unbothered by the turn of events. She continued to explain herself to him as the plants grew high, animals running between the stalks, and Halton felt himself smile as he watched it all joyously unfurl. If only he had a way to capture the unravelling as it happened so he could never forget it.

"Mae—" he started.

"Do you see now?" she said. "There's no nothing anymore, because nothing is everything."

ACKNOWLEDGEMENTS

—————————— ✣ ——————————

Special thanks to Michael Kelly, Richard Gavin, Helen Marshall, Nathan Ballingrud, and s.j. bagley for their support and friendship while these stories were being written, and additional thanks to editors C. M. Muller, S. T. Joshi, and Paula Guran for commissioning some of these works for their respective anthologies.

Inspiration for and help with these stories came in part from a wide variety of sources, including: The Guardian; Wikipedia; Lynda E. Rucker; Wired; *The Thing*, issue 4; Yves Tourigny; Business Insider; Environmental Graffiti; Steven Millhauser; Angela of Foligno (by way of Eugene Thacker); Nine Inch Nails; Peter Straub; my neighbours' dog; Robert Aickman; Kelly Link; The Allan Gardens Conservatory; Jeffrey Ford; Leonard Cohen; and many other places and people I'll likely recall only after you read this.

—Simon Strantzas, Toronto, June 2018

ABOUT THE AUTHOR

───────────── ✂ ─────────────

Simon Strantzas is the author of *Burnt Black Suns* (Hippocampus Press, 2014), *Nightingale Songs* (Dark Regions Press, 2011), *Cold to the Touch* (Tartarus Press, 2009), and *Beneath the Surface* (Humdrumming, 2008), as well as the editor of *Aickman's Heirs* (Undertow Publications, 2015), a finalist for both the World Fantasy and British Fantasy Awards, and the winner of the Shirley Jackson Award. He also edited *Shadows Edge* (Gray Friar Press, 2013), and was the guest editor of *The Year's Best Weird Fiction, Vol. 3* (Undertow Publications, 2016). In 2016, he co-founded the non-fiction journal, *Thinking Horror*, which is dedicated to exploring the literary field of horror and its various philosophies. His writing has been reprinted in a number of annual best-of anthologies, and published in venues such as Nightmare, Cemetery Dance, and Postscripts. His short story, "Pinholes in Black Muslin", was a finalist for the British Fantasy Award, and his collection, *Burnt Black Suns*, a finalist for the Shirley Jackson Award. He lives with his wife in Toronto, Canada.

Lightning Source UK Ltd.
Milton Keynes UK
UKHW011954181219
355642UK00001B/75/P